SUMMER OF THE DANCING BEAR

May it inspire
you in your
own work
Bianca

ESSENTIAL PROSE SERIES 93

Guernica Editions Inc. acknowledges the support of
the Canada Council for the Arts and the Ontario Arts Council.
The Ontario Arts Council is an agency of the Government of Ontario.

SUMMER of the DANCING BEAR

Bianca Lakoseljac

GUERNICA

TORONTO • BUFFALO • BERKELEY • LANCASTER (U.K.)

2012

Michael Mirolla, general editor
Lindsay Brown, editor
Guernica Editions Inc.
P.O. Box 117, Station P, Toronto (ON), Canada M5S 2S6
2250 Military Road, Tonawanda, N.Y. 14150-6000 U.S.A.

Distributors:
University of Toronto Press Distribution,
5201 Dufferin Street, Toronto (ON), Canada M3H 5T8
Gazelle Book Services, White Cross Mills, High
Town, Lancaster LA1 4XS U.K.
Small Press Distribution, 1341 Seventh St.,
Berkeley, CA 94710-1409 U.S.A.

First edition.
Printed in Canada.
Legal Deposit – First Quarter

Library of Congress Catalog Card Number: 2011945664

Library and Archives Canada Cataloguing in Publication
Lakoseljac, Bianca, 1952-
Summer of the dancing bear / Bianca Lakoseljac.

(Prose series ; 93)
Issued also in electronic formats.
ISBN 978-1-55071-361-9

I. Title. II. Series: Prose series ; 93

PS8623.A424S86 2012 C813'.6 C2012-900004-3

For Jovanka Ivanović

whose love bound the family that bent reality
during the birth of the country that no longer exists

Chapter I

Searching The Wells

my dress in rags
jewels of stardust
my home gypsy carts
i sing and dance
for copper coins
and i sell cookie hearts

(Summer 1960)

PERCHED HIGH UP in the crown of an old cherry tree, eight-year-old Kata sat in her hideaway, humming a tune. The melody repeated itself in her thoughts, gathering resonance from voices in the past until it reached hypnotic proportions and she felt that she could touch it – touch the voice if she kept her eyes closed and carefully extended her hand out into the summer breeze.

For the last two nights, she had been listening to music drifting over from the distant gypsy caravan. She could identify the sorrowful duet of violins, the deep echo of the gigantic double bass, and the imposing rumble of the accordion that, to her dismay, drowned out other instruments. And then, well into the night, when the caravan seemed to be sleeping, she discerned a gentle singing voice she thought must belong to a beautiful gypsy fairy. It was carried aloft by the sweet, melancholy notes of a violin, but not like violins she'd heard played from house to house earlier in the night. Sitting on the window ledge in the moonlight, hidden from her sleeping Grandma and the world, she watched the long shadows swaying over the courtyard's flower garden and wished the crickets would stop the incessant chirping that muffled the gentle melody. She hoped the voice would return every summer, and that someday she might steal out into the night and find the singing fairy.

* * * *

But now, from her post in the cherry tree, she wished the mystique of the previous night had not dissipated in the haze of afternoon heat. Below, the fruit orchard sprawled on her right, and the two-storey yellow brick barn loomed on her left. The main house, glaring in whitewash, stood behind her, the guesthouse in front. The courtyard between the houses seemed overstuffed with the two linden crowns towering over the exuberant flower beds down in the shade and a blazing rose garden in the sun-drenched circle in the middle – all enchained by the rusty iron fence and gate.

Kata revelled in her seclusion under the cool canopy of boughs, as she inhaled the familiar bittersweet greenness of the foliage. Spotting a bead of leaching cherry sap, she scraped it off the bark and nibbled on the tart, gummy substance. She found the odd shrivelled cherry the robins had missed, hidden beneath drooping clumps of leaves. She gazed through the branches at the fields. Then, through the sluggish sway of the wheat, a cloud of dust twisted up like a small tornado, staying close to the well-trod path. Finally it popped out of the field, the dust dissipating to unveil her friend and classmate, eight-year-old Miladin.

He was riding his horse – a long broom fashioned from twigs. He held the broom-handle between his legs, the branches trailing behind. Head cocked to one side, neighing loudly, whipping the branches behind him with a stick and shouting "giddy-up," he sprinted to the gate. As she watched his thin arms and legs flail out of sync with his body and his slightly oversized head wobble on his thin neck, she felt a twinge of guilt for secretly naming her new string puppet after him.

The large iron gate squeaked as he pushed it open and galloped through.

Hoping to remain unnoticed, Kata carefully climbed to a higher row of branches. But Miladin headed straight for the tree.

"Whoa!" He commanded his horse to stop next to the rope swing suspended on a branch below her, and continuously jogged in place while hitting the broomstick behind him and shouting: "Whoaaa! Whoaaa boy!"

He finally dismounted and tied the rope he used as reins to the wooden seat of the swing.

"Your horse better not rip my swing off!" Kata shouted.

"I was gonna tell you something, but now I'm not." Miladin struggled up the smooth bark of the tree. Eventually, he reached the fork of three thick branches and sat across from her, separated by the tree trunk.

She scowled: "You're sitting in Maja's chair."

"Well, she isn't here, is she?" He widened his eyes and puckered his lips wryly and Kata marvelled at the soft dots of mauve bordering his pupils.

Rolling her flute between her palms, she raised it to her lips and blew a low ominous note.

"Ha! You think I care? I'm not afraid! There is no magic in that flute."

They staged their usual ritual of spiteful remarks. Then Miladin began to climb down.

She stuffed the flute into the bodice of her faded flowery dress and followed, careful not to step on his knuckles gripping the branches below her.

"So aren't you gonna ask me?" Miladin blurted as they faced each other at the base of the tree.

"What news do you bring now, Hermes?" she snapped, imitating the wobble of his head and rolling her eyes, feigning boredom.

"That's name-calling. You broke the rule!"

"It's not! My grandma said you're just like Hermes! He was a god, you know! Flying around, bringing news! It's not name-calling!"

Violet eyes lit with excitement, his thin face crinkled in mischief. He hunched his back, chin jutting, and clasped his left fist with the palm of his right hand. She thought he looked like a barnyard rooster, ready to take on any and all comers.

"Everybody's searching," he whispered, with a devilish grin.

"Searching for what?" she asked.

"I'm not gonna tell you."

He mounted his broomstick horse and rode off.

"That's just like you!" she shouted into the cloud of dust billowing behind him.

She returned to her perch in the cherry tree and watched him vanish into the path in the wheat field, until all she could see was the shimmer of hot air above the expanse of yellow.

And then, to her astonishment, the field transformed into the *Wheatfield with a Reaper*, a painting she had recently seen at the Vincent van Gogh exhibit during a class excursion.

The exhibit surfaced in her memory – she, face to face with Van Gogh's masterpieces, heart pounding, hot air rising to her throat. Her classmates pushed and played silly games, obstructing her view, oblivious to her need to bask in the vibrant colours and the frenzied curves and the warmth of the swirling sun and the swaying wheat. She needed to immerse herself in the landscapes that blazed under the summer heat, penetrating her vision, her whole being.

Back home, she had gone to the well-thumbed picture book of Dutch painters Grandma had given her. Gazing into the paintings, she had realized she was a new person. For her, blossoming orchards, sunflowers, irises, wheat fields, the sunshine, the clouds, the well-trod path leading to her friend Maja's house would never again be the same. Van Gogh's icy-blue stare had pierced her own vision and opened a breach through which all life took on a new meaning. All things, animate and inanimate, were infused with new light and shadow, and with the swirl of a brushstroke were instilled with a mystical power. For the next little while she existed in a frenzied state. Her body dwelled on a farm in the little village of Ratari, but her mind drifted amongst the paintings in the National Art Gallery in Belgrade, 40 kilometres away, absorbing the aura of a genius whose hands had painted ... no ... created ... breathed life into the images that now possessed her.

The wheat field below began to sway, and the *Wheatfield with a Reaper* came to life. She closed her eyes and the inscription under the painting appeared on the canvas of her vision: *Van Gogh described the 'all yellow, terribly thickly painted' figure as Death, who reaps humanity like a wheat field. The yellow symbolically derives its power from the sun, which is the painting's source of light.*

That is precisely how the field before her now appeared. Complete, with reaper – except that this reaper was swinging his scythe back and forth, back and forth – harvesting the wheat.

She slid down the tree, ran across the yard to her grandmother, who was sitting in the deep shade of a linden, and asked who was the reaper harvesting the wheat. Grandma looked at her curiously. She paused, removed her spectacles, set aside a bouquet of herbs she was carefully tying with a string, and finally answered: "Today is Sunday, my little swallow. No one harvests wheat on a Sunday."

"But there is a reaper in the field behind the barn," Kata whispered. She ran – cutting across the rose garden, barely missing the razor-sharp thorns, oblivious to the rosy hues of rumpled petals she usually collected – back to her perch in the tree.

But now the reaper was nowhere to be seen – just the oscillating mirage in countless shades of gold.

She slid down again, ran to her grandma's room, and retrieved the book on Dutch painters. She flipped back to the painting to ensure there was a reaper in the canvas. And yes, there he was – about to swing the scythe, and as always – frozen in his stride.

"Did you see him swinging his scythe, Deda Mihailo?" she heard her own timid voice. Warily, she peered into her grandfather's black-and-white photograph, still hung above Grandma's headboard fifteen years after his death. If his all-seeing eyes, if his all-knowing presence could not reassure her, who could? Didn't Grandma say that he had built this large estate, planted almost every tree with his own hands, and that he watched from above all that transpired on his land? Didn't Grandma ask him to give her a sign each time she was, in her words, in dire need of his guidance?

Kata considered asking her mother about the reaper in the painting, but quickly dismissed the thought. It was easier to talk to the ever-calm face of her grandfather. Although he had died before she was born, through her grandma's recollections she felt she'd known him for as long as she'd been aware of her own existence. She'd been heedful of his dreams and aspirations, his successes and even his failures, his ultimate folly, in Grandma's words – of allowing himself to be killed. In fact, she felt she knew him better than her own aloof father, even better than her unpredictable mother. Her parents taught grade school in the nearby town of Obrenovac and spent their weekends and school breaks on the farm. Living with her grandmother, she was accustomed to their absence. During the summer, she dealt with their presence by keeping out of their way. This was easier than she first thought. They existed in their own worlds, separate from each other and separate from hers, as if they were all complete strangers.

She waited patiently, flipping through the pictures of paintings, recalling the canvasses from the gallery, glancing at her grandfather's image on the wall. But he gave no sign. He continued overseeing with those serene eyes, a likeness of which she would sometimes glimpse in her mother's when she was unaware of being observed. His portrait remained steadfast in its role of family timekeeper, stamped in the corner with an imprint, *1945, Belgrade Photo Studio,* reminding everyone of the time no one could ever forget – the end of the war, and the year of her grandfather's disappearance.

Clutching the book against her chest, she ran back out. As she stood on the high verandah unsure where to turn next, whom to ask, her gaze drifted again to the wheat field in the distance, beyond the barn.

She stood motionless, sweat flooding her forehead. In the distance, where the reaper had been, now a dozen people or more were holding hands, linked in a human chain, sweeping the field. They shifted and swayed, flattening the sea of yellow below them, hollering, undistinguishable sounds floating on still air.

"Kata, do you hear that? Can you see anything from up there?" Grandma rose from her chair, hand shielding her eyes against the sun, gazing into the distance.

"I'm here, Grandma! On the verandah! You see it too? You hear it?"

Grandma dropped the herbs into her basket and hurried toward the verandah, head cocked to one side, listening. Her words raced ahead: "What is it? What do you see, Kata?"

"Over there!" Kata pointed at the advancing, faceless figures.

Grandma picked up the pace. She was short and appeared child-like, with the handle of the huge willow basket slung over her arm, and the kind brown eyes, too large for her face, wide with apprehension.

Kata stepped down and stood by Grandma under the two tall cypresses Grandpa Mihailo had planted long ago. They looked over the barnyard as the human tide approaching through the wheat field moved closer and closer – wailing – louder and louder.

A neighbour, a recent bride, marched through the iron gate, clutching her uplifted apron.

"She's gone!" the young woman cried, her handsome features twisted in terror. "Gone! She's nowhere. It's the gypsies, I tell you! She's gone. My God!" Her dark curly hair had long escaped the red kerchief that sat, awry, on her head.

The fine wrinkles tightened around Grandma's eyes, pulling up the loose skin on her cheeks, leaving her sun-bronzed face taut, her thin lips pale. The willow basket that seemed attached to her arm fell to the ground and rolled on its side down the grassy slope toward the rose bushes.

She placed her arm around the young woman's shoulders: "From the beginning, Roza. Sit down." Grandma pointed to a rough-hewn wood bench under the old lilac tree, her typically calm voice betrayed by a faint tremble. "Tell me. Who's gone?"

"The baby! Angela's baby! Vanished!" Roza remained standing, wild-eyed.

"Calm down, Roza dear. In your condition, you shouldn't over-excite. She must be somewhere."

Roza laced her fingers protectively over her lower belly: "How did you know?"

"You're glowing, dear. Everybody knows. We're all happy for you and Alex."

"She's gone, I tell you!" Roza repeated. "She's nowhere."

"Where could a two-year-old be gone to, dear? I'll come with you to Angela's."

"Nobody's there! Everybody's searching! My mama always said... some day those gypsies... we're searching in vain, I tell you."

"Are you sure, Roza? Have they looked – "

"Am I sure? Didn't you know? The whole village is in an uproar! Searching everywhere!"

Roza waved her hand toward the looming commotion, the pale swelling of her large breasts spilling over her low-cut dress, held together by translucent round buttons ready to pop off with every fretful word.

Grandma encircled Roza's waist and led the way toward the gate. Although the top of Grandma's head barely reached Roza's shoulder, she kept up with the young woman's stride, the bun of salt and pepper hair fastened tightly at the nape of her neck bobbing in rhythm.

Kata trotted behind, eyes glued to the gigantic fuchsia flowers and green leaves of Roza's dress, the thin fabric rising with every step, accentuating Roza's muscular calves. "The giant's wife," she muttered. "Sleeps in a beanstalk in the sky."

The chorus of sobbing voices became louder.

"Go away," Kata whispered, holding her temples, hoping to block the wailing. Shielding her eyes from the light, she observed the wave of figures silhouetted against the setting sun, trailed by long shadows, as they came into focus: familiar faces, gaunt with panic, dread, rage ... mouths wide shouting ... at the sun ... at God ... at gypsies.

In the midst of the turmoil, village elder Papa Novak was assigning tasks, his guiding voice rising over the hubbub.

"Go search the pig sty! Take two men and go! Hurry, hurry! We have much to cover before dark."

"It's done," a man answered. "I checked the closer ones. A toddler couldn't be this far."

"Turn over the straw!" Papa Novak fired commands left and right.

"I'll check the chicken coop," a woman called out.

"You two! Go look through the haystacks! Take them apart!"

"You! Check behind the barn! Climb the manure pile!"

"Has anybody been to the gypsy camp? Has anybody even looked there?" a woman cried out.

"And the three of you, go search the orchard! Sweep the tall grass!"

"God knows how far she is by now," an older woman wailed. "Crippled already. Smuggled out to another clan. Never to be found."

"They're clever that way, those vagabonds. Slippery like eels. Know how to get away with any crime," another woman lamented.

"Check the pig puddle! Poke in the mud! But careful with the pitchforks!" Papa Novak commanded as Kata watched him setting up the search parties, his gangly form towering over the crowd. He was an imposing figure with his unruly clumps of hair, bushy eyebrows and long beard snow-white against his red face, his deep-set black eyes flashing. In the midst of panic he remained calm, arms raised as if conducting an orchestra, ensuring each person followed the score.

A thunderous cracking in the sky sent tremors through the dry earth. The shouting subsided. Kata stared at the whirl of dust spiralling toward her, at the dark clouds churning above, reaching for the tossing linden crowns. Bales of hay rolled across the barnyard. Screeching geese flapped their huge wings and staggered to a lean-to against the barn. A cow mooed mournfully and a horse neighed in a prolonged quaver. As if on command, the villagers lifted their faces to the sky.

"Where on earth did this come from? Well, I'll be! All that humidity, and now this! Can't remember this much heat!"

A shower of ice pebbled the crowd, moist whiff of the storm and the musky scent of dust filling the air. People stared at one another, at the clouds, and ran toward the barn as one crack after another shattered the sky and rain poured through the screen of hail. Large puddles filled with icy marbles flooded the barnyard. Kata found herself in the barn immersed in steam rising from the many bodies that towered over her, their dankness mingling with the comforting musk of horse tang in her nostrils. Mesmerized by the storm, people stood under the shelter as they had done many times during the harvest. This time there was a shared sense of foreboding.

"An-ge-laaa! An-ge-laaa!" Roza cried, running out into the storm.

"No, Roza! Come back here!" a man bellowed.

"Stop her, Alex!" a woman yelled. "She'll lose the child!"

Bent forward against the wind, Roza ran out toward a frail young woman. All eyes focused on Angela staggering into the barnyard, rain rinsing the mud from her waist-length brown hair, from the clinging fabric of her once-white dress.

"Come inside!" Roza gripped the other woman's arm.

Angela yanked herself from Roza's grasp as if fighting off an attacker.

"Come back in, Roza," Alex exclaimed, encircling her shoulders as he drew her under the shelter.

Angela continued waving, shouting into the storm. Two men stepped out, each taking an arm, and pulled her into the barn.

"No! Oh God! My baby!" Angela screamed.

"Let her be, Ivan!" Papa Novak called out.

"Don' tell me what to do, Novak! She's my daughter, ain't she?" The older of the two men waved his cane as Angela slumped on the floor.

"She's looking for her child, Ivan," Papa Novak said. "Leave her be."

"Don' preach to me, Novak. This ain't your big city school!"

Papa Novak raised his arms in despair. A long-retired history professor at Belgrade University, most villagers still called him Professor out of respect. Ivan used it to scorn.

"We're looking at all the wrong places, Father," the younger man cut in turning to Ivan. "Let's get to the gypsy camp."

"I'll find those murderers. Who's with me?" Ivan sucked the words in through his clenched teeth, black hair like brushes poking out of his flaring nostrils. Then he spat the cud on the barn floor.

Kata peered into his face. She could not see his eyes behind the furrowed brows, just two sunken dark pits and a deep groove running down from each, liquid trickling through them as if somebody poked his eyeballs with a stick and made them leak. She shuddered and averted her eyes.

"Let's find those goddamn swindlers, those goddamn cradle robbers," two other men joined in.

Grandma put herself in front of Angela's father: "The child will be found, Ivan. Let's keep looking. The police searched the camp, I hear. Found nothing."

He rushed past her as if she were invisible. The three younger men followed.

"Let's get 'em, I say. Before they take off. I'll find that child if it's the last thing I do." Ivan nudged his son with his cane and the small army marched into the storm.

Angela ran back out into the rain. She dropped to her knees in a puddle of hailstones. With both fists, she began pounding her chest. Grasping the front of her dress, she tore it open. She continued beating her bare chest while kneeling on the ground, long strands of muddy hair hanging down her face and shoulders. Clasping her hands in prayer, she raised her face, words torn by the wind: "My baby… my baby…"

Roza lunged forward, but Alex tightened his embrace: "You must be careful, Roza." He wrapped one arm around her shoulder and with the other caressed the small protrusion of her lower belly. Her determined jaws softened into a shy smile. "Yes, Alex," she exhaled, as she looked at his face. Two young women ran to kneel next to Angela and began praying. A few others joined in. Kata stayed with the older women in the barn who were in a huddle, hands clasped, eyes upturned, lips moving. The men stood silently, some chewing long straws, and some shaking their heads in the eerie hum of whispered prayers.

Kata weaved out of the barn and knelt on the soggy patch of grass next to the women. The hailstorm had subsided, with stray pellets driving through the pouring rain and the rupture of thunder. She stared into the sky – the lightning zigzagging through the heavens, the leaden mountains receding and gathering among the shrouded giants with flashing silver prongs. She glimpsed a shadow of Saint Ilija riding his chariot, his whip snaking through the clouds, six wild horses foaming at the mouth, sparks flying from their hooves. Through the churning vapour above and under and all about him, he dispensed justice in bolts of lightning – just like the icon on Grandma's bedroom wall, next to her grandfather's portrait. She glanced at the women kneeling next to her. Do they see him? Are they not afraid of his anger? But their eyes were closed, mouths barely moving. As she looked back up, Saint Ilija had vanished, moved on with the receding thunder to unleash his wrath on other sinners. She put her hands together and began to pray:

"Please Saint Ilija, please God, find Angela's baby. I'll never sin again. Ever." Following the motions of the woman beside her, Kata lowered her head and kissed the wet ground.

Angela prayed frantically, first with chin on her hands, then beating her chest, then bending forward and kissing the ground. She seemed unaware of the sheets of rain, the thunder rumbling in the distance, and the tree branches whipping the turbulent air.

* * * *

Grandma's prayer was long that evening. In bed, her hand drooped heavily while caressing Kata's hair in tune to their bedtime song – a term they used for outgrown lullabies. Soon, Grandma's soft singing turned into noisy puffs of air. Wide-awake, Kata climbed out and opened the bedroom window, listening for the gypsy-fairy song.

But all was eerie and still. Even the crickets seemed to be sleeping. She set her fingertips on the holes of the flute and blew gently. A shriek! Horrible! Worse than the screeching peacocks. Worse than the screeching gate.

Cold sweat and shivers coursed through her body as the pounding of her own heart thumped in her head. She threw the flute out into the shadowy darkness. It hit something with a clank, followed by a cry. A baby's cry?

"Who stole Angela's baby?" she whispered. "Could it be the fairy with the beautiful singing voice?" She pressed the palms of her hands on her temples. *Stop. Stop the pounding, stop the thumping.*

It was the flute, she knew. The flute had gone bad. It no longer played beautiful tunes. But now it lay out in the darkness. It could do no harm.

All was calm again. She inhaled the freshness of the night air, stared at the stars in the pale sky, and squinted at the man in the shiny moon. Nothing but a smothering silence. Did the previous day even happen? The frantic villagers, Angela's prayers, Saint Ilija's bolts of lightning, the reaper swinging his scythe – on a Sunday?

* * * *

The next day, Kata hurried outside to help with the morning chores. But they were done. And the sun had already climbed above the tree crowns. Bathed in the morning light, Roza stood in the barnyard in a clean white dress sporting big yellow flowers and green leaves, talking to Grandma. The clean brown chickens were fighting over the worms wiggling on the washed earth; the clean white geese were flapping their huge wings. All clean and new, new and clean … did yesterday even happen?

Roza's voice rang out: "It's my little brother! My poor mama, God bless her soul, must be turning in her grave. I said I'd take care of him. Raise him like my own child. But he doesn't listen!" She was pulling Grandma by the arm and leading her toward the gate.

"Yes, yes, let's go, Roza, dear. I'll talk to them."

Roza adjusted the kerchief on her head and continued. "That brother of mine! Climbing down the well before I got there! You've got to stop this! That old well could've collapsed and buried him. And now it's Alex! Wants to climb down! He's a big man! These are old wells!"

Kata trailed a few steps behind.

"Some people are careless. A toddler could climb on a pail and fall right in the well if the lid's off." Roza led the way to a shaft framed with wide wood planks.

"You can't go down, Alex. You've done your part. And where's that brother of mine? I'll give him a piece of my mind!" Roza pushed her way through the men carrying ladders and ropes, all heading toward the well. Papa Novak walked ahead. A group of boys, with Miladin in the lead, followed closely behind.

Alex began tying together the ends of two wooden ladders. "This well's quite deep," he called out. "We'll need one more." The men attached the third one. They lowered the contraption into the well by tying it to the large plank straddling the well mouth.

"I'll go in," Roza's brother announced.

"Over my dead body!" Roza shrieked, pulling him away by his shirt collar.

"Only sixteen and older," Papa Novak cut in. "Don't worry, Roza. They began without me. I wouldn't let a 14-year-old go."

He turned to the others: "All right boys! You'll take turns. It's cold down there."

Three boys stepped out of the group, elbowing each other out of the way. Miladin jostled his way amongst them, stretching his neck, perching on his toes.

"You boys don't look sixteen to me," Papa Novak said, chuckling. "But it's mighty brave of you. You can show your courage another time."

"But I can do it! I'm not afraid!" Miladin stepped forward, with a swift glance at Kata. She turned away, pretending not to notice.

"I'm sure you can, young man. But we need somebody a little taller."

Miladin's face turned red. This time Kata made sure she met his glance.

Alex began uncoiling the rope slung over his arm: "I'll go in!"

"You're too big for the narrow bottom of the well, my son," Papa Novak said. "And a little heavy. Too much weight on the ladders."

A slender young man of average height stepped up to the task. Two men tied a rope around his waist, holding taut the other end as he began his descent into the pit.

"Angela's brother's going in first. Everybody stand back!" Alex announced. "You boys don't get any closer," he said to Miladin and his group. "And you stay here next to me," he cautioned Roza's brother.

Grandma took Kata's hand. "And why are you here, child? Forgotten you're a girl?" She pointed to Miladin's group. "Don't you even think about running through the village like those boys, led by our little Hermes."

* * * *

Kata followed her grandma's orders to avoid the search party but she could not stop thinking about it. In fact, that's all she thought about. She had never seen a dead person and the thought of being faced with the drowned body of the little girl in a flowery dress made her chest ache, her stomach churn.

A few hours later, as Kata was helping pick cucumbers in the vegetable patch behind the barn, Roza returned. Grandma looked up: "Oh, dear. I wonder if they found her."

"Nothing so far," Roza bellowed. "Angela's brother almost drowned. Sudden gush of water from an underground spring. Rose faster than you can blink. If it wasn't for Papa Novak, we would've pulled a drowned body out, all right."

Grandma crossed her heart and murmured a prayer.

Roza stepped carefully between the cucumber vines. "They're on their way here. Those boys have no fear. Still competing for the number of times they get lowered into the well – 'number of wells,' they call it. Little Miladin's the scorekeeper."

Grandma shook her head. "Boys. At least Miladin's using his math skills. Mighty clever of him."

"Not just boys! The men are at it, too! Placing bets, I tell you! Egging those boys on! Bad examples. Those men are betting on those boys' heads." Roza pulled a cucumber off a vine, wiped it on her apron, and bit off a large chunk.

"And now it's that low-life! Leading with the highest number of wells," she said as she chewed. "You know, the one that loves his beer. He'd sell his mother for a drop of home-brewed *slivovica*."

Grandma frowned: "Stefan's just a young man who's lost his way a bit, Roza dear."

Roza swallowed. "Sure! Just like his father. Drinking. Chasing after young gypsies. Besides, our village low-life is used to getting his way. Used to bullying others. Why stop him now? When he's doing some good."

Grandma compressed her lips and slanted a censorious look at her neighbour.

Roza made a sad-clown face and daintily slapped the back of her left hand with the fingertips of her right one. "Got my baby brother to place a bet for me. I bet a hen and a dozen eggs that low-life's going to win." She glanced about as if revealing a great secret. "Well, that and a pack of my favourites. Alex doesn't know. He smokes, too. He can't tell."

Grandma shook her head and pressed her lips even tighter. Then both turned toward the approaching search party.

"I better go," Roza said. "Find that poor girl, Angela. Get her to eat something. Refusing food, they say. Killing herself with worry."

Kata had a quick decision to make. *You're just a girl! Afraid to see a dead body, aren't you? Aren't you?* Miladin's taunts echoed in her head.

Kata hid behind the main house, close enough to hear the voices. If they found the body, she could scurry off without being seen. But if nothing was found, she could come out and join the onlookers. She listened to every word and every sound, ready to run at the slightest hint of being discovered. The men were pounding with something that sounded like a wooden mallet, remarking that the brick walls of the well were as strong as the day her grandfather Mihailo built them.

"Don't be afraid, Stefan, my son," Papa Novak said, "This well's built to last."

"No fear, Mr. Novak, no fear. Let's get on with it."

Kata knew that Stefan must be the man they called the low-life. Yet she sensed something enchanting in his voice, as if it drifted from a fairy tale. She could listen to this voice forever, follow wherever it went. But the voice was disappearing into the well. What if her grandfather's well wasn't that strong after all? What if it collapsed? And the voice she could follow forever plummeted into the pit, gone forever?

She listened for the voice, but all she could hear was Miladin announcing the score, laughing with his friends, showing them where to stand for the best view. She knew he hoped she would hear him bossing others about. So she remained hidden. But then she heard Papa Novak: "Anything down there, Stefan? Just drag the pail once or twice and climb up, my son. You've done your best."

She listened for a response from the pit.

"Do you hear me, Stefan?"

She thought she heard panic in Papa Novak's call. She ran out from behind the house and dashed toward the well. Two hands grabbed her just before she reached the ladder.

"Oh, no, my princess," Papa Novak said, holding her back.

She saw the top of a head with wet, curly black hair ascending from the well. Heavy eyebrows appeared above slightly blood-shot brown eyes gleaming on a wide, sunburned face. There was a charming gap between his front teeth, water streaming off his strong shoulders.

"I'm all right, Mr. Novak. Nothing down there." The enchanting voice had returned.

She gaped at his magical presence. For a moment, their eyes met.

"Don't worry, little girl," he said casually while the onlookers encircled him, patting his shoulders and offering words of praise.

She gave in to the urge to run away, as far as possible, as fast as possible. She thought she heard Miladin calling after her, but could not face the prospect of talking to anyone. Not just now, when she needed to figure out what had just happened.

I… found the voice from the well, she thought. *And the voice… belongs to a prince… from the Princess and the Frog… He is the prince. He just needed to be… kissed. He looked… with all the people gathered around him… patting… his shoulders… he looked…* lonely. She sat on her grandma's bed and, realizing she'd just uttered the word *lonely* out loud, clasped both hands on her mouth to prevent more sounds from escaping.

Then she closed the palm of her hand, smelling like the earth she had crouched on, and kissed the top of the fist. It felt smooth, so she shut her eyes and imagined that she was about to kiss her frog-prince as he ascended from the well.

She wondered what would be the best place to kiss him. Grandma had taught her never to kiss older people on the lips. *Some people are not very considerate,* Grandma had said, *but you should always turn your cheek for them to kiss and never let them kiss you on your lips. It's not hygienic.* Kata had seen grownups kiss their own child on the lips and thought it a disgusting habit. She should not imagine kissing him like that. He wouldn't like it. She considered his sunburned forehead, but then recalled Grandma kissing her on that same spot every night before going to sleep. No, that would be like being kissed by one's grandma. She could pretend-kiss him on his cheek, but then thought of her Aunt Agata who kisses everybody on the cheek so loudly the whole village can hear her. And she repeats the loud smacking of her lips, so her pale peach lipstick that smells like stale boiled eggs remains plastered on one's cheek.

Eyes still shut, she envisioned his features, searching for the spot on which to place her kiss. He had big brown eyes. Had anyone ever kissed him on his eyelids? No one had ever kissed her that way. She envisioned him again and again, ascending from the well. There was no point imagining him as a frog. His presence was deeply etched in her mind, and she did not wish to change a single thing. His eyelids were closed now and she was leaning over the ladder. She puckered her lips, and then relaxed them a little to make them feel softer. She made a gentle smacking sound on top of her tight fist. *Kissing him could be better than eating cherries,* she mused. *He will always be my prince.*

She opened her eyes and thought back on the amazing events of the day. She retrieved Grandma's rose-coloured lipstick from an armoire drawer in the guest room. Its faint scent reminded her of the rose petals in the garden that every year heralded the arrival of summer. She applied it liberally to her lips. Then expertly guiding the scissors she used for making her doll's garments, she cut a sleeve off a faded yellow shirt. Carefully, she pressed her puckered lips on the sleeve. The imprint was satisfactory. She folded the fabric and placed it in the top drawer of Grandma's dresser, adding to her collection of souvenirs.

This is my first kiss, she declared. *I will remember it, forever.*

* * * *

That evening, Grandma dunked a bouquet of dry basil in holy water and sprinkled it about the house and all over Kata while murmuring an incantation. She threw a pinch of salt over Kata's left shoulder, then over the right one, and a third toward the yard, ushering evil spirits out of the house. Thus cleansed and snuggled in bed close to her grandma, Kata recited a prayer and crossed her heart. But soon the nightmares began. First, a white bundle floating deep down in the well was calling to her, and she woke up screaming. Comforted by her grandma, she fell asleep again. But this time she saw her grandfather's well crumbling while, she knew, her prince was down in the pit. She jerked up in bed, determined to remain awake. Yet, the next moment her prince's face was ascending from the pit. She could see his brown eyes smiling through wet eyelashes. She opened her own eyes. Morning sun filled the window and Roza's voice carried clearly from the yard: "It's Stefan! That low-life, I tell you! I knew it'd be him!"

Kata ran outside, legs wobbly, breath drowning in hot air.

"It's him, all right," Roza hollered. "I won five hens and enough eggs to feed the village. And six packs. Think of that!"

"And they found nothing?" Grandma asked, cutting her off.

"Zilch! All that searching in vain. Risking all those young lives. But the low-life's now a hero. Highest number of wells."

Grandma placed her hand on Roza's arm. "Let's go over to Angela's. Let's see how that poor girl's holding up. Barely sixteen, and already been through hell."

"I was just there! Took some roast chicken to her! My Alex likes roast chicken for breakfast. And he likes my apple strudel first thing in the morning. All steaming hot, smelling heavenly, a dead man would rise from his grave for a bite. Angela didn't even look at the food or me. We used to be friends!"

Roza stuck a fork into the baked chicken she was carrying in a roaster. "Here, take this!" she said to Grandma. Then she turned to Kata, pushing the pot into her hands. "Take it in. Go eat it. While it's hot!"

Kata walked toward the kitchen, holding the roaster away from her face. She opened the oven and shoved it in. But even that wasn't far enough. So she ran outside, away from the smell of the chicken that would wake up a dead man from his grave.

"My prince is safe," she whispered. "And a village hero!" Breathing freely, she hopped on one foot a few times and then the other in make-believe hopscotch, wishing she could fly with her lungs full of sweet air.

Over the next few days, she hoped the baby would be found and the village would return to normal. But the search continued.

A sense of gloom settled over endless days of speculation, permeating the dreams that invaded her fitful slumber. She existed in an ominous never-never land, as if sinister characters from winter stories and fairytales now roamed the countryside, turning it into a realm of chaos and threat.

Chapter II

The Spring Of Bad Omens

(Spring 1960)

"I HEARD THE THUMP... I heard the thump..." Kata gasped as she ran, inhaling the morning air so crisp and thin. She envisioned it penetrating her bones, packing them with air bubbles, each stride becoming longer and longer, lighter and lighter, as if she were flying over the blades of grass slashing her bare legs. She stopped, lifted the dew-soaked hem of her dress and wiped the sweat off her face. She stared ahead at the corner of the woodlot where the soldier had been killed... and shuddered.

"Grandma will be looking for me," she said firmly and turned back along the grassy path through the field, young corn stalks barely to her knees, her once-white canvas running shoes squishing with every step. The first rays of sun flooded the fields and tinted the eastern sky a pale rose.

"I heard the thump," she whispered to the two peacocks, each a cluster of tarnished brass feathers encased in the iron gate.

She lifted the rusty ring off the gate-post and slipped it on her left arm as if it were a bracelet. She licked her index finger and rubbed it gently along the green stone-eye imbedded in the bird-head profile. Then she settled her face into a reverent pose and recited: *Open your eyes the blue peacocks of India, once made sacred to Hera, queen of the heavens, and do the fan dance!*

With both hands, she lifted the gate just high enough to clear the ground, pushed it open, and squeezed through. After replacing the ring, she gingerly brushed the palm of her hand over the green stone eye and the intricate brass train and chanted: *Go to sleep the blue peacocks of India, once made sacred to Hera, queen of the heavens.*

Stepping carefully between the clumps of dewy tulips and clusters of hyacinths in the garden, she bent down and began lifting the broad leaves and pink and blue blossoms. "Where is it? Where, where ..."

"There you are!" Grandma was holding a sack of chicken feed in her hands, ready for morning chores. "Why are you up so early, child? It's Sunday. No school." She stopped. "You're soaked. Better go and change into dry clothes."

Upon Kata's return, Grandma continued her inquisition. "Where have you been so early? And without asking." She cocked an eyebrow at her granddaughter.

Kata knelt in the garden and inhaled the familiar perfume of a blue hyacinth. "I'll put it on your dresser," she said, picking the blossom.

Grandma wiped the wood bench under the old lilac tree and sat down. "Come over here, child. Sit down. Where did you go?"

"For you," the girl said, handing the blossom to her grandma and kissing her hand. Then she snuggled close: "Please, tell the hyacinth story."

Grandma smiled, proudly. The custom of kissing the hand of the elderly as the sign of respect was an old one. Her granddaughter was one of the few village children who practiced it, willingly.

"I see you're not about to tell me, are you? Well, then, a story about Hyacinthus it is, if you promise never to run off into the fields by yourself, early like that. A *vila* could see you and cast her evil eye on you." Grandma wrapped her arm protectively around the child.

"The *vila* that dances all night and makes magic in the woods?" Kata asked.

"That very one."

"But I didn't go in the woods."

"Don't you play smart with me," Grandma said.

Her face relaxed as she explained that these stories were a little like a religion Greek people believed in a long time ago, before Christ was born. And that she added her own twists to them, just for fun.

"Once upon a time," she began, in her mysterious storytelling voice, "there lived a young man far, far away in Greece. His name was Hyacinthus." She described his beauty, which became known around the world. She told of Apollo, god of music and poetry who admired all beautiful things, and who loved Hyacinthus with all his heart. But Zephyrus, god of the west wind, fell hopelessly in love with Hyacinthus.

"What does that mean, fell in love hopelessly, Bako?"

"It means that, even if he knew that love would bring pain and sorrow, he could not stop."

"I'd like you to tell me the story in exactly the same way," Kata pleaded. "I don't like it when you change the words."

The kind face crinkled in a curious smile: "I don't change them on purpose, dear. I change them because of the way I feel at the time. Sometimes I think of my Mihailo. If I knew that he'd be killed and that I would be left alone, would I have still married him? Sometimes my own feelings end up in the story."

"And would you have, Bako?"

"What's that, dear?"

"Would you have married Deda Mihailo?"

"Yes, I would have, my love. My answer is always the same. Yes."

"Do you still miss him, Bako?"

"Every waking moment, my love."

"Even when you're telling me stories?"

"When I'm with you, my little swallow, my heart is full. But you can miss somebody and still be happy with other people. I'm always happy when I'm with you. Don't you ever forget that."

The story continued: "With Zephyrus in such a state, the weather around the world changed. It was either too cold or too hot. Like when we pray for the rain, but it doesn't come and the wheat and corn dry up. So people began praying to Zeus."

"Zeus was the most important god," Kata announced.

Grandma nodded. "Hearing so many prayers, Zeus asked all gods to investigate. But the gods knew just how much Zephyrus loved Hyacinthus, and could not snitch on one of their own. It would've been the same as snitching on one of your friends, like Maja or Miladin."

"I would never do that."

"And neither could they. Crops wouldn't grow, and famine overcame the entire earth, people dying of hunger, everywhere. As bad as the potato famine in Ireland. Worse than the Great Depression in America and Canada."

"Is that where Deda Mihailo may be hiding? America or Canada? You said so. You think he'll come back some day?"

The eyes softened: "I pray every day that he might walk through that gate and see you. He would be so proud. You are his spitting image, in body and soul, my little butterfly. You have his energy, his enthusiasm. But you also have this... this natural curiosity. It's a gift, I know. But sometimes I... worry about it."

She returned to the story: "River Acheron became jammed with souls travelling to the House of Hades. The oracle of the dead, who guarded its bank, fell into a deep sleep."

"Like our watermelon farmer? The one we saw sleeping by the Sava? Remember Bako? When you came on our school trip?"

Grandma sighed. "Ivan drinks, dear. Sleeps wherever he happens to fall, until somebody finds him and drags him home."

She continued the story: "More and more souls kept arriving and the river groaned from all the weight. Hades heard it and demanded an explanation. So the River Acheron asked Zeus to meet one of her nymphs at the dark gorge where the watercourse enters the underworld. That was a scary place. Dark and mysterious."

"I sure wouldn't want to be that nymph," squeaked Kata as she pressed herself even tighter against her grandma.

"I don't blame you. But the nymph wasn't scared of Zeus. She was at home in that dark and mysterious place. And she was very beautiful."

"As beautiful as Angela?"

"Could be, dear."

"Did she have a baby, too?"

"Maybe, dear."

"Did her baby have a father?"

"Must've. Everybody has to."

"Angela's baby doesn't have a father."

"God is her father, dear."

Grandma got the story back on track: "The beautiful nymph hoped to use her feminine wiles to soften Zeus' heart. And Zeus was very, very handsome. No woman could ever resist him."

"And why not, Bako? Why could no woman resist Zeus?"

"Hmm... You certainly know how to ask questions, my little swallow. You can add this one to your list of puzzling questions, dear. You'll understand some day. When you grow up."

"But my list is getting longer and longer. And I see no answers."

"Zeus was in one of his bad moods. He was a little like your father when he has words with your mother. Moody."

Kata shook her head to dislodge the quarrelling voices from her thoughts. "I hate it when they fight. Sometimes when I sleep in my own room I can hear them, shouting."

Silently she summarized Zeus' character: *The most important god, irresistible to women, and moody like my father*, she listed, folding a finger for each trait.

Kata held her breath. This was the part she adored – when Grandma puts on her romantic voice and describes the old willow that couldn't draw Zeus out of his bad mood.

And sure enough: "Under the gigantic willow tree with the crown reaching up to the sky and the weeping branches tickling the ripples of the river Acheron, the nymph played Zephyrus' sad love song to Zeus."

Kata closed her eyes, feeling the cool seclusion under the canopy of weeping branches, deafened by the water surging into the bottomless gorge that led to the underworld. The nymph was tiptoeing from rock to rock, swathed in mist rising above the rushing water. From somewhere far away the storytelling voice continued: "She wore …"

The nymph's transparent gown of morning dew shimmered with all the colours of the rainbow. She loosened her dark glistening hair so it fell to her knees. She sat on the rock's deep green moss and surveyed her surroundings with brilliant turquoise eyes. Raising a flute to her rosy lips, she began to play Zephyrus' sad tune.

"And what did Zeus do, you ask?" The storytelling voice interrupted Kata's vision: "Well, believe it or not, he got upset. He accused her of using her feminine wiles to soften his heart."

Kata opened her eyes as the nymph and the gorge with green moss and the rushing water and the gigantic willow tree vanished into … the underworld?

"Zeus ordered Zephyrus to resume his travels, at once. Zephyrus begged Hyacinthus to join him. But Hyacinthus preferred to listen to music, especially the lyre and the flute."

"Like the flute you gave me? The one you got from a gypsy?"

"Yes, dear."

"The gypsy who helped you when you broke your hip? The blacksmith?"

"That very one."

The story continued: "And Hyacinthus liked to read poetry, especially by Homer, just like you like to read fairytales. But most importantly, he liked doing all these things with Apollo."

"Apollo was the god of music," Kata interjected.

Grandma nodded. "He was Zeus' son. Made sure that everyone, human and divine, obeyed his father. Because, as we all know, Zeus had to get his own way."

Number four. Kata folded another finger: *Had to get his own way.*

"Apollo also talked to prophets and oracles and warned people of future events. But sadly enough, he wasn't able to foresee Hyacinthus' future."

"And why not, Bako?"

"Well, I really don't know, dear. Maybe he couldn't bear the thought of losing him. And sometimes things just happen."

Why could Apollo not foresee Hyacinthus' future? Kata resolved to add this point to her List of Puzzling Questions.

"Zephyrus became enraged with jealousy. Evil thoughts filled his soul. He tried to fight them. But the blood in his veins turned to poison. When he saw Apollo throwing a discus, he blew at it, causing it to change its course and kill Hyacinthus. From Hyacinthus' blood sprang this beautiful flower, and Apollo named it Hyacinth."

Kata knew that at this point in the story the romantic voice would drift off, and Grandma's face would slump into the forlorn look she adopted while talking about her

Mihailo. *Not the right time to ask questions about evil thoughts.* And then she heard a noise, like a bird thrashing its wings. She darted into the garden and lifted a blossom.

"I found it! It's not under the cherry tree. It's here!" Kata yelled.

Grandma approached cautiously.

"Oh! Just a dead bird."

Then she pushed the hyacinth aside with her foot and revealed a whole heap of feathers. "It's a … swallow …" she said in a faltering voice. She stared at the child. "What do you mean it's not under the cherry tree? Did you see somebody do something to a swallow?"

"No, no! I came to look for it under the cherry tree. But it wasn't there."

"Why did you come to look for it? Did you, or did someone else … who?" Grandma was not smiling. Kata wished she never had to see that dreaded look – the look that infused those kind eyes with fear.

"I thought it would be here, under the cherry tree."

"Why would you think that?"

"I heard the thump! Just before I woke up. I saw a swallow. It fell off a cherry tree. It was awful! Awful! And now, if I close my eyes …" Kata closed her eyes. "Thump! Thump! Thump!" she yelled and stamped her feet.

"You saw it fall? Just before you woke up? Are you playing games with me, child?"

"No! No! Honest, Bako …"

"Did you see it in a dream perhaps?"

"It was so real! I got up and came to look. And then I couldn't find it. And then I ran and ran … But … now, it's here …" Kata felt hot tears welling.

Grandma remained quiet, a look of dread fixed on her face.

"I touched the feathers … I touched them! I can still feel them … tickling my fingertips. They're tickling my fingertips …" Kata was stomping her feet and wringing her hands.

Grandma embraced the frightened child: "Oh, dear, dear. It's all right. It'll be all right."

"You think I would kill a swallow, Bako?"

"No, of course not. I just thought... how would you know to come and look for it? But now I think I understand."

"I know killing a swallow is a sin. Everyone knows that!" Kata said as she followed her grandma to the barn.

Grandma leaned a tall ladder against the barn wall. Carefully placing her foot on the first rung, she shook the wooden structure with both hands to make sure it was stable, and began her climb to the swallows' nests.

"Can I, please, go instead of you?" Kata asked. The only climbing Grandma ever did was the five verandah steps, always holding her lower back.

"Not this time, dear," came the answer from above. "If you touch the nests, the birds would abandon them and their young."

Grandma reached the nests clinging to the rafters over the horse trough and looked into each. She carefully removed one and brought it down. "A couple of dead young," she said and carried the nest to the fire pit in the barnyard, quick flames turning the dry little bundle into ashes.

* * * *

That morning at breakfast, Grandma made a solemn announcement: "Kata found a dead swallow in the flower garden. This is a bad omen. The second one. I don't like the looks of this."

"I'm certain you'll tell us all about the first one," said Kata's mother. Staring at her scrambled eggs, Kata knew her mother would pout her lips and flutter her eyelashes, while carelessly tossing her long hair.

"Well, that's a given, dear," Grandma said. "Don't you remember the gander attack? On this very child? If I hadn't been close by, holding that shovel..." She heaved a sigh, then continued: "That gander's been vicious this spring. Protective of its young like never before, frightened of something. If that's not an omen, a warning of some kind, then I don't know what is. They could cripple a small child with those large wings, or peck it to death."

"You've warned the whole village, I'm sure," her mother said with a smirk.

"Sure did. And people tell me their geese are nastier than ever, hissing and flapping their wings. It's a warning, dear."

As if two bad omens were not enough, a few days later Grandma saw, perched in the pine grove that sheltered the farmhouse from the fields, an owl hooting in the middle of the day.

"Everybody knows that sighting an owl in daylight forebodes death," she announced. "Animals sense danger much better than people."

Three bad omens could not be dismissed, she concluded, and became gravely concerned about impending evil. It did not escape her observant eye that two out of the three seemed linked to her granddaughter.

Her mother's answer was simple: "The girl spends all her time in the flower garden, in the barnyard, or sitting up in the tree tops. So she notices more things than anyone. It's natural."

And Kata's father, who dismissed any talk of bad omens as old wives' tales, simply put his hand out in a gesture that everyone understood to mean "stop talking."

Grandma ignored the disrespect and mocking. Her mother's commands to "stop looking for bad omens; do not fill peoples' lives with fear; leave remedies to the medical doctors" were not so hurtful compared to some others. Kata had a clear memory of one in particular.

"Keep your witchcraft out of my house, woman," an old man had growled. "An' yourself. Out of my house."

"Let go your anger, Ivan," Grandma pleaded.

"I'm the master of this house, aren't I? I decide what's done aroun' here."

"A child is a gift of God, Ivan."

"Don' meddle in my family, woman."

"Embrace your family, Ivan. Your daughter and your grandchild."

"Don' tell me what to do!"

"Your own flesh and blood, Ivan. Accept the gifts of God with grace."

"Whad'ya know about grace, old woman, 'bout God's love an' sweet Jesus? In the good ol' days, you'd be burning at a stake. Out!"

The old man stood and leaned on a cane that was slightly bowed and dotted with lumpy growths. He propped himself against the back of a chair and banged the stick on it and for one horrible moment Kata feared he would attack her grandmother. He continued hitting the chair and shouting, the din of it all thundering in her head. She closed her eyes and in her phantom vision saw his large ghostly frame looming over her, his white bones rattling like the skeleton that high school students shook to frighten first-graders.

"You better do as Father says," Angela's brother scattered the apparition in Kata's head, his voice the sound of something shattering, like a glass vase full of water that once slipped out of her hands and fell on a cement step. "Here, I'll help you out."

"I don't need your help, young man. About time you start using your own head, wouldn't you say?" Grandma stepped over the threshold, her old hen gait now spry. "Remember what I said, Ivan. A gift of God."

As they walked along the crumbling plaster wall of the house, an elderly woman poked her head out of the side window: "Thank you for helping my daughter, and God bless you," she said. Her face was a wilted version of Angela's. Her large eyes were kind, as if she were a suffering saint icon framed by the weathered window.

A few days later Angela had run over to Grandma's house, holding the baby wrapped like a mummy against her shoulder.

"Colic? All gone. Baby's sleeping all night. It's fennel tea from now on, and chamomile. Thank you."

"Give my regards to your dear mother," Grandma said and slipped a few pouches of herbs into Angela's hand.

Others were equally grateful: "That spider bite? The swelling's down." "My cow's giving more milk than ever. You're a miracle worker."

Grandma could forecast the weather by "reading" the sky and smelling the air, and she could predict events by examining her own dreams or the dreams of others. Kata observed the preparation of every concoction, the incantation of every prayer, hoping to learn the craft some day.

* * * *

Faced with three bad omens, Grandma watched her granddaughter's every move: she forbade her to go unaccompanied to the library, the village store, Miladin's house, or even to her friend Maja, who lived closest to them.

"It pretty much covers all the fun things," Kata told Maja.

And seven-year-old Maja's advice? Kata mulled it over and over, but was still unable to make sense of it: "Maybe nobody's going to die. Maybe your owl ate some coffee grinds."

"Coffee grinds?"

"That's right! From the garbage pile. Behind your barn."

Maja's words had a calming quality Kata sought, along with some sense of impossibility, a missing link that could not be grasped.

"That doesn't matter," Kata said. "Grandma knows best. An owl in the daytime? That's a bad omen."

Chapter III

Dispelling Bad Omens

As WEEKS PASSED, Grandma continued dispelling bad omens, while the whole village buzzed with the excitement of having a new bride.

Although she was local, until a few months ago she was just Roza, the handsome, hard-working daughter of a farmer at the far side of the village. But now she was Kata's neighbour. And once she was promoted to the status of a new bride, all eyes were upon her: Is she pregnant, yet? Is she a good cook? Does she keep a clean house? How is Alex treating her? Will he get used to having a woman in the house? Does he know how to be a husband?

After all, he'd never had a guiding hand. His father had been killed in the first year of the war when Alex was only four. And his mother died when he was fifteen, so he took over the farm and, with Papa Novak's guidance, had been running it for the past nine years. The pride of this village! Will she bear an heir? What an honour that would be.

And Roza? Roza surpassed everyone's expectations. She was all a wife could be: she cooked and she cleaned and baked bread in the old brick oven Alex's father built in good times before the war; she carried large pails of water for the cattle; she fed the chickens and cleaned the pigsty; she milked the cows and made cheese curd that she sold at the market in Obrenovac every Saturday; she baled hay and piled it under a thatched shelter for winter feed. She hoed and planted the vegetable garden and was already sharing young spinach with her neighbours. Her bed sheets hanging on the line were so white the passing villagers stopped their horses and buggies just to admire. She even revived the old rose beds that were once her mother-in-law's pride and joy. If only Alex's parents could see their son now, the neighbours crowed. They would be proud.

The villagers were certainly pleased with the newlyweds. That's all anyone talked about. Even Papa Novak, who dispensed praise sparingly, boasted about them. Alex and Roza, Roza and Alex, twirled in Kata's head. The importance of finding the right person to marry could not be underestimated. And very soon, Kata forgot all about the bad omens. All she thought about was whom she would some day marry.

Would I have to do all those chores? She wondered. The first time she met Roza, really met Roza – outside of seeing her in a white veil and what appeared to be a very large white dress, she was chopping the head off a beautiful red-tailed cockerel. Kata had witnessed Grandma and Mother kill a chicken many times, but she somehow managed to close her eyes and count or chant aloud until it was all over. This time, there was nowhere to run. She stood, both hands holding the warm apple cake Grandma had sent to the newlyweds.

Roza shoved the flapping bird on the chopping block. She held the chicken's head with one hand, pressed her foot on the body, swung the axe with the other hand and *thump*. Roza straightened and – severed head in one hand, foot on the feathery body with a bloody wiggling neck – said cheerfully: "Kata, isn't it? Spitting image of your mother. Grandma's princess, aren't you?"

Roza lifted her foot off the headless chicken and it began flapping about, jumping in the air and falling down like a bouncing football. She tried to catch it. Eventually, the feathery body settled on a grassy patch, twitching to the chattering of curious robins that had quickly gathered around.

Since then, Kata was hounded by the notion of having to be a bride some day and having to do all those chores if she wanted the villagers to like her. She made a mental list. She could do all of them except one: killing a chicken. Every way she imagined, it seemed dismal. She found herself awake at night, thinking of methods. She could place it on the chopping block, press her foot on the flapping wings, hold the chicken's head with one hand and the axe in the other – and close her eyes.

She now had her eyes closed and then *thump*. She opened her eyes. But instead of a chicken's neck, she saw a stump of her own bloody arm with no hand, wiggling. She screamed until someone was shaking her shoulders.

"Wake up, dear," Grandma's voice soothed. "You're having a bad dream."

Kata now began thinking of all possible excuses for not killing a chicken. But they were hard to find. And then, unbidden, the answer came to her. Grandma had invited the priest to bless the house – this was a vital step in dispelling bad omens. To thank him, she had given him a chicken.

"A well-fed one," commented the priest's helper who drove the horse and buggy and carried all the parcels of food the villagers gave to the church. "I'll get it all plucked and ready for your wife, as soon as we get home." He shoved the bird in a wicker basket and hoisted it on the back of the carriage.

"I think we'll keep that one," the priest said. "It's a young hen. Soon it'll be laying eggs."

Relieved that her chicken's life would be spared, Kata followed the priest into the house. Holding a bouquet of dry basil in his hand, he dunked it in the bowl of water provided by Grandma. He sprinkled each room, chanting in a drawn-out voice. Kata caught a few words, "Aaaall the saints... blesss this house... briiing prosperity..." while counting on her fingers how many roasted chickens could fit into the priest's large belly. All the while the helper's words, "I'll get it ready for your wife," swirled in her head.

Now, she stood very close to the priest. "Your helper always kills chickens for your wife, Father?" she asked timidly, looking up at his puffy, red face, searching for the beady eyes buried in the small head that seemed wedged into his black robe.

"Well, yes, Kata," the priest answered with a grin that lifted one side of his cheek and exposed the pointy canine in his upper jaw. Then he smiled, and to her surprise revealed a row of white teeth, unlike many other villagers whose teeth were yellowed, brownish, or missing altogether. Still holding the dripping bouquet in his hand, he sprinkled a sign of the cross over her head. He then tapped the top of her head with the same wet herb: "Clever girl. Doing God's work in this village. Reading to the elderly. We're all very proud."

"Never? Your wife doesn't have to kill chickens, ever?"

"Not unless she wants to. And I've never heard her say ..."

With a cheerful, "Thank you, Father," Kata ran off, back to her tree perch to mull over what she had just heard.

I never have to kill chickens! Ever!

* * * *

The following Sunday, dressed in a pleated navy skirt and a white blouse, a huge white bow tied at the top of her head, Kata waited to be summoned by Grandma for the weekly visits with elderly friends and relatives. She usually read newspapers to ease the burden of those with failing vision. She rather enjoyed these readings that opened doors into an adult world that seemed, often, as bizarre as fairytales. While many of the words she read were unfamiliar to her, the discussions they incited offered her a glimpse into events beyond tiny Ratari that could seem enchanting or just plain frightful. On occasion she was allowed to take certain clippings home, and some of the more interesting ones she saved in a wicker trunk under Grandma's bed.

Grandma usually brought along small gifts: homemade cookies; a bowl of fruit from the orchard; or freshly roasted and ground Turkish coffee and a small bag of sugar cubes.

"Let's go, Kata. You can read to our Professor first. Then we'll go on to the others."

Papa Novak was one of her favourite reading customers. As always, he welcomed them warmly, as if he'd been waiting for them all day. He recited his usual praises with as much enthusiasm as if it was her first visit. He stood with his right knee bent slightly forward, head held high, arms raised in wonder. He had this grand yet tragic look about him. With his bushy white hair in upright clumps, Kata thought he looked like Hamlet's father, the ghost of a murdered king in a Shakespeare play she had seen at Belgrade Theatre with her class.

"Look how you've grown up!" Papa Novak exclaimed, although only a week had passed since they'd last met. "You've been reading to us for about... two, three years now? Since you were about five years old. You are God's little miracle. Going to be important. High in society when you grow up."

And then the question came, the one Kata had been anticipating for a whole week.

Papa Novak looked at her under his furrowed eyebrows and, as every other Sunday, inquired: "And what would you like to do when you grow up, young lady?"

"I know what I am going to be!"

"You do?"

"Yes, I've decided."

"Tell us, then. We're all ears!"

She straightened up and raised her head as if about to recite a poem, and answered: "A priest's wife."

He waited as if he had not heard the answer. Then he cocked his head to one side: "What did you say, Kata?"

"A priest's wife," she repeated proudly. "I want to be a priest's wife."

He paused, and laid down his newspaper. "Well, that's an honourable … profession, now, isn't it?" His large white moustache twisted in a grin. "And why do you want to be a priest's wife, Kata?"

"Because I wouldn't have to kill chickens," she blurted out. "His helper does that. I could never, ever do that because the dead chicken would look at me with its glassy eye. The glassy eye that doesn't blink and doesn't see anything!"

"My little princess!" Papa Novak shook his head a few times. "You don't have to marry a priest just for that. You'll be living in a big city, and you'll buy your chickens all clean and ready to cook. That's what the city folk do."

"I don't want to live in a big city. I like feeding the chickens and picking cherries with Grandma and riding my horse Kidran. Aunt Agata in Belgrade has none of that."

"Nothing wrong with marrying a handsome young man of the cloth, Professor." Grandma cut in, the title high-pitched to make her point stand out. "They're good to their wives. Since they can only marry once – that's the rule of the church, as we all know. A good rule."

Papa Novak gave Grandma a perplexed look.

"Didn't you tell me, some time ago, you wanted to be a teacher, Kata?"

"Yes. But now, everybody's asking my teacher why she's not married. And when she's going to be."

"That's because that teacher of yours should marry while she's still young. While somebody still wants her!" offered Nana Novak, who had been sitting quietly in her rocker.

Kata sank into her chair. Nana Novak had a way of glancing sideways, her grumbling interrupted by guttural coughing. In her presence, Kata always felt she was in the wrong. She didn't know where to place her hands, where to look. Even while reading, she was acutely aware of the reproving looks that caused her voice to falter.

A faltering voice was something Kata feared, especially when reading to Papa Novak. Reading to him was a privilege. Unlike other elderly people, he would have already read most of the articles, eager to recount the events. Sometimes he would ask her to choose: "Now, what will it be, Kata? An editorial? An exposé?"

Then he would quiz her to ensure she remembered the meaning of these words. On other occasions, he would ask her to read a particular excerpt he thought she would find interesting. And to her surprise, the stories he pointed out were most challenging and amusing. She sometimes wondered why he would ask her to read those articles he'd already read. Once, she found the courage to ask. His answer was equally puzzling.

"Every piece of news, every story, takes on a different meaning when read by a different person. I like to see your reaction to the events." But what pleased her most is when he added, with a wink: "And most of all, I like hearing the music behind your words, my little princess."

Ever since then, Kata had been acutely aware of the sound of her voice. She practiced, reciting passages aloud, listening for the music. But she could not hear it. Nevertheless, knowing that he did made her feel as if she could fly, as if she had magical powers no one knew about.

"And what's wrong with marriage, Kata?" Grandma asked. "Everybody has to marry, some day."

Grandma taking Nana Novak's side? Kata felt her chest squeezing the air out. Not letting any new air in. She may not be able to emit any sound.

"Nothing's wrong," said Nana Novak on Kata's behalf. "You're one of the lucky ones. Miladin comes from an old, well-off and respectable family. It's all arranged."

Kata's face felt scalded, as if she were one of the Roman snails she'd seen Grandma drop in boiling water in preparation for a special dish. She recoiled into her snail shell, feeling only her eyelids blinking. She could say nothing, nothing.

"Old customs!" Papa Novak said. "Who follows them? Have you forgotten when we were young, Nana?"

"Miladin's a good boy," Grandma said. "But I wouldn't let my girl near that family, seeing his poor mother. A slave to all of them."

"You know about that, Bako?" Kata heard her voice, like the air escaping from the snails in boiling water.

"Know about what, dear?"

"Miladin's mom. I saw it."

"Saw what, dear?"

"The door was open. I heard his dad shouting. But I walked in, just in the doorway. Then I saw his mom wiping the blood off her mouth. Her eye … all blue and swollen. Then his dad was shouting again. I ran …"

The others listened intently with leaden faces.

Grandma was the first to speak: "That's one troubled family. I've talked to Miladin's father. He says a wife shouldn't provoke. Vera provoke him? That poor woman …"

"It's the *slivovica* doing all the damage," Papa Novak cut in.

"She left him a few times," Nana Novak added. "Vera. Left the kids."

"I told him to stop drinking," Papa Novak scoffed.

"She came back pretty quickly. Each time."

"Missed those darling children. Who wouldn't?"

"There's your value in marrying a priest. Has to be good to his wife."

Grandma propped her arms on her hips. "My dear Lord! Is this called progress? So many drunks and wife abusers. Our young girls fear for their future instead of looking forward to it. My Mihailo was what I call a real gentleman. Never so much as raised his voice at me. Brought me little gifts, even flowers from the fields. 'A flower for my flower,' he'd say. Brought silk for my dresses from abroad. I still have some in the armoire, wrapped up with sprigs of lavender to save from moths. When you're older, Kata, we'll make a dress for you from Grandpa's silk."

Kata realized that a long rehashing was on the horizon.

"My Mihailo. At least if I found his body I could give him a proper burial, to have a grave to visit. Instead, I sit at an empty grave! I talk to an empty grave!"

* * * *

"Your empty grave," Grandma sighed and passed her hand along Grandpa's headstone, "waiting for me. Waiting to relieve the burden of this life." She handed Kata a few candles to be lit. They recited prayers and sprinkled wine over the crumbled earth and the coarse grass and the wild pink carnations with powdery leaves. This was Saint Ilija's day, Grandpa Mihailo's patron saint. Grandma spread out a linen tablecloth from her hope chest and set places for three, complete with silver cutlery she'd hidden from the communists. Then came the food – cabbage rolls and roast chicken and freshly baked apple cake. They dined from their own plates as well as the absent Grandpa's while Grandma reminisced about the good old days.

Roza approached, walking between mounds and tombstones. "So many people, like a fair. My poor mama and papa must be smiling in their graves, God bless their souls. To see all their neighbours." She laughed and scorned at once, and Kata wasn't sure whether to smile or look sad. Which was appropriate? So she picked up a piece of cake and offered it to her.

Roza's eyes flashed with fear: "No! Take that back the same way!"

"Never pass the food over the grave, dear," Grandma said. "That's a bad omen. Somebody could die in the family, or in the village."

Roza propped her hands on her hips. "Now, circle the grave three times, and keep your eyes downcast 'til you're done. Or the first person you look in the eye is doomed, my girl."

Kata did as she was told, and when she stopped and looked up, she met Angela's gaze.

Roza stepped up to the approaching woman and placed her arm around her shoulder: "Let's go visit your dear sister's grave."

Angela nodded, her arms crossed on her chest, shoulders slumped. The two walked away, stepping over the mounded earth as Roza's voice trailed over the headstones: "Her blessed soul in heaven soaring like a swallow…"

* * * *

Grandma heaved a sigh then continued. "Some people think he was killed by the Nazis for hiding our Jewish friends, the lawyer's family from Obrenovac."

"The communists, Jovanka," Nana Novak said. "Many people think so. Easier to confiscate his land that way. Agrarian Reform."

"The same people who professed progress? Freedom and equality for all? What equality? What progress? Drunkards and wife abusers. And killing my husband who stood for truth and hard work." Grandma scoffed at no one in particular. "But if it's the Nazis, well, that wouldn't surprise me. If they could execute thousands, including school children in Kragujevac…"

Kata closed her eyes, pressed her hands over her ears, and blocked the words out. But the vacuum cracked and let another voice in – her teacher's. It was her grade one excursion.

Some of these pupils were your age.

In the darkness of her vision, the tombstones glittered in the autumn sunshine, as far as her phantom eye could see.

They were marched out of their classrooms, lined up, and shot. The teacher's voice rang out, clear as a church bell. *It was in retribution. That means punishment, for the ten Nazi soldiers that were killed in this area. And the twenty wounded.*

A hundred people for every dead soldier. Fifty for every wounded. But here, in Kragujevec, they killed five thousand. That's five and three zeros. The voice was firm. *We all must remember the date, October 21, 1941.*

"October 21, 1941. Five and three zeros." Kata never forgot.

No end to the tombstones. Everywhere. Some huge, shiny ones. Black granite, the voice had said. *Letters of the alphabet, scribbled: a, b, c. Notes, 'I love you, mom.' 'Don't forget me, dad.' Poems beginning with, 'Here lies little Nada,' 'Here lies little David,' 'Here lies little Kata.'* Kata remembered the first four lines on that tomb:

as the winds blow
the rain and the snow
my heart will sing
waiting for the spring

And then four more that she had unsuccessfully tried to forget:

but the spring won't come
into my tomb
and the birds won't sing
the upcoming spring

" – hustled the children and the teachers from their classrooms, and shot them," Grandma's voice jogged Kata back to the present, "and anyone else they found, whole families. While the world watched. As if there was no God. And no laws of humanity."

Kata surveyed her surroundings. Nana Novak was scrunched up in her rocker, eyes half closed. She was shrunken, her breathing raspy like a cat-purr. Most of the time she said nothing. Then she would cut in as she pleased. Will she say something? Even her hurtful words would be better than having to remember the other four lines in the song – the four lines that burrowed their way into Kata's mind – *the four lines that do not even exist* – *unless I let them in. Unless I let them be remembered.*

"If it's the Nazis that killed my Mihailo, than somebody in this village must've snitched."

Grandma's voice was stronger. "Our families have lived in this village for centuries. And if I'm breaking bread on Mihailo's Saint's Day with the scum that snitched on my husband and had him killed, with his murderer, well, that's worse than death. I'd like to at least know who my enemies are. But what vexes me is that he allowed himself to be killed, by anyone.

"'Go hide, Mihailo. Like so many others,' I said to him.

"'Why should I hide? I've done nothing wrong, Jovanka, my dove.'

"'Men are vanishing, Mihailo. Men of position. Wealthy men, like you.'

"'And admit to guilt? I am an innocent man.'

"'People know, Mihailo,' I told him. 'They know about Braća Baruh. They know you were friends with Boro. About your involvement with the choir.'

"'This is our village, my dove. Our home. We're simply helping friends.'

"I thought he was the smartest man on earth. Too clever to allow himself to be killed... and leave me here... and break my heart, forever."

Papa Novak had heard this recital before. As always, his expression swung between sorrow and pity, but with such tenderness that Kata felt as if she could hear his heart cracking.

Grandma sighed. "Who am I to complain, stir up old anguish, again and again? You lost the apple of your eye, your heart and your soul."

Papa Novak lowered his gaze, his features set in a sadness Kata had not seen before, as if in the last few moments he had aged 100 years.

"The price of war is our children, my dear. We pay with our children. That's the price of war." His voice was glacial.

"I have a tummy ache. Please, Bako, can we go home?" Kata asked.

"Yes, dear. You can read next Sunday. We get carried away. Old people, old wounds."

Relieved, Kata bowed to Papa Novak and kissed his hand. As usual, he also bowed to her, bashfully, his kind eyes smiling, as if none of the war-talk had happened.

And then came time for Kata, forced by custom, to kiss Nana Novak's hand. This part she minded. Bitterly.

Every other time she somehow managed by closing her eyes, thinking happy thoughts. But so far, this day had been dismal. Images of Miladin's mother's bruised eye, of the empty hole in the ground below her grandfather's tombstone waiting for Grandma, of a war-devil killing children, mingled in her head.

Cautiously, she approached Nana Novak's rocking chair. Her eyes focused on the arm in a brown sweater that resembled a crocheted tablecloth, with a dark navy shirt sleeve protruding from it, with another brown shirt sleeve peeking out from the navy one and from it a skinny, leathery hand with two prominent black moles. Gazing at the moles, Kata moved her face, ever so slowly, toward the hand. She could see the knotted blue veins bulging through the leathery skin littered with brown patches. On the index finger, the nail that had remained black since last summer had grown even longer. Now it seemed to have curled under, looking more like the black claw of a strange animal Grandma called a pig turtle, the one Kata and Miladin had pulled out of a mud puddle in the marsh last spring. She remembered Grandma saying that they should not have stuck their hands in the deep mud, that they could have been bitten. And when Kata had asked if anyone had ever been nipped by a turtle, Grandma had sighed and said: "Do you want to be the first one?"

As she got closer she could smell the putrid warmth of cooked cabbage that always clung to Nana Novak. Now, it reminded her of the stale mud hiding the turtle. She recalled that the turtle did not even have the bony shell she'd seen on other turtles. Instead, it had a leathery back with crusty patches, just like the hand she was about to kiss. And then she saw the black claw move.

I can't kiss the turtle! She screamed, and ran out of the house.

At home she hid under the bed in the guestroom – and waited. She knew the drill.

Grandma would come home and look for her everywhere. She would call her name, first from the flower garden, then from the dining room next to the guestroom. With sighs of exasperation, she would walk in, sit on the bed, and then explain to the flowers on the table, or to Kata's portrait on the wall, or to Kata's doll, how the granddaughter Grandma is so proud of had embarrassed her today. She would list all the things the girl did wrong. Then she would make clear how things should have been done. Then she would offer forgiveness, if only the child would promise never to do bad things again.

Kata knew this was her cue. She would give her word from under the bed. Then she would sheepishly crawl out. She would be asked to repeat, word by word, what it was she had agreed to. After all the proper words were recited, freshly baked cookies and linden tea would be served.

This time, however, was going to be different. Kata knew that she could not promise to kiss Nana Novak's hand the next time, or ever again.

So she lay under the bed, her back stretched on the wood planks, listening to the voice from outside.

Grandma is under the cherry tree, the young one by the guest-house window. Now in the dining room. Now at the door. The doorknob squeaked. Kata turned on her side facing the door and listened. The beige-socked feet on the pine planks headed toward the bed. They stopped near Kata's head.

Sit on the bed, Grandma! Sit on the bed!

But the feet turned away and headed toward the door. Kata froze. *I won't even have the chance to explain. Is she never going to forgive me? Did I embarrass her that much? I'll promise to kiss the stinky turtle, even if it bites my face.*

She was about to crawl out, when the footsteps stopped. She held her breath. The feet turned around, ever so slowly, and headed toward the bed again.

Grandma sat on the bed and in a calm voice announced: "From now on, my granddaughter does not have to kiss anybody's hand. It's a new world now. And some of the old customs are just that, old. Not all, just some. Are you happy with that Kata?"

"Yes! Yes!" The voice shouted from under the bed.

Chapter IV

The Dancing Bear

THE SUMMER OF 1960 arrived, and so far the bad omens had remained just that. Grandma was relieved. But she was still watchful. After all, three bad omens called for three times the caution. Since then, the priest had blessed the house three times and had concocted three bowls of holy water. Grandma had been dunking the bouquet of dry basil into the bowl, motioning a sign of the cross, and casting droplets all around the house and the barn, cleansing all.

She sprinkled the gander that now hissed very seldom; the young goslings that were catching up in size with their mother; the swallows' nests under the barn roof; and even the pine tree where the owl had been spotted. Kata received the cleansing every morning and evening, before kissing the dark wooden cross engraved with Jesus' image and sipping a teaspoon of the same holy water from the white bowl. All the while Grandma whispered prayers, her lips moving silently wherever she went, whatever she did. She made sure that her granddaughter made the sign of the cross without shortcuts – pressing the thumb, the index finger and the middle finger together, then touching her forehead, her belly button, the right side of her chest, and the left side of her chest, all in that order.

Grandma was pleased – it all seemed to be working. Gradually, she relaxed the rules. Kata was allowed to visit friends. Since the summer break had begun, she was even allowed to go to the library and the village store on her own. But the daily rituals continued and the bowl of holy water remained on the table.

The wheat harvest was on. The gargantuan thresher had begun its deafening journey from farm to farm. At the outskirts of the village, it was already gathering the early grain. For the next month, everyone would keep track of the thresher's whereabouts. Helping hands moved along with it, taking on tasks that were assigned and reassigned from one household to the next.

Women took turns preparing food. All who came along with the thresher, including the ragged hordes of children, were fed well. The farmers in line for the thresher counted the number of days left to complete the harvest. Scything was now the main priority. A dozen or so reapers swung the long curving blades with their wooden handles, cutting the large fields, waves of wheat rising and falling like a sea of gold.

Kata, who had just celebrated her eighth birthday, was assigned a new chore. She carried pitchers of water straight from the well to the fields. She watched the reapers stop to cool down, taking long swigs, spilling the dregs onto the stubble for good luck. They mopped the sweat from their brows. Some drew stones from their pouches and whetted the scythe. Others rolled the wheat between their palms, blew off the chaff and bit the grain. They nodded at each other and spoke in low grunts that rose from some deep pleasure within as if the earth was proclaiming God's blessing.

"Kernels full, healthy."

"Plenty of sunshine."

"Just enough rain."

Talk buzzed about the upcoming fair in Obrenovac. The wheat harvest had an air of festivity with the villagers welcoming the respite from everyday chores. Kata knew that any day now gypsies would begin setting up caravans of horse-drawn carts in the countryside. In Ratari, they usually camped by the crumbling bridge over the creek that drained into the river Sava. During their stay, some of the gypsies attended the fair, peddling their wares. Others went through the village and, for a small fee, offered to read fortunes or play a song on their violins.

It was early Friday afternoon and Kata's parents had already left for the market in Belgrade. She was in the courtyard, using a small willow basket to collect rose petals for flavouring preserves. Once in a while, she glanced at her grey tabby, Remi, dozing on the wooden bench under the lilac tree. He was on his back, legs spread wide shamelessly, exposing soft white fur on his belly, with white front paws bent as if they were broken: the left paw was carefully placed over the left eye and the right paw over the right eye. His flat, grey nose with black dots and pink nostrils encrusted with dry milk appeared squashed between the paws. His plump body seemed to be spilling over one side of the bench, as if at any moment it would tumble off into the dusty hollow beneath. But he seemed unconcerned, snoring, his long white whiskers dancing to the tune of the chirping crickets.

Kata heard the gate squeak and saw Miladin approaching. With a finger across her lips she whispered, "Shhh." But he paid no attention.

"I saw a dancing bear!" Miladin exclaimed.

Remi opened his eyes and yawned lazily. He hopped off the wooden bench, twitched his whiskers, and glared.

"You woke him up," she hissed.

"Didn't you hear me? I saw a dancing bear!"

"You saw what?"

"Twice! I saw it twice today! I saw *cigani*, you know, gypsies. With their wagons and the whole thing. And they have a dancing bear."

Kata pressed both hands on her chest, trying to stop the loud thumping of her heart. She didn't want to give Miladin the satisfaction of knowing he had brought exhilarating news.

"Some people gave them eggs and bread," he said as he stomped his feet and strutted along the rose garden, imitating the dancing bear. "So the bear can dance. But they want a chicken. You think your grandma – "

Kata could no longer contain her excitement: "She will! I'm sure."

The two now had an urgent agenda. They found Grandma. She nodded in agreement, and the three went off into the barnyard. Kata and Miladin poured some dry corn kernels into the tin feeder. They threw handfuls of the corn up in the air. From all around the barnyard, the chickens ran toward them, clucking excitedly. Miladin quickly closed the gate, and they now assessed several young fowl they had trapped.

Grandma pointed to the one with a clump of upright burgundy feathers, tipped with black, at the top of its head. "Let's catch that one."

The cockerel began to crow, walking sideways with head tilted, puffing its wings and circling a cluster of young hens.

Miladin was imitating the cockerel, puffing out his chest and crowing. "I want an old *Ciganka* to tell my fortune."

"Fortune-telling? For you? I think not! My mama, God rest her soul, always said those swindling gypsies will do anything! To sway your young mind! To get into your pocket!" Grandma, Kata, and Miladin turned, startled. Roza was standing behind them, hands in a red apron.

"Didn't see you coming," Miladin said, frowning.

"Little Miladin," Roza stretched the words as if she were tasting them. "Showing off. In front of a girl."

"And look at you!" She now turned to Kata and feigned a spitting: "Tpp! Tpp! Tpp! A young chickadee! Don't you let any gypsy cast the evil eye on you, you hear?"

Roza walked over to the fire-pit Grandma used for cooking poultry-feed. She scraped some ash with her index finger and drew a stripe across Kata's forehead. "This will ward off the evil eye."

"Here, Roza," Grandma called. "Help me get that cockerel, will you?"

"You wouldn't want any gypsy boy looking at her," Roza said. "Casting his spell with a love potion. I know a woman, got a headache potion from a gypsy. Made with water from many wells. And some bird spit and a feather from a swallow's nest. Worked like a charm. No headache, ever. They have a love potion…"

"No worry, Roza, dear, about an evil eye, or a potion," Grandma replied. "They have better things to do."

Roza looked uncertain. "No harm in making sure! My mama always said they have their place in this world. And we have ours. As long as we all know our place and don't mix."

With Roza's help, they cornered one of the cockerels. It offered little resistance as Grandma tied its legs with twine, placed it in a wicker basket, and fastened the lid. The rooster squawked and thrashed about. It tried to crow, but only a muffled croak escaped from the basket.

"You could sell this cockerel for 2000 dinars, instead of giving it to those lazy gypsies," Roza continued: "Used to work for my papa, God bless his soul. Those vagabonds. Hoeing and weeding the corn. Ate more than their labour's worth. Brought whole families. Sang and danced all night. But the next day, in the field? Moved like snails."

In the distance, they heard a man's voice bellowing" "Dancing bear! Come and see the dancing bear! This is your lucky day!"

Kata and Miladin ran toward the approaching band of gypsies.

"Over here! Grandma wants your bear to dance!" They shouted as they raced along the rutted path toward the road that snaked from one farm to the next. Grandma opened the wide wooden gate leading to the yard and waved the procession in.

Kata and Miladin strained to see the star of the show, the Dancing Bear, encircled by the cheerful band of gypsies. Children of various ages ran alongside the group, barefooted, some wearing only shorts, their long hair bouncing around suntanned faces. Two women held a wooden stick suspended between their shoulders. Colourful cloth bundles tied in a knot were slung over the stick, the bulging contents swinging to and fro.

Other women strode along in colourful dresses and skirts, their dark long hair hanging loosely or carelessly looped in buns or ponytails. One propped a toddler on her hip, supporting its back with her hand. She was chatting with another woman carrying a straw basket, the type villagers used for carting groceries. Another toddler's cherubic face and round little arms protruded from the basket.

A third woman wore a flowery frock. The top part of her bodice was unbuttoned and her right breast hung out with a baby's mouth firmly attached to it. It was difficult to tell where the baby's chubby cheeks ended and where the plump breast began. With her arm the mother easily supported the baby's weight, as if carrying a loaf of bread. Chatting happily with another woman alongside her, she kept gesturing with her left arm as if unaware of the cargo on her right one.

Kata stared at the untanned part of the woman's breast. She had seen women nursing many times before, but usually while reclining comfortably in a sofa or a chair. This woman seemed oblivious to the baby on her arm. Yet suddenly, she lifted the baby up, pushed her breast inside her bodice, and without bothering to button up, propped the baby on her left shoulder and gently patted its back, while continuing her chatter. A few moments later, she placed the baby in the straw basket that had been slung on her arm, and supported the basket on her hip.

"Look at that baby! Fresh like an apple! Plump like a dumpling!" Roza laughed joyously as she ran out toward the road, waving the neighbours in. Kata thought it strange that Roza's voice was not scolding, not even a tinge.

As the group got closer, the rattle of the chain and the metal caught Kata's attention. Two men held the two chains fastened to a metal rod that led the large, brown bear walking sluggishly in the middle of the group. The rod was attached to a metal collar around the bear's neck. A burly, middle-aged man in faded black pants held one chain. The upper part of his body was clad in a tattered leather vest over bare skin. He was covered in dust from head to toe, as if someone had sifted dry earth over him: particles clung to his chest hair, his wide black moustache, and the tangled dark hair protruding from under a brimless felt hat.

A golden eye feather? From Hera's peacock? Kata could not believe her eyes. An iridescent blue and green peacock feather poked through a rip in his hat crown. In his other hand, he held a wooden stick striped by freshly peeled bark. His gait was confident, head held high, a mischievous shine in the dark eyes. Insolence shaped his proud face, and his demeanour exuded energy and strength – all fairytale-like under a frosting of brown dust. Kata instantly named him Gypsy King.

The crowd with two horse-drawn gypsy carts entered the barnyard, Roza close behind waving her hands and shouting: "Menagerie, menagerie, they're here!" A train of village children followed, most barefoot and scantily dressed. If Kata hadn't recognized their faces, she would've thought they were part of the gypsy band. Other neighbours neared, calling out and waving for yet others to join them.

Gypsy King raised his head and assessed the gathering. He handed the stick to the older man beside him who'd been holding one of the two extensions of the chain.

Gypsy King passed the chain from his right hand to the left. He flexed the bulging muscles of his right upper arm on which a tattoo of a dancing bear was etched, with the word *GRIZZLY* vertically next to it.

Miladin grasped Kata's arm. "Look at that tattoo! Look at *GRIZZLY* on that *Cigan's* arm! Those muscles, they're huge!"

And then, below Gypsy King's prominent nose and drooping moustache, a broad smile showcasing a glint of gold tooth greeted the crowd. Kata wondered how such a fierce face could radiate such a welcoming grin.

"My name is Grizzly, and this is my little brother, Hungaro," he announced in a deep voice, pointing to the man next to him. "That's not really his name, but we call him that 'cause he was born in Hungary. Some people like to call 'im Scarecrow." He glanced sideways at his audience as the villagers broke out in a wave of laughter. Hungaro shook a clenched fist in mock threat.

"I'm also big brother of Wild Bear," Grizzly continued, pointing to the chained bear. "I rescued him as a cub and we've been together ever since. This wild beast has a gentle soul. And he'll dance for you if you ask him."

The children shouted: "Dance, bear! Dance!" They frantically elbowed each other for a closer view.

Grizzly raised his hand and shouted: "Please, parents! You must keep your children at a safe distance! I said he's a gentle soul, not a lamb! He's a wild animal and his name is Wild Bear for a good reason!"

"Dance, Wild Bear! Dance! Dance!" squealed the village children.

"I'll sing him a song," Grizzly said, "and this magnificent, majestic bear ... yes, I said this majestic bear, will dance for you!"

Hungaro, holding a chain section in one hand and the wooden stick in the other, stood on guard, glancing watchfully over the growing crowd of villagers. He smiled the same broad smile as Grizzly, but there were dark gaps where teeth once stood.

And then all eyes were on Grizzly, who stood poised, *like an actor performing on a stage*, Kata thought. He raised a hand above his head and snapped his fingers. Two musicians stepped up, one with a fiddle and the other with a flute. They began playing lazily, then suddenly quickened their pace. Another musician, walking a large double bass that appeared taller than him, joined the duo. The music subsided to a near-whisper, and Grizzly's deep voice filled the air:

dance for me, my wild bear
dance with your body, dance with your soul
dance with all your wild mighty
until your spirit starts to soar

Slowly, the bear lifted a paw off the ground.

dance for your mighty master and his sons
his dutiful wife, her frail sorrow
dance for his bashful, innocent daughter
his morning glory, his virginal swallow

The bear lifted a second paw, first unsteadily, and then more assuredly.

and if your heart was to break and fall
dance with your heartless, divine soul
dance until your master's soul is high
until the swallow soars in the sky

The bear was now standing on its hind legs, shifting its large mass from one foot to the other.

and if the swallow's heart was to break and fall
dance for her heartless divine soul
dance until your master's soul is high
and your divine roar fills the sky

The crowd was hollering, laughing, clapping, and shouting:

"Lift the other one, bear!"

"Dance like this, bear!"

"You crazy, crazy bear! Dance, dance, dance!"

The village children were jumping up and down, contorting their limbs and faces while trying to follow the rhythm. Kata stared at a four-year-old who was screaming and rolling in the dust. She thought at first he was throwing a tantrum, then realized he was laughing. The frenzied audience clapped and shouted more instructions to the bear.

The gypsy group huddled to one side, some swaying to the music. Their children sat on the ground, cross-legged, their tanned, slender bodies pressed tightly against the adults' legs.

Hungaro stood before the bear. With one hand he waved his wooden stick as if it were a baton and he a concert conductor, while with the other he held the metal rod with the chain attached under the bear's muzzled chin, forcing it to keep its head raised.

"Look at those flies under the bear's chin! You see it?" Miladin shouted over the noisy crowd, as he poked Kata with his elbow.

"That poor, poor, bear! What is that?" She yelled back into his ear and pointed at the festering sore, wet fur smudged in gooey yellowish substance, covered in a swarm of flies.

"Maybe it's from that metal thing," he shouted back. "Somebody said that's a muzzle, so the bear can't bite."

From the swarm of people, a cane eased out toward the bear. The next moment, it stuck out farther, poked at the bear's chin and landed on the sore. The bear's roar cracked through the chorus of Grizzly's song, the bass's thump and the villagers' laughter.

The bear lifted the front paws even higher and growled again. Then it dropped first one paw and then the other and yanked at the chain. The three men holding the chain stumbled, before quickly regaining their balance. Two others rushed to their aid. They led the bear into the large cage on wheels.

"Who did that to the bear?" Kata shouted angrily. Without a word, Miladin turned and ran from the crowd.

"Come back," she called after him. "Stop hiding."

Grizzly was no longer singing. With clenched fists, he was advancing toward an old man who was limping away, thumping his cane on the dry earth. Grizzly caught up to him and grabbed him by the shirtsleeve. Another gypsy seized Grizzly's arm as two others placed their hands on his shoulders, pleading restraint.

The old man straightened up and waved the cane in his raised hand. Another villager stepped in and clutched the stick just before it could land on Grizzly's head.

Papa Novak made his way among them and placed his arm on the old man's shoulder: "Come now, Ivan. Let's talk like men, let's reason."

A young man ran through the gate and pushed into the crowd: "You'll pay for that, gypsy! For attacking my father!" Angela's brother's voice rose over the throng like a trumpet. He grabbed Grizzly by the shoulder. Two villagers took hold of the young man's arms, trying to calm him down. The whole group shifted to the side, shouting.

Papa Novak raised his hands above his head: "Hold it, now! Hold it!" He let go of Ivan and turned to the crowd encircling the shoving trio. The group parted and let him in, threatening voices yielding to calm. He patted Angela's brother's shoulder. "Help your father home, son. Don't start a brawl."

The young man shook off Papa Novak's arm and walked off brusquely. Papa Novak turned to Ivan, led him to a tree stump and pushed him gently down. He seemed to be comforting him.

Kata peered at the burled knots on Ivan's cane, the same one that poked the bear's chin. *Why is Papa Novak comforting*

Ivan? Why isn't he upset at him? She spotted Roza talking to a neighbour and joined them.

Roza waved her arm toward Ivan: "Broken-hearted. Shamed. By his own daughter."

The neighbour nodded. "Disgraced her father, Angela did, and with a gypsy, they say."

"Lost her chastity."

"No decent man will marry her."

Roza fluttered her fingertips on her chest, daintily, face beaming. "My Alex got himself a virgin bride. A cherry. Everybody knows."

"That we do, my dear sister," the other woman said, boasting. "We saw your white sheets with your blood on them, waving in the breeze." She waved her hands in the air, simulating the wind. Kata moved closer to Roza, ensuring she did not miss a word of this *forbidden* talk.

The neighbour pointed to Angela. "There she is now, trying to console her poor father. Should've thought of him before she gave in to desire."

Angela took her father under the arm and, with Papa Novak's help, walked him through the gate. The whole time Ivan waved his cane angrily.

Roza leaned over and whispered to the neighbour: "Killing a gypsy. The only way, people say, to avenge his daughter, to reclaim her honour. *His* honour."

The musicians changed their tune and quickened the pace as another fiddler joined them. The melody rose as the instruments blended in harmony, weaving a tempestuous tune Kata had not heard before. A young gypsy woman pulled the elastic off her loosely-tied bun and shook long, dark hair that fell to her waist. She flipped the hair away from her face and preened, using her whole body. With a few quick steps, she edged into the circle where the bear had danced, hands raised above her head and fingers snapping. Everyone turned her way. Then she swished her skirt, revealing multicoloured layers along the bottom that resembled a dahlia blossom. A bare-chested gypsy man stepped up, replicating her brisk steps in time with the melody. The woman began to sway her hips and thrust her breasts forward. The tune was hypnotic, and Kata wished it would go on forever. The man followed the woman's steps, rhythmically, one moment facing her and the next striding to her side, his muscular arms and chest gleaming with sweat. They trailed each other, holding their gaze, as if one dancer's vision flowed from the other dancer's eyes.

Roza stood with her bare feet in dust, hands propped on her hips, eyes focused hard on the dancers. She leaned over to a neighbour. "See him? Eyes like a devil." She thrust her chin toward the dancers. "Must be careful not to look a gypsy in the eye or you get weak in the knees."

Kata stood on tiptoes to see the man's eyes, but he was turned the other way.

"See her, the dancer?" the neighbour said to Roza. "A gypsy, yes, but still a woman, can't resist him."

Roza shuddered. "Whooo! Gives me the shivers just to think. They can read your mind. Make you do things you'd never do. You'd rather burn in hell. But you'd do anything... when you're under their spell."

She swayed one shoulder then the other, quickening her pace to follow the dancers' rhythm. Then she caught herself and stiffened. Crossing her arms tightly across her ample bosom she whispered to the neighbour: "They say, that one, with the devil's eyes, is the father."

"Whose father?" Kata asked.

"Angela's baby. Who else?" Roza snapped. "You're just a girl. Shouldn't listen to grownup talk."

The villagers egged the dancers on, some stamping their feet to the tune, some humming, and some calling out, "Flamenco! Flamenco!" One elderly farmer was shouting "cha cha cha!" while dancing in circles, fingers snapping. With the farmer's checkered brown shirt hanging loosely over brown pants, Kata thought he resembled the bear more than the dancers. Other farmers were leaning on shovels and rakes, laughing and clapping.

Kata stared at her neighbours' faces, all parched from the sun, a jumble of grins with white and yellow teeth and dark gaps, faces she'd always known. Then she glanced at the group of gypsies who weren't dancing, huddled around a few baskets, each filled with a baby. Their tanned faces were also parched and smiling – the same jumble of grins, the same white and yellow teeth and dark gaps.

They don't look scary, the gypsies. I am not afraid of them, of the stories. They look the same as ... Roza ... or any of the neighbours.

Through the mingling crowd, she spotted the lone figure of a boy – no, young man. His black, unruly hair cascaded in ringlets to his shoulders, some drooping over his face. He pushed his hair to one side enough to show one eye – the green of oak leaves high up in the tree crowns at Vila's Circle. The narrow bridge of his nose arched over thinly drawn lips the colour of overripe cherries. A square chin with a deep dimple heightened his angular features.

"Go and mix a pitcher of cherry juice, Kata," Grandma's voice interrupted.

Kata stared, blankly, as if the voice was coming from far away.

"Go, go, and hurry up! Bring it out, quickly!"

Kata ran through the barnyard to the kitchen. She found the pitcher and a bottle of sour cherry syrup. She was glad the water pail was nearly full, saving her the scary task of having to draw water from the well.

Between each pour of the red drink into glasses, she craned her neck hoping to catch a glimpse of *him*. But he was nowhere to be seen as the grownups were taller than her and tiptoeing through them only yielded a better view of their necks. She ran back to drop off the pitcher in the kitchen. Taking a shortcut, she jumped over the rocks bordering the fire-pit in the barnyard. The next second she was sprawled on the cracked earth, a sharp pain piercing her shin. The shattered fragments of the pitcher were scattered about, as the last drops of red liquid rolled into wobbly bubbles of ash and dust.

"Are you hurt, little girl?"

"Can you stand on your leg?"

Kata tried to look up, but, blinded by the sun, she could only squint through one eye and then the other. Through the green hue revolving in her vision, she could make out three gypsy women leaning over her. One was brushing the dust off her dress, another picking up the shattered glass around the rocks. A tin flask was pulled out of a large bag, and a ray of sun caught in the metal slashed through the whirlpool in Kata's vision that was now turning orange. Some liquid was poured over the scrape on Kata's shin. The smell was unmistakable. It was *slivovica,* Grandma's first-aid remedy as well, and it stung.

"Give me your hand," a gentle voice beckoned.

Two large, almond-shaped eyes and a halo of reddish-black hair bent over Kata. She placed her hand into the firm grip and was lifted.

As the rainbow hue began fading from Kata's vision, the women walked away, chatting constantly. And then the auburn halo turned around, and smiled.

"You have a strong hand, little girl. Sign of a strong character. You will have *many* adventures."

The compassionate voice, the drawn-out enunciating of each word, sank deeply into Kata's mind and engraved itself in her memory.

The women blended into the crowd. Kata tried to follow them with her eyes, but all she could see were village women handing food items. Roza cradled a loaf of bread wrapped in a dishcloth. Nana Novak held a greasy brown paper bag with what Kata knew had to be a slab of smoked bacon. Miladin's mother also had a brown paper bag. Suddenly the bottom of the bag gave way, releasing shiny apples, red on one side and green on the other, to a patch of dry grass. The gypsy woman holding a straw basket with a baby's face bobbing over its side bent down and helped Miladin's mother pick up the apples.

Is she the one who lifted me up, Kata wondered? But she wasn't carrying her baby, then. And her hair was now hanging down, lopsided, over one shoulder. Kata was not sure.

Another gypsy woman gathered the hem of her flowery skirt to create a makeshift sack and began filling it with apples. And then Miladin's mother looked about fearfully and walked away, taking a shortcut through the orchard. Kata glimpsed an approaching figure and realized it was Miladin's father.

The pain in Kata's shin had become intense to the point of nausea but all she could think about was whether *he* had witnessed her fall. Spotting an empty wooden crate nearby, she turned it over and sat, observing the crowd.

Grandma was in the middle of the gathering, pulling the squawking cockerel out of her wicker basket. She handed it to an elderly gypsy who shoved the bird under her arm to prevent its wings from thrashing. Kata thought her grandma seemed quite transformed, talking exuberantly with the elderly woman, motioning with her hands, without the measured manner that was her habit when speaking to people she did not know. Was this gypsy an old friend? She scanned the group again, hoping to catch sight of him.

And then she spotted him next to the horse and wagon just outside the barnyard. He was seated on a gigantic upturned copper kettle, so new that the sun on it was blinding.

The pain in her shin had subsided and she hobbled toward him, eagerly, as if she had seen an old friend. Then she stopped, feeling as though her body still lunged forward. *Unladylike,* Grandma's reproachful voice rang in her head.

She stood, motionless as an icicle hanging off the eaves trough. Their eyes met. She felt the ice cracking, falling from her limbs, blood rushing back to her face. She moved one stiff leg forward and then the other.

"Hullo," she said huskily from a throat suddenly gone dry.

He remained seated on his throne, head cocked to one side, a wry smile on his face, left eyebrow raised in a questioning gesture.

She moved a step closer and smiled. "My name is Kata!" she announced, the sound of her own voice now back to normal.

"Hello Kata," he replied flatly.

"What's your name?"

"What's *my* name?" he repeated. She sensed irritation in his voice.

"Yes, what's your name?" she asked again, thinking that if this was Miladin she would not be so polite.

He paused, looked at her with renewed curiosity, then smirked and shook his head.

"Just because I'm younger doesn't mean you should make fun of me," she said. For a moment, she considered walking away but her feet refused to move.

"All right." He rose, lazily, as if ready to walk away himself. Then he paused. He appeared even taller than before.

"I'm Lorca. Pleased to meet you, Kata."

"Wow! I've never known anyone by that name!" She extended her hand toward him, but he looked at it without moving. "I'm Kata," she repeated, still holding out her hand.

"I know. You told me."

She finally dropped her hand. "I just wanted to say 'hello.'"

"And you did."

"Well, nice meeting you," she said quickly and hobbled away, feeling she had stretched the conversation as far as it could go.

She returned to the kitchen hoping to find Miladin, but he wasn't there. In her mind, she tried to replay the sound of Lorca's voice. She couldn't describe it, at least not precisely. First, she thought that it was like touching velvet ... soft. But then she realized it was more complicated than that. More like touching corduroy – it had ribs in it. Then it came to her. It was like caressing Remi's chin and feeling the tiny rows of dried milk under her fingertips. Lorca's voice was soft, but slightly raspy, with bumps and rough spots. It was scratchy ... with an edge she could not describe.

She picked up a plate of cookies from the table and carried it outside. The crowd seemed to be the same as when she'd left, cheerful and loud. Lorca was seated on his copper throne again. He was holding a thin wooden stick, tracing figures in a patch of dusty clay. Another man sat on the ground a few steps away chewing on a blade of dry grass and twirling a twig in his hand, and yet another was leaning on the cart, one leg crossed over the other, puffing on a cigarette.

They seemed not to notice as Kata approached.

"Would you like a cookie?" she asked, looking at Lorca. A smirk of boredom returned to his lips.

"Oh, it's you again. Kata, right?" Black eyelashes lifted and the deep green eyes stared ... deep into her soul.

Her heart thumped; and her head spun; the air in her chest became stuck, right in the centre, with nowhere to go. *Those spindly legs, and bony knees.* Her mother's voice mocking. And now her bony knees were visibly wobbling. But an even more terrifying notion struck her: *He's a gypsy. He can read my thoughts. Just like gypsies read fortunes. He knows I ...* Her hands holding the plate felt weak and unsteady. At any moment she could drop the cookies. And, unlike the apples, they could not be picked up.

"Would you like a cookie?" she said, her voice emerging in a squeak. Unsteadily, she held out the plate.

"Did you get your parents' permission to bring them out?" Lorca asked in a serious grownup tone.

"It's fine. They're not home."

"So you didn't ask, then," he repeated, curtly.

She glanced at the other two men hoping they'd come to her rescue, but they paid no attention.

"My grandma doesn't mind." Her voice was now almost back to normal.

"You must *ask* before giving things away," he said and resumed scratching figures in the dust.

Forgetting the pain in her shin, she turned sharply away and walked toward Grandma, who was still talking loudly and gesturing.

"Pass them around, and don't forget the kids," Grandma called out.

Within seconds, the many hands of the villagers and the gypsies had emptied the plate.

Kata stared at the empty plate and then sought Lorca's face through the crowd. Their eyes met. And for the first time she saw him laughing wholeheartedly and shrugging his shoulders as he pointed at the plate. She walked slowly back to the kitchen and placed the dish on the table.

Outside, the cacophony of voices seemed to be subsiding. A feeling of disappointment overwhelmed her. She felt as if all the great expectations of the morning had been shattered, and only the unfitting fragments, like cookie crumbs on an empty plate, or shards of the broken pitcher around the stones, remained.

Chapter V

Foretelling Of The Future Husband

AFTER THE BEAR-DANCE letdown, Kata needed the comfort of her treasures. And there they were – *Huckleberry Finn* and *Tom Sawyer* among other enticing titles – arranged on her grandma's dresser. There were more on the night table, and some on the old trunk, and even on top of the armoire – just the way she'd placed them a few weeks back when the school break began. Each time she picked up one of the books she relished the memory of how they'd come to be hers.

"I'll be receiving a new order of books and need to make room on the shelves," the teacher told her. "You're my helper this summer, so you get first pick."

Books were scarce and expensive, and borrowing from a library was a treat, Kata knew. But owning a book was the greatest privilege of all.

"Are you sure, Miss Pavlova?"

"I'd be pleased to know they're well used. So you may select from that pile, any books you wish."

Any books you wish, any books you wish, resonated in Kata's head as she moved books from the enticing piles she inwardly labelled as the *must-have* pile to the *maybe* pile to the *don't want to leave behind* pile, and then changed her mind and began all over again.

"Have you made your choice, Kata?"

"Yes, Miss," Kata answered and crossed her fingers, secretly, to prevent bad omens for telling a lie. She knew she wanted them all. For the first time ever, she felt as if she were one of the hens in the barnyard greedily fighting over corn kernels. She wanted to grab all the books and scurry home with them, where she could read and reread them as many times as she wished, press wild violets and lily-of-the-valley between pages as bookmarks, peek at certain passages or pictures on a whim, even at night, by the window in the moonlight, undisturbed by the outside world.

The teacher flashed a coy smile: "You want all of them, don't you?"

They placed the books in a cardboard box and, with pieces of jute, tied it to the basket over the back wheel of a bicycle. The rest were stuffed in two cloth bags. The teacher pushed the loaded bike and Kata walked next to her, insistent on carrying a bulging bag in each hand. As the handles began cutting into her palms and her fingers tingled, she felt more and more exhilarated, with each step grasping the heft and the wealth of books that she now owned.

This new sense of ownership stunned her. Only that morning, she'd never expected to have this many books, not just now but ever in her life. Her surroundings appeared oddly foreign to her, as if she were seeing the wheat and the clover fields for the first time, as if she were walking on the wind swirling the dust around her, rather than the bumpy road she'd always known.

Miss Pavlova pointed to a clump of wild chamomile flowers and said, in her high-pitched musical tone: "*Matricaria chamomilla*. That's Latin for chamomile. Are you interested in botanical names, Kata?"

"Oh, yes! That sounds like singing."

"They're easy to remember. '*Matricaria chamomilla*.' Now you try it."

Kata repeated the words. And suddenly, she heard the music in her own voice. The same music Papa Novak heard? The words simply turned into a melody.

She tried to remember similar mysterious names, but managed only a few. *Achillea millefolium*, the milfoil flower, she repeated over and over again, planning to impart her new-found knowledge to her grandma, who used chamomile and milfoil in making tea for Kata's tummy aches and winter coughs. Knowing that lavender was one of her grandma's favourite plants, she made sure she could recite *Lavandula vera* as easily as her own name.

"See that brownish bird with a white stripe under its neck? Under that clump of clover?" the teacher asked.

"Wow! It has another white stripe that looks like a hair band."

"That's a quail. See how she blends into her surroundings? To keep safe from predators."

Predator, that's the word, Kata thought. She stopped and stared at her teacher. *A blue bruise, all puffy and swollen. Predator. That's what he is. Miladin's father.*

"What is it Kata? You look flustered."

That teacher of yours should marry, Nana Novak's voice echoed in Kata's mind. She shook her head and dispelled the voices, the images.

"I hope you don't get married. Ever, Miss," she blurted out.

The teacher laughed: "What is this about?"

"Nothing. I wonder why people have to marry."

"Hmmm ... So they can have children, is one reason."

"Angela has a baby and she's not married."

"Well, yes ..."

"Is that why people say bad things about her?" Kata said.

"Well, they shouldn't," said the teacher. Her voice rose, and the last word cracked like a dry branch underfoot, "chu-dnt." Her brown eyes darkened and her thin nose aimed higher than usual while her face stiffened – like a quail watchful for predators.

"Here! Let me carry those books. They're too heavy for you," she said, in a voice Kata recognized as pretend chirpy.

"Please, Miss. I like carrying them."

Miss Pavlova quickened her pace. As she placed her weight first on one spindly leg and then the other, her knees seemed to bend in at the front and bulge out on the back, just slightly, the way birds walked. Her shoulder-length hair was pinned behind her ears, with bangs standing up in a puff over her forehead, like the cap of a skylark. And now Kata recalled her teacher's singing in the classroom – sweet and melodious.

"Well, here we are. Where would you like these books?"

Kata looked around. They were home.

* * * *

Hidden in the guestroom, Kata appraised the front cover of *Tom Sawyer*. She flipped to the first page. Somehow, the words that usually reeled her in seemed ineffective: lifeless black symbols imprinted on a white page. Instead, she was drawn to the picture of a scrawny boy on the cover. What was the real Tom Sawyer like? He appeared to have a smudged, freckled face, and muddy pants. He did not, in any way, resemble Lorca.

She thought about the boys from school. They were usually silly, or aggressive, or annoying. Some were dirty – not just dusty or dressed in patched clothes. The ones with unwashed faces, sleep crusts in the corners of their eyes and un-brushed teeth – these she despised. And those who bullied the younger and weaker kids or worst of all those who belittled girls.

The courteous boys who were her friends never made her feel awkward and light-headed, and most of all, disheartened – the way Lorca did. He mocked her every time she tried to get to know him. What made it more painful was that *she* was accustomed to doing the rejecting.

She crawled deeper under the starched white sheets of the guest bed and inhaled the soapy sweetness of sun-dried linen. This room remained cool even on a hot summer day, and after a quick bath in the lukewarm water Grandma had left in the washtub to heat in the sun, Kata felt refreshed and glad that the major part of the day was over – the thrill of the dancing bear, the indignity of the broken pitcher, and most of all, her exasperation with the young man who wouldn't talk to her. It all reminded her of walking in the dark and stepping into potholes, bumpy and unpredictable. The bruise on her shin, resembling a potato that had turned blue after being left in the sun, pulsated with a dull pain.

* * * *

Where are you? The voice from far away sounded familiar. Kata opened her eyes, jumped out of bed, and barked a sharp "ouch" as her bruised shin hit the bedframe. Maja's voice floated up again. Kata limped to the open window and waved to her friend. She noticed Grandma and four other women in the shade of the linden. Katia recognized the two grandmothers – Maja's and Miladin's, sitting on a wooden bench. The third woman was Nana Novak. But, with only a glimpse of the fourth woman's back, she was unable to guess her identity.

Most elderly women in the village wore their hair either in a tight bun tied at the nape of the neck, like Grandma, or in one or two braids pinned tightly in a circle wound around the top of the head. Nana Novak was an exception. Her hair-bun looked as if a scraggly grey-feathered bird were perched precariously on her head. The fourth woman, the one Kata couldn't recognize, had long grey hair with black streaks that spilled out from under a blue kerchief, over her shoulders, ending at her knees. And then she turned and Kata realized who she was.

"That's the gypsy my grandma was talking to at the bear dance," Kata said out loud, just as Maja entered.

"How do you know?" Maja's asked.

"Because I saw her there," Kata replied as she ran toward her friend and hugged her tightly.

Although Maja was only a year younger, she was almost a head shorter than Kata, and smelled like baby powder and warm milk. She wore a faded cotton dress, the original pink still evident in the seams and creases. Kata released her friend from her embrace, amazed as always at Maja's clear light brown eyes, and the gentleness in her softly squared face: straight nose; full lips; silky, shoulder-length, light brown hair; and rosy, flushed complexion. It would be many years before Kata would realize why only one word – sublime – would adequately describe her friend, and why she thought Maja the most beautiful girl she'd ever known.

The two friends had much to tell each other. They spoke in spurts, completing each other's sentences, questioning, exclaiming, every once in a while clapping their hands in unison and jumping up and down.

Maja told of her morning at the market in Obrenovac, where her mother sold cheese and eggs; of picking out fabric for her new dress; and of the gypsies with the dancing bear at her house later the same afternoon. Kata talked about the same group of gypsies and of course Lorca, who – to the unbearable disappointment of both girls – had not shown up at Maja's house. After a brief debate the girls agreed that Kata was in love.

"But isn't Lorca a girl's name?" asked Maja.

"No!"

"Are you going to marry him?"

"I don't know. Do you think he wants to marry me?"

"You never said you liked any of the boys. And now you want to marry Lorca? What are we going to do?" Maja bounced a few times and clapped her hands eagerly, as though the marriage ceremony was planned for the following day.

"He doesn't like me," Kata said morosely. "He wouldn't even talk to me. At first, he wouldn't even tell me his name."

"But you don't know he doesn't want to marry you. Maybe he does. How do you know?"

"He probably thinks I'm just annoying."

"But you love him. Don't you?"

Kata wondered whether all this enthusiasm was a good or a bad thing. Maja, who was Kata's voice of reason, was persisting, with unusual exuberance.

"He thinks I'm just a child," declared Kata.

"Is he old?" asked Maja with such a mixture of surprise and shock that Kata blushed. "Well, is he? Otherwise, why would he think that? You never said how old he is."

"I dunno," Kata shrugged.

"He is?" Maja's face betrayed her dismay. "How old?"

"Just old. Maybe even as old as ... your brother."

"He's seventeen? And you still like him? My brother's just awful."

"Lorca's not like anybody else."

"You can do what Ana did, my brother's girlfriend. She told me she's going to marry my brother, but she said not now, but she will, she knows for sure, and I can't wait, she's pretty."

"How does she know?"

"A gypsy read her palm and told her she's going to marry a rich man."

"A rich man? I thought you said your brother."

"That's right. But Ana told the gypsy that she wants to marry my brother, not that rich man. And guess what the gypsy said? 'Your future husband is not rich now, but he will come into his riches.' Can you believe that? My brother is going to be rich some day and he's going to marry Ana." Maja's rosy complexion was even more flushed.

A sense of unease settled in Kata's stomach. *Where is that gap, that missing link?* She thought it best to leave it alone. Besides, she would be accused of ruining everything. Instead, she asked: "How do you know it's all true?"

"Because the gypsy told her how to find out," Maja answered quickly. "For sure."

"I need to find out, too!"

"We need a mirror, and we have to pick a little branch of rosemary. Just like we make boutonnieres for weddings. But this one can't be decorated, just plain."

"And then?"

"We need to pick some creeping charlie," Maja said. "You put everything together under your pillow. Before going to bed. But first, you look at yourself in the mirror. Then you turn the mirror over and hide it under your pillow. The gypsy told her the rosemary and the creeping charlie must be tied together with a piece of fuchsia ribbon, to make it look happy. But not all decorated or the spell gets ruined. Then you say the magic words to make the spell work. Then you go to sleep. And don't talk to anybody before you go to sleep. Or you'll break the spell."

Kata waited for further instruction, but when none came, asked: "And then what?"

"That night, you will dream your future husband. And she did. Ana did. She dreamed my brother. So, you see? It's all true."

"But how do I know what to say?" Kata blurted out. "The magic words. What are they?"

"Magic words?"

"Yes! What's the chant?"

"Oh, that? I don't know. Ana didn't tell me. She can't, you see. The magic words are secret. If she tells me, the spell would be broken."

"Broken? Then how can I do it?" snapped Kata, plunking down on Grandma's old hope chest.

Maja's face was solemn. "What do we do?"

"Maja?" a voice called from outside. "Where are you? Time to go home!"

"Got to run," Maja said. "I'll come over tomorrow, so you can tell me if you dreamt Lorca. If you're gonna marry him."

"How? I don't know the magic words!" Kata cried. But Maja was already out the door.

Chapter VI

That Other World

THE SPRIG OF rosemary and the creeping charlie tied with a piece of fuchsia wool lay safely under the pillow; Grandma's rectangular mirror face down next to it. Kata picked up the tiny mirror and looked. By the pale flicker of the kerosene lamp, the cutout of her face stared back at her so close from the other side, it was as if she could touch it. But her fingers stopped on the cold glass surface.

The large single eye peered at her through the flop of dark hair. She shut her eyes and with her fingertips traced her own features – they were all there. And when she re-opened her eyes, the eye was still staring at her, as if from another world, as if it was magic. Magic… the magic words… she needed them now.

Eyes squeezed shut again, *Matricaria chamomilla, Achillea millefolium, Lavandula vera* echoed in her head. Kata whispered the Latin names. Again, she could hear the music. *They have music. They are magic. My magic words.* She smiled. She had just completed her ritual. She replaced the mirror, ready to sleep.

But sleep would not come. She missed Grandma's bed, the rhythmic breathing next to her. At last, she heard faint singing, far out there in the darkness. Had the gypsy fairy returned? A distant refrain, like a lullaby, led the way to the land of dreams.

* * * *

Glad to be awake, Kata pushed aside blobs of images that popped up and burst like soapsuds, leaving fragments of her dreams. They tugged at her thoughts and beckoned her back under, to escape the bleakness of her sun-drenched room with the white metal bed, the white bedspread over white sheets, and the sheer white curtains blinding her vision. She shut her eyes, blocking out the austerity of her room.

Write them down, dear – Kata heard Grandma's voice in her head – *then sometime later, you can read them. Dreams can be messages from beyond.*

Kata wrote down the first image she recalled: "The dead swallow is under the blue hyacinth."

There was something eerie about the swallow. She lifted one wing, then another, and unsteadily took to flight. But Kata knew that the bird was dead. There was more. The deep hues of red and green and blue shimmered on her feathers. The feathers grew longer, shaping a figure of a woman in a transparent gown like a rainbow. *The nymph from Grandma's Hyacinthus story?* The nymph looked at Kata with her turquoise eyes and, just like in the story, raised a flute to her lips and played a sad tune.

Kata's visions were becoming words: "The sky is turning into a white light, burning my eyes."

She felt a sense of dread. Her whole body shivered under the cold spell of the white light. She continued writing as the images appeared and disappeared behind the lace curtain that was being blown by the wind through an open window, as if playing hide and seek: "I open the book on my lap and see the dancing bear. He lifts one foot, then the other and walks off the page. He is in the fields far beyond, bounding through the golden wheat."

Kata left the white room and tried hiding in her favourite tree crown, but the shadows stalked her. She continued writing. Then she read the lines. They seemed nonsensical. She scratched out some. Numbered them in the same order as they occurred the previous night. Rewrote them. Again and again. By late afternoon, they began making sense:

the dead swallow under the blue hyacinth
flutters her wings
colour shimmers on her feathers

i look up
and the swallow is playing a flute
i look down at the open book on my lap
at the picture of the dancing bear

and he steps off my page
brown and furry and playful
a large, light-as-air teddy bear
leaping through the golden wheat
following the swallow
into the white light

She went back in and hid the notebook in the top drawer of Grandma's dresser. Had the magic words from the night before gone awry? Could she not simply forget the whole thing? But the images resurfaced, one moment fairytale funny and the next terrifyingly alien.

Was this dream a bad omen? Had it to do with the man she would some day marry? She re-examined her marriage options:

Would it be a village priest? He would be young and handsome, and he would, of course, have a helper to kill chickens.

Or would it be someone educated, who would respect me, as Papa Novak said?

Or could it be someone with a hissing voice, like Miladin's father, who yells at Miladin's mother and punches her in the eye?

Or could it be someone like Grandpa Mihailo, who allowed himself to be killed and left Grandma with a broken heart?

Or would it be someone like my father who doesn't believe in 'women's idle talk,' and looks above my head when he talks to me?

Or could it be someone kind and funny, like Professor Papa Novak, who reads all the newspapers and knows everything? And best of all, who looks like an actor in Shakespeare's play?

Or would it be ... could it be ... someone who would make my head spin and my knees wobble and my hands so weak that I might drop the cookies in the dust? Could it be someone ... like Lorca?

Recalling Lorca's refusal to tell her his name, his refusal of a cookie, and his refusal to even talk to her, she concluded that Lorca was ... moody, like Zeus. How does one talk to someone who looks like Lorca and makes her feel the way he does, but who is moody like Zeus? But why is he so gloomy? Other gypsies seemed happy, smiling and singing and dancing.

She gazed toward the bench in the garden and saw Grandma hunched over the low wooden table sorting the herbs into her willow basket. She was peaceful. The day before, talking to the gypsies, she was uncommonly chatty, even cheerful. It was unlike her.

Kata walked over to the bench. "Why do gypsies make you happy, Bako?"

The serene features lifted in surprise. "Hmm. I never realized. I think you might have something there."

Grandma paused for a long while and then said: "With gypsies here, I feel as if I'm living in my other world. Where Mihailo is alive. Everything was better then."

Kata shut her eyes and tried to picture that other world. But she could not see it, could not see herself in it. And yet, she could see the dancers from the previous day and she could hear their music.

"Did gypsies play their music in your other world? When Grandpa was alive?"

"They certainly did, my little swallow. That music you heard, after the bear danced? That's for us, the *gawdjo*, the farmers. That's what they play at weddings or at town fairs. They keep their most exquisite melodies, the ones that have a special meaning to them, only for their own people. Music is part of their soul, their whole being."

"How do you know all this, Grandma? Have you ever heard it?"

"Certainly have. When Mihailo was alive and they worked for us during harvest time. They're close families. We always welcomed their children and their elderly. In the evenings, they would sing and dance. They'd ask us to come and listen."

Grandma was transposed into her other world, this time into a wonderful and magical corner. Kata wished she could have prolonged the moment, but Grandma's face quickly settled into its usual sadness.

"It's their philosophy of life, my Mihailo used to say. They own nothing and have everything. Now, think of that."

"What was their special music like, Bako?"

The clouds on the melancholy face cleared again.

"Can't describe it, dear, in words. After hearing gypsy music, words are … hollow."

Kata closed her eyes and listened. And there it was, she could hear it – from the previous summer and every other summer as far as she could remember – the gentle singing far away in the moonlight. She did not realize that she had finally forgotten her distressing dream.

Chapter VII

The Cookie Heart

THAT EVENING, KATA crawled into bed earlier than usual. It was only dusk. After the restless night in her own room, the muffled sound of Grandma's feet on the wood planks was as comforting as the lullabies she used to sing.

Grandma knelt on the floor next to the bed and began her long evening prayer.

From the courtyard, Roza's voice broke through the calmness: "Where's everybody? Gone to bed with the sunset? Like the chickens!"

Kata winced. Grandma did not like interruptions during her prayers. But Roza continued calling.

Grandma rose slowly. She walked to the door and opened it, her long nightgown outlined in the dusk: "They're all at the market, dear. Staying for the week. It's been a long day. We're off to bed."

Roza cut in, drowning Grandma's words: "All day I spent! Brewing Turkish coffee! Dishing out my apple cake to neighbours! Come over, I said to them. The old gypsy's coming. Telling fortunes."

"We'll talk tomorrow, Roza dear," Grandma said.

"This can't wait! It's that old gypsy of yours. Where is she? I come to talk to her."

Kata jumped out of bed and squeezed in next to Grandma.

"The women came," Roza said. "The gypsy looked at their palms. Told miracles. Miracles! But when I put my hand out? Nothing." Roza stood with her palms upturned, staring into one and then the other. "Hardship, she said. Prepare for hardship! Then she got up and left. Her great grandson, she said. Leaving. Had to see him off. What about me, I said. I don't need a fortune-teller for that. I live hardship! Lived it all my life. After my poor mama died…"

"Calm down, Roza dear. What gypsy are you talking about?"

"She's a sorceress, I tell you! For all I know, she could've put a curse on me! Goya. Her name's Goya. I saw her here at your house. Not long ago. So I'm here to ask her to take the curse off me. She said I had a good heart! What good is a heart with a curse on it?"

"Goya's long gone, Roza dear," Grandma said, firmly. "Get hold of yourself."

"She put a curse on me, I tell you! The moment she walked out, I knew. I dropped my *buklija*, my old clay jug. My dear father, God bless his soul, used it to invite my wedding guests. Filled it with best *slivovica*, all decorated with rosemary sprigs, every person in the village drank from it – and they all came to my wedding. How could they not? My *buklija* was as good as they came. And now it's broken! Then I looked for my ducats! Three of them! Belonged to my dear mother. My dowry to my Alex! How many brides have three ducats to bring to their husbands? Ha? They're nowhere. Nowhere! Those thieving gypsies. Stole my ducats! Put a curse on me…"

"Stop it, Roza. Now!" She took Roza's extended hands with upturned palms and placed them at Roza's side.

Kata was stunned. Grandma never used this tone of voice with a neighbour – only with Mother and that very seldom.

"Think, now, Roza. Where did you put your ducats? Hide them somewhere? Before the gypsy came? Retrace your steps."

Roza's eyes opened wide. Her lower lip dropped, leaving her mouth agape. She slapped her forehead with the palm of her hand and gasped. "Oh, my dear Lord!" She ran off.

"She just remembered where she hid them," Grandma said with a sigh. "Goya doesn't put curses. She's a healer, the true *Chovihani*. My *pen*, my sister in spirit. We've both had a tough life. Lost our husbands, our protection. But we're surviving, each in our own way." She stopped suddenly as if only now remembering Roza was no longer there. Then she shook her head a few times, closed the door and returned to bedside. She inhaled deeply, settled her face back into the same reverent pose, and continued praying.

Kata was almost asleep when Grandma climbed into bed and said: "Goya went to say good-bye to her great grandson, going to be a university student in Madrid. Only 16. Skipped two grades. Tall and handsome like an angel. She's so proud."

Kata's body tensed. With effort, she dismissed the sudden notion. But it crept back, invading the hidden crevices of her thoughts, until her mind burned with anxiety, like the red-hot iron tongs that hissed when dunked in sugar tea. She sat up in bed. Goya's great grandson is ... Lorca?

"Most gypsies don't like sending their children to school," Grandma said, as she struggled out of the high bed. "But in Goya's family, education counts."

At the armoire, she climbed unsteadily onto a chair and brought down the basket piled high with bunches of herbs. She reached in and pulled out a package wrapped in white paper, tied with a thin purple ribbon.

Grandma held out the package. "Here, this was left for you. I almost forgot."

Kata looked at the package, her thoughts still trying to solve the identity of Goya's great grandson.

She pulled on the longer end of the purple ribbon, silky and wiggly as if it had a life of its own. Then she slowly unwrapped the white covering to reveal a powdery pink, semi-transparent, scented, paper. She rubbed the wrapping with her fingertip and the object felt smooth, like a perfectly polished surface. Carefully removing the pink paper, she stared at ... a puzzled face with flushed cheeks, dark bushy hair, and bewildered eyes. She almost didn't recognize the disarrayed reflection of her own face in the mirror.

"Goya said to give it to Kata," said Grandma, sounding far away.

Gingerly, the way one handles precious objects, Kata lifted the gift by the string: a cookie-heart necklace – with the largest pink heart made of the hardened dough that she'd ever seen and a round mirror imbedded in its centre. White tulips and purple violets and green leaves of icing encircled the mirror. She stared, puzzled by the mysterious gift yet bedazzled by its size and colours as it swivelled on the satin cord.

"Are you sure this is for me, Bako?"

"Goya was very clear."

"But why? Why would Goya ..."

"It's not from Goya, dear. She was just a messenger. She said you'd know who the giver was." Grandma looked surprised. "Don't you?"

* * * *

Kata sat up in bed and listened to her grandma's even breathing. Stealthily, she tiptoed to the window, and opened it. Ever so carefully, she perched on the wide wooden ledge. All was calm: the soft moonlight and the long shadows stretching across the courtyard. The invisible crickets chirped on and on. Here, enfolded in the safety of the night, she could relive the last two days, sort out the events.

Far away, a gentle melody floated on the tepid night air:

my dress in rags
jewels of stardust
my home gypsy carts

i sing and dance
for copper coins
and i sell cookie hearts

A violin wove its haunting tune and the refrain resumed in a quicker tempo.

i'm a poor gypsy girl, just a poor gypsy girl
with no ducats of gold
but my heart and my soul, soar with a swallow
it can't be bought or sold

Sleep? Where reality ceases to exist and only the floating lightness of being wafts effortlessly from one castle in the sky to the next? Not for Kata. Not on this night.

Chapter VIII

The Holy Water

ALL AROUND, THE reverent eyes of the saints looked down from the large icons looming on the walls. Kata dipped a silver spoon into the bowl of holy water and brought it to her lips. The liquid was cool and soothing. She lifted the dish and began drinking, swallowing large gulps.

First, you cross your heart, kiss the cross, and clear your thoughts. Then you can sip a teaspoon of the holy water. Otherwise, it's blasphemy, dear. Grandma's voice was reproachful in her head.

The next moment, Kata was standing in a puddle of holy water, watching the bowl as it rolled across the boards. It took awhile for reality to sink in.

She crawled under the table and sat between the wooden lion claws. She squinted and made the tiny cutout leaves and miniscule flowers dance in the white embroidery of the tablecloth above her.

Water... Holy water... Where can I find a bowl of holy water?

The answer came to her. She ran to the well, drew a pail of water, and filled the bowl. In the guestroom, she retrieved a paper pouch of incense, the tiny copper burner and a box of matches from the armoire. She lit the incense and the intoxicating smoky fragrance filled the air. Slowly and reverently, she crossed her heart and kissed the wooden cross lying on the table. She recited words she had heard the priest chant – "bless this house" – and dunked the bough of dried basil into the bowl of water. Next she lightly sprinkled the walls and the furniture, just like the priest. Then she set the bowl on the table.

Head hung low, she walked out into the courtyard, feeling odd. Everything about her seemed changed, somehow foreign and distant. The linden leaves fluttered gently, secretly waving to her. The grass, covered in morning dew, shimmered like a wobbly mirror that didn't quite reflect her face. But could that large, glittering surface see her? The swallows, wings swishing in perfect semi-circles, called out, spreading news. And the sunflower, looking at the ground from its twisted stalk, snuck a sideways peek at her. Did everything know what she'd done?

If this morning had begun strangely, it was only a prelude to a series of events so bizarre it would be forever the day every resident in Ratari would remember.

It was the third day after the dancing bear, the day the two-year-old girl disappeared. The whole village embarked on a frantic search. All eyes turned to the gypsies. The stories that had been told and retold over the years became infused with new life as if now somehow they'd all been proven true.

The police searched the gypsy camp several times. The villagers, led by Papa Novak, searched the wells and the pig barns and the haystacks, and the wheat fields flattened by that day's storm, and the green cornfields, and the farm woodlots. All in vain.

Day in and day out, gloom clung to Kata like the smoke of the burning incense that had been sticking to her lungs, blocking out the air, since the morning she had committed blasphemy of the worst kind. She existed in a state of hollowness. Until now, Grandma had been able to ward off bad omens. But on that day, sprinkling holy water and chanting prayers was futile. The holy water was not holy. And it was all Kata's fault.

In the days that followed, dissent grew among the villagers. Some were so certain that the gypsies had stolen the toddler they no longer questioned if, but only how and why. They asked the police to search the gypsy quarter in Obrenovac as well as the shacks clustered along the main road to Belgrade. Some were certain the toddler was being smuggled to a distant hideaway, and may have already been crippled. Others thought that the investigation was too narrowly focused on the gypsies and that other possibilities were being overlooked.

Angela, the toddler's mother, searched incessantly. She could be seen day and night, wandering the fields and yards. Villagers simply allowed her to roam through their homes to appease her torment. She appeared to have stopped sleeping or eating. Within a few days, her clothes turned ragged, her eyes sunk deep in her skull, dark hair in tangles around her face and shoulders. She walked aimlessly, calling out "my baby ... my baby ..." One whole side of her skirt was torn off. Caked blood from an unattended dog bite streaked down her leg.

She was seen searching the rose bushes at the edge of the forest where gypsies had been picking rosehips for making jam. Thorns scratched her face and bare arms and legs, as if someone had scribbled all over her. She continued walking barefoot through farmers' fields, blouse unbuttoned, chest exposed, mud encrusted on her tattered clothes, calling her child.

Chapter IX

The Lullaby

"SUNDAY," KATA WHISPERED as she pulled down on the rope that lowered the tin pail into the well. "A whole week since the bear danced. The priest will make *real* holy water. The bad omens will vanish. The baby will be found."

Over the scraping of wood against metal she heard another sound – a faint sorrowful tune swelling from the pit below, then fading away. Kata reflected on the many fairies and witches and devils and the innumerable mythical dwellers of the well. She rushed her task, the quicker to flee the humming well.

After filling the pitchers, she poured the remaining water into the barrel that emptied through a contraption of pipes into a pig puddle nearby. She stopped, still holding the pail in the air. The faint lilting melody neared and she heard the words:

sleep my little baby
sleep in the night
sleep in your cradle
under moonlight

She listened and searched for the voice.

and if the moon hides
beneath its lore
sleep under the stars
my angel's soul

Angela was sitting against the tree trunk by the puddle. She was covered in mud, as if she had rolled with the pigs. The few remaining green branches of the mulberry mingled through the dry tree-carcass above, casting a ragged shadow over the puddle. Kata took a pitcher and cautiously approached the woman. But the voice continued:

and if the stars hide
when swallows fly
chase the swallows
into the sky

"Would you like some water?" Kata asked timidly. She lifted the pitcher toward Angela's lips: "Here, just a sip. It'll make you feel better. It's a terribly hot day."

But Angela just chanted:

chase the swallows
my angel's soul
sleep in the stardust
of gypsy lore

Carefully, Kata tilted the pitcher until the water was touching the woman's lips. *That's good, she's drinking,* she thought, but the woman's voice never faltered.

Kata saw the water trickling down the woman's unbuttoned blouse, carving rivulets in the mud smeared across her breasts. Angela continued singing... and humming... arms crossed over her lower belly, gently rocking.

* * * *

That afternoon, Kata vomited all she had taken in. She stayed awake that night, staring at the white ceiling, or chipping the plaster off the wall next to the bed. The next day, she continued chipping the plaster off the outside walls, chipping, chipping, chipping, and vomiting every drop of chamomile tea Grandma coaxed her to sip and every bit of chicken soup and every drop of water.

* * * *

"Make sure you pack all your pretty clothes, child," Grandma said, "and some of your favourite books." She filled large bags with tomatoes and carrots and bunches of herbs in the spaces between. Papa Novak came to help carry the bags to the bus station.

"A change will do you good," Grandma said as they walked along the familiar path through the fields.

"Three days with no food or drink," Papa Novak added. "You can't survive much longer. No nourishment in chipping the plaster."

"Look," Kata shrieked, pointing at a pair of rubber boots with pant legs stuffed in them, lying across the path. The pant legs were connected to a man slumped on the ground, his head and upper body partially concealed by the corn stalks.

"Dear, Lord. What now?" Grandma groaned and rushed toward the man.

Papa Novak followed and the two declared in unison: "It's Ivan."

They raised his head and poured water over his face as he grumbled and finally drank from the bottle they brought to his lips.

"He'll sleep it off," Papa Novak said, picking up Ivan's cane from the path and placing it next to him. "He'll need this when he wakes up. *Slivovica*. As always."

"Goddam grizzly," Ivan groaned and rolled over, snoring.

"As much as we all feel his pain..." Papa Novak said, shaking his head.

"Fell off a horse, as a young lad, people say," Grandma added. "But some think different. Got an early start at drinking, picking fights. Once, he was found beaten, almost dead. Rumour had it, to avenge a girl he raped, somebody's sister, they said."

"How do we know what to believe?" Papa Novak raised his arms, exasperated. "That's a cross no man wants to bear."

"You think Angela paid for her father's sins?"

"It's a terrible thought," Papa Novak said, rubbing his chin. "But he's always managed to avoid paying for his own. There's something Machiavellian about the man."

They shook their heads, resuming their slow trek to the bus station.

During the two-hour trip to Aunt Agata's in Belgrade, Grandma spoke little and Kata slept during much of it. She awoke here and there, her eyes resting on the rushing mosaic of fields and trees and even vineyards, which were rare in her own village. She saw it all from above, floated over it in her cushy plastic chair that reclined back like the dentist's and allowed for a full view through the large glass window. Each time she fell asleep her dreams blended with reality. One time it was her cherry tree rumbling along the road to Belgrade with her perched high up in the crown, while Remi purred loudly – until she realized it was the humming of the bus engine. Next it was the smoky voice of Elvis pouring out of the bus radio, rocking and rolling along the bumpy stretch of the road and she woke up fully, wishing Maja were there to hear it. Then it was Chubby Checker singing The Twist and she perked up, wiggling in her seat and humming along.

She felt that, as soon as she entered this bus-world that rumbled along the paved roads connecting the big cities, everything changed. Things outside of it had nothing to do with her as long as she stayed in this capsule and in her elevated seat. Before long, the bus stopped and everyone got off. She stepped back into the real world and her aunt was kissing her on the cheeks, one, two, three times.

That evening, Kata announced that the chicken soup tasted yummy, and Grandma was pleased. But she still fussed over her granddaughter and a new network of worry lines had settled on her face.

"She's still a child ... can't be left alone ... can't be trusted to just anyone," Grandma said.

Then she announced her return home, alone. Kata was to stay a bit longer until, in Grandma's words, the village calmed down.

* * * *

Although Kata's health quickly improved, she constantly sought news from the village. Three days and three nights at her aunt's home was the longest she had ever stayed. She missed her grandmother.

But soon, because she could talk to the farmers, she began enjoying the daily trips to the market to buy fresh produce. She also looked forward to visiting various exhibits. Her aunt's friends took turns accompanying her to the Belgrade National Art Gallery, where she happily spent hours memorizing images and their inscriptions. She recited them daily in her thoughts so she could impart her knowledge to Grandma. And she especially enjoyed the evenings at the National Belgrade Theatre. Her aunt, a theatre critic, was always in possession of free tickets and happy to see every play.

To Aunt Agata's surprise, Kata chose *Hamlet* for three evenings in a row, although she had seen it with her class a year earlier. And to Kata's surprise, her aunt no longer wore the pale peach lipstick that smelled like rotten eggs. She now wore a shiny, translucent one that had a burgundy hue and tasted like cherries. All the while, the grownups avoided the subject of the missing toddler as carefully as if they were playing "dodge the ball."

Kata looked forward to her mother's weekly visits, but only for news about Grandma and the village. Conversations about the missing child were carefully guarded. But the hushed voices in the next room never failed to draw Kata to the door.

"Where is Kata?" her mother asked. "She could hear us."

"She's in my room, reading. Loves her books," her aunt replied. "Did something happen again? You seem troubled."

"They found her."

"Angela's baby?"

"No, no. Not the baby."

"Who, then? Who did they find?"

"They found Angela."

"Angela?"

"Yes. In a neighbour's well. Drowned."

Chapter X

Evil Eye

PAPA NOVAK PULLED Kata's suitcase out of the luggage compartment and placed it on the gravel shoulder of the road. He straightened up and gave her a wide smile.

"Welcome home, my girl. Had a nice long visit with your aunt, I hear." He waved to the driver as the bus rumbled away, leaving behind a whiff of diesel fuel.

"Kept good company with all those artsy friends of Agata's," Grandma said cheerfully. "She's become a big-city girl. The Art Gallery one day, the theatre another. Goodness gracious, hope she remembers how to feed the chickens."

Kata slung a bag of books over one shoulder, clothes and souvenirs over the other and ran to the rutted path between two cornfields, inhaling deeply the scents of late summer, her eyes absorbing the green and gold of the fields below. They had not walked long, when Grandma dropped her large straw bag on the ground.

"Dear God, there she is again!"

Papa Novak placed the suitcase on the ground, the worn leather the colour of the dry earth. He waved his arm in greeting.

"Good day, Roza."

"Good day, Professooor," Roza said glancing at them with suspicion before cautiously approaching. "Shhh. He's asleep. Take a peek! Here. Just a quick one," she whispered, holding out the bundle in her arms. "Isn't he handsome?"

"Yes, yes, Roza dear," Grandma said. "We're just on our way home from a long bus ride – "

"Well, if you don't want to see him," Roza cut in.

Kata stepped forward and perched on her tiptoes, about to peek into the swaddle of rags. But Roza yanked it away.

"You! Spit! Spit three times. I said, spit!" She jutted her chin out, her face turning a furious red. "Don't you cast your evil eye at my baby! You spit first! You hear?"

"Go ahead, Kata," Grandma said. "Just make the motion, dear."

"Tpp! Tpp! Tpp!" Kata spat toward the bundle while keeping her distance.

"What are you waiting for?" Roza said, her eyes glaring. "Look! I said look! You all want to see him, but you're all afraid to look."

Wearily, Kata leaned over and peered into the bundle of folded garments. Then she stared at Roza, before turning towards Grandma.

"Ha! What'd I tell you?" Roza said deliriously, whole body quaking with wild laughter. "Alex's heir! The handsomest of them all! My Alex! The proudest father on this earth."

Kata stepped back quickly, her eyes on the white patches expanding through the purple on Roza's forehead and cheeks.

"Gotta bake bread. Milk those cows. Can't stand here all day talking to you. You all wanna see him." Roza turned and walked away hurriedly, her voice scolding the summer air.

"Her baby…" Kata said.

"They didn't tell you, did they, my girl?" Papa Novak said. He picked up the suitcase and began walking ahead. "I'll let the two of you talk."

Grandma took Kata's hand. "I told them not to tell you right away. To wait a little."

"I don't understand. I know about Angela, but what's – "

"There's more to it, dear. We thought we'd give you a nice long break from all of this."

"There is no baby in there. Just some clothes."

"It was in Roza's well, dear, where they found Angela." Grandma propped her arms on her hips and sighed: "Roza lost the baby that same day. She bled through the whole village. Wouldn't let anyone come near. By the time Alex got back from the fields, it was too late."

For a moment, Kata felt as if the fields spun all around her, blending colours and sounds into a jumble. She crouched down and placed her hands over her face – and now she saw it all from another angle – from above, from the cushy plastic chair in her bus-world, where Chubby Checker sang *The Twist*. She glided along a paved highway to a place with theatres and art galleries and vegetable markets where potatoes came from a bin rather than the hard earth, and her aunt's apartment where water came from a faucet rather than a singing well. She felt Grandma's arm around her shoulders, lips planting kisses in her hair, murmuring prayers. She took Grandma's hand and pressed it against her own cheek, and the two stood up holding on to each other.

"But what's in the bundle, Bako?" Kata asked.

"Nothing, dear. Alex's shirts. She cradles them, gives them her breast. Thinks it's her child."

"Aunt Agata said Roza wasn't well."

"She wanted to tell you."

"She said I should think about things that make me feel happy. About the plays I'd seen and the paintings. And I should come to visit her again very soon. But she didn't tell me..."

"Hard for any of us to explain, dear. Roza comes every day and cooks for them, for Alex and her brother. Goes back to her parents' house to sleep, all alone. The farm's been run down, overgrown for years now. She carries bread in her apron, back and forth, wanders the fields day and night."

"I didn't know."

"I hoped to spare you some grief. Hoped things would get better. But it's not to be."

"I'd rather know."

"In time, dear. You'll know more than you can bear."

Chapter XI

Angela's Baby?

(Summer 1964)

"GO IN AND get the nipples," Grandma said pointing to the pharmacy, "a dozen or so. That calf hasn't suckled for a few days now. We'll likely have to bottle-feed it for a while."

Kata did as instructed and came back out, excitement rising in her chest. The next errand on the list was what she'd been waiting for – an early gift for her twelfth birthday, just a few weeks away: a pair of store-bought shoes.

This was the first time Grandma had agreed to such impracticality. She firmly believed that comfortable shoes were one's single most important item, and had to be made of soft but durable leather by the only shoemaker in town who, in her opinion, measured up to the task. The procedure was tedious. First, one's feet would be measured, a template traced and cut out of cardboard and then the leather would be chosen. Children had no say, for only adults could discern the quality of such a pricy item. Three weeks later, the shoes would be ready.

Lately, Kata had been very unhappy with the type of shoes she was forced to wear. Sure they were comfortable and kept her feet dry and warm, but they certainly detracted from the look she had been trying to achieve.

Every time she glanced in the mirror in the guest room, where she could see her whole body, she thought she'd make a better clown than a girl.

Her mother's voice echoed in her head: *Too tall for her age, too skinny, too flat-chested.* She wondered how Grandma saw beauty, to call Kata such endearing names as *my princess, my butterfly,* and Kata's favourite, *my swallow.* The last two she could relate to the most. She wanted to do so many things at the same time, she often wished she could fly. And when Grandma called her these names, she actually felt beautiful, felt she could do anything.

But then she'd stand in front of the mirror and grimace at her skinny scarecrow legs stuck in her father's old work boots. "You're a clown," she'd yell into the mirror. "You'll never look like Lena. Ever."

Lena had a curvaceous body, with a round behind and chubby legs and little feet, and breasts already bulging under her sweater.

Every time Kata checked under her blouse, she was bewildered by her breasts' refusal to show any sign of expansion. She had overheard Lena's chitchat with another schoolgirl.

"My breasts are as big and firm as the largest apples on our apple tree," Lena lisped in the childish voice that caused all the boys to swarm around her.

"You're lucky," her friend replied, disheartened. "Mine are already the size of small melons. All the boys are asking them out. My breasts, not me. As if I'm nothing but a walking pair of blubbers. I just wish they'd stop growing."

Kata was perplexed. Since her eleventh birthday she'd been checking hers daily. Then she realized that perhaps her fixation had jinxed them. So she'd stopped looking and only occasionally, in bed at night, she would pass her hand, as if by chance, across her chest. But the little bumps under her nightgown remained the size of green plums she often picked from her neighbour's trees along the road to school. So she'd given up hope of growing breasts, and thought that she should try to change other things, the ones she could, like the clunky shoes.

Each time she went to the shoemaker, he would insist the shoe needed a little extra toe-wiggling room. For her growing foot, he'd say with a wink. Her *growing* foot? How terrifying.

She remembered the times she'd looked forward to visiting the shoemaker, believing he was a magician, with black, bushy hair crammed under black hat and long white sideburns extending all the way to his chin. He'd recheck all his measurements through an eyepiece, and nod with satisfaction. He had an assortment of dark wood boxes with leather samples in some, spools of thread in others, shoe horns and all kinds of strange looking do-jiggers in yet others.

He used to tell his favourite story, *The Elves and the Shoemaker*. And he, like the shoemaker in the story, made sure that every pair of shoes he made was as perfect as if it were his last. Each time Kata bent her toes or arched her foot to make the shoeprint just a little smaller, he would catch her trying to trick him. He would gaze at her over his eyepiece in mock disapproval, and start retelling the story, stressing his pride in his workmanship.

But now, the story had lost its appeal. The good magician had been transformed into an unyielding evil sorcerer who refused to acknowledge just how stylish the store-bought shoes were in comparison to his frumpy, comfortable, and so annoyingly durable ones.

After a winter spent watching Lena prance around the classroom with a pair of store-bought, brown suede boots that came all the way up to her knees, Kata became determined. Her new spring shoes? They would be store-bought.

But it appeared she did not need a new pair, since the previous pair had much toe-wiggling room.

To make matters worse, Lena wore her suede boots even in spring. She'd walk indolently, the suede folded in pleats so the top of the boot reached only halfway up her calf, dragging her feet as if her boots were the least important part of her attire. But the other girls knew better. They knew the foot-dragging helped Lena draw even *more* attention from the boys. They whispered behind her back:

"That's not lisping, that's baby talk."

"She's doing it for the boys."

"She's the living, breathing, *puss in boots*."

So here was Kata, in town for one important purpose: Grandma would buy her an early birthday present, a pair of red, pointed-toe shoes with a narrow little heel that would make clicking sounds when Kata walked nonchalantly past Lena's desk at school, as if her shoes were the least important thing on her mind.

She recalled the way they looked and felt when she and Maja tried them on. Since that time, she could even hear the clicking sounds of the little red heels in her dreams. She could see the pointed red toe protruding under an oversized red bow with a shiny silver buckle that stretched along the whole width of the shoe. She had been doing the chores diligently and making promises, most of all promising not to be disappointed when her birthday came. She could hardly believe that she and Grandma were here, in town, on their way to pick them up.

Since they had gotten up early, they looked forward to the special breakfast at the town bakery: a fresh piece of *burek*, a pastry made of thinly-layered dough filled with meat, cheese, or apples. While Grandma preferred the cheese-filled *burek*, Kata hoped they wouldn't run out of the apple one. They rushed because this was a popular breakfast item for townsfolk as well as those coming especially to the market.

The streets were a jumbled mass of horses and buggies, buses loaded with people, and a few automobiles, all claiming priority in the cramped space. A bus driver stuck his face out the window and began yelling at a farmer to move his horse and wagon. Unconcerned, the farmer continued to unload what appeared to be a gigantic necklace of chickens. Each chicken's legs were tied to a segment of a long rope, as if they were strung on a clothesline. He was passing this string of chickens on to his wife, who seemed about to lose her hold on the squawking mass of flapping wings and fluttering feathers.

Another farmer now stopped his horse and wagon right in front of the bus. He began unloading potatoes with young shoots growing right through the sack. Seeing the chicken farmer's dilemma, he dropped his sack and ran over to help. A bright blue Volkswagen Beetle was stuck behind the bus. It beeped rhythmically as if to accompany the teenaged accordion player who was leaning against a hydro pole. The young musician squeezed the bellow pleats open and shut, fingers of his right hand dancing on the keyboard, the left ones caressing the studs. His eyes were closed; chin gently leaning on the bellow, foot tapping to the rumbles of the accordion. A few copper *dinars* lay in a greasy, wide-brimmed hat at his feet. The bus driver, head now swollen red with rage, shouted obscenities, while through open windows several passengers joined in, waving their arms and hollering at the farmers.

Grandma led the way, masterfully, away from the throng of shoppers and vendors. Following as if she were still a little girl, Kata walked behind with her neck craned, gaping at the market scene. The crowds were now partially blocking her view, but she caught a glimpse of the chicken farmer. He was untangling himself from the squawking wings and feathers, smiling with his single yellow tooth, and with one free hand waving at the bus driver and his load like a movie star acknowledging his fans.

They were walking toward the bakery when Grandma pointed to a middle-aged gypsy woman with a child she used as a beggar. The child, propped up with a cardboard box behind her, was sitting on a pile of rags on the sidewalk.

It was difficult to tell the age of the little girl. She could have been about five or six years old. She was so thin that her skin appeared transparent and bloodless, stretched over her face as if it were a mask. She was blind, but the most frightening part for Kata was that she appeared to have no eyes. Her eyelids were closed as if they had grown together – or as if they were glued. They seemed hollow, as if she had no eyeballs. A yellowish tear oozed from the outer corner of each eye. A dark yellow sticky substance, the consistency of beeswax, was clumped on her sparse eyelashes. Her right hand seemed completely bent backwards at the wrist. It remained frozen in that position as if it were broken, as if it could not be moved. Her legs could not be seen from the rags piled around her. She looked like a stump, stuck in a pile of rags, a living head with brown, matted hair hanging to her shoulders, a broken wrist extended in a begging manner. A lidless shoebox sat in front of her.

The woman called loudly to passers-by to have pity on this unfortunate child, cursed by God Almighty, and to give generously if they wished to save their soul and help the hungry. Every time someone threw in a coin, she grabbed it eagerly. Then her eyes resumed searching the faces of people approaching her, and she began her wailing refrain again. On the sidewalk in front of her lay a greasy paper bag with chunks of smoked bacon and half a loaf of bread. She kept stuffing chunks of bacon in her mouth and taking large bites of bread. She chewed continuously during her rant, grabbing coins while the child next to her sat quietly, hunched in its pile of rags. Every once in a while a whimper escaped its pale lips, and a nervous twitch flitted across its glued eyelids. Occasionally, the stump that stood for its body seemed to shiver, causing the rags to tremble.

Grandma's face was a frozen mask – the look Kata dreaded – as if the face belonged to a stranger.

"God help me," Grandma said as if speaking to herself. "Even I can't help but think... that it just... could be... She could be about that age."

Kata squeezed Grandma's hand even harder, afraid of becoming separated from what provided all her warmth and security.

"Do you really think... this could be her, Bako?"

"I don't know. God forgive me I could bet my life they had nothing to do with it. But who am I to say? They are people like all others. Good people and bad people. When so many in the village think that gypsies had *something* to do with it..."

"But if they didn't, who did? Somebody must've..."

"And when I see something like this God forgive me I see that poor woman, Angela, wandering the fields. Sometimes in my dreams, she comes to me. As if she has something to say. But she says nothing, just like when she was alive. She never really spoke much to anyone. Such a sad young woman."

"You dream about her, Bako?"

"Yes, dear. Something in her eyes as if she needs to tell me something... I never see her mouth. As if she's incapable of speech."

"Have you tried asking her, Bako?"

"Asking her, dear? This is in my dreams, my little swallow. And she seems so troubled. But of course she would be. Nothing seems to make sense. What am I saying?"

"Maybe you should try asking her."

"It never lasts long enough. And I have no control over my dreams."

"You taught me how to try and control my dreams, Bako. When I have nightmares. Remember? I just thought, maybe..."

"And her poor mother finally died, God rest her soul. She is better off dead."

They had walked almost a whole block now, leaving the beggar child behind. Kata felt ill, the gut-wrenching pain spreading to her chest and her head, weakening her legs, as if they would, at any moment, fold under her. She led Grandma toward a bench.

"If she's not crippled by the gypsies, why would she be like that?" Kata asked. "The beggar child."

"Oh, my dear girl. There could be so many reasons. Sometimes, young women get pregnant out of wedlock. Try to abort, out of shame, fear of parents, of gossip. But if it doesn't work, and a child gets born, it could be crippled because of damage. There are so many reasons." Grandma sighed and added: "Just like in our village. Not long ago, you were only four or five years old..." She stopped, then said: "Better leave that alone..."

"Please tell me, Bako. I am not too young. I'm almost twelve."

"A young woman in our village... Well, not *any* young woman. It was Angela's older sister." Grandma brushed a palm over her forehead. "People say she inserted needles in her womb. Died from infection or from bleeding, nobody knew for sure. The family hushed it up. Said it was some kind of fever."

"Angela's older sister?"

"Yes, dear. Roza was friends with her, best friends. She took Angela under her wing after that, took the place of her older sister."

"Do you think that's her child, Bako? The gypsy's?"

"I don't know her story, dear. But when a gypsy uses a child as a beggar, everyone suspects it's been stolen and crippled. It's all so heart wrenching. Besides, how do we know she really is a gypsy? It would be an easy disguise for any woman trying to escape, even from her own family."

Once home, Kata went into Grandma's room, opened the top dresser drawer, and took out the pink cookie heart. She unwrapped it, narrowed her eyes and scrutinized the wobbly image that peeked at her from various contorted angles, searching, shrewdly, for a glimpse of… what?

You made that holy water that wasn't holy… it's all your fault, the image in the mirror taunted. *But I repented. To err is human, to forgive divine,* Kata told the mirror. *And I gave up the red shoes. That's another penance. Isn't it?* She felt bizarre, ashamed of her secret, of her bickering with the mirror. Yet, looking into it made her feel that she was doing something useful.

* * * *

"Kismet. It's kismet, I tell you," Roza had hollered as she ran into the barnyard early one morning, a few days after the disappearance of Angela's baby. "You can't change your fate. You can run and hide all you want, but fate will find you. It finds all of us."

"What now, Roza dear?" Grandma had sighed.

"That poor Angela. First her sister. Then that orphaned child of hers. And now her dear mother has taken ill. Doesn't look good, they say."

"Dear God. The tragedy that's befallen that family." Grandma began gathering herbs in her basket, ready to leave.

"Don't go. Ivan doesn't let anyone near. He's barred the house. Stands with a shotgun at the gate."

"That tyrant. I've no fear of him."

"Searched the gypsies. Ivan and his son and a few others."

"Can't be, Roza. That's a raid. Against the law." Grandma slipped the willow basket off her arm and placed it on the grass.

"Whose law? Tied those gypsies with ropes! Whipped them with horsewhips!"

Grandma turned pale. "Angela's poor mother took ill, you say. No wonder." She walked through the gate and headed toward the encampment. Kata followed.

"To get them to confess," Roza yelled behind them.

The scene had been unlike any other: overturned cartons of costume jewellery, boxes of heart-shaped cookies, embroidered skirts and blouses. Bales of hay lay scattered, torn tarpaulin and a heap of rubble that once was a cart were strewn along the riverbank.

Papa Novak was there.

"Convinced the police, finally, to let the gypsies leave. But not until this happened," he said. "Somebody could've planned this heinous crime during the town fair. So easy to shift the blame."

Over the years, rumours about Angela's baby had never ceased circulating throughout the village. One was about the gypsy who was found face down in a foot-deep creek that fed into the river Sava. Some suspected an angry mob had killed him after discovering him wandering the fields at night. Others wanted to believe that drunken gypsies had fought among themselves. No name had ever emerged. He was simply referred to as the gypsy who drowned the night after Angela's drowning. Gossip also had it that the dancing bear had been found dead. No one knew for certain if that was true, nor how the bear died, nor why. An even stranger thing was that the police seemed to have no leads.

Chapter XII

The Peacocks Bring News

(Summer 1966)

"K*AAA! KAAA!*"

The blue peacocks of India, once made sacred to Hera, queen of the heavens, Grandma's voice whispered. Kata found herself in a courtyard filled with colossal pink roses as tall as trees, bordered by blue morning glories reaching to the sky. A peacock, its magnificent train framing a glossy blue head and neck, postured and strutted. The elongated tail coverts tipped with eyespots of turquoise and gold shimmered as the peacock quivered its fan and rattled its quills at a small harem of peahens. "The fan dance," Kata murmured as she yawned lazily and stretched her hand over Grandma's pillow.

She opened her eyes and realized that she had again spent the night in Grandma's bed in the guesthouse where no one except guests had slept since Grandma's death two years earlier, just before Kata's twelfth birthday.

Kata leapt from the bed. *I better sneak back to my own room before Mother sees me looking like this.* She ran her hand down the outgrown dress rumpled from sleep and yesterday's wear, trying to smooth the fabric.

Then she heard it, again – the thin, hesitant squeaking of the front gate, as if someone was trying to steal through.

Who could this be? They could wake my mother. Nervously, she stepped out to the front verandah. Since Grandma died and her parents took over the running of the farm, she'd devised new means of keeping out of their way. Most of the time, she was successful. Her parents spent much of their time in the fields or at the Belgrade market.

As she glanced about the peaceful courtyard awash in morning light, the fear of her mother's reprimand dissolved into melancholy. The lilac tree – with the twisted branches she once sat among as a child – seemed weary with age. The cherry tree – with a rope swing no one used any longer – gave off an aura of loneliness. She felt like a complete stranger in this place she'd always known, this courtyard veiled in mist, infused with the fragrance of linden blossoms.

Stop the fantasies. Stop romanticizing the past, Katarina. She could hear her mother's voice in her head. *Your fits of melancholy are like a disease, distorting your sense of reality.*

Kata shook her whole body – like her dog Samson after running through the marsh – hoping to dispel the gloom that enveloped her.

The front gate squeaked again. She ran to it, but there was no one in sight.

Crouching down, she fastened the laces on her white runners, ready for her morning run along the rutted path through the fields. Two hands grabbed her shoulders from behind. She shrieked and spun around.

Miladin's roguish laughter greeted her: "I saw them! Under the bridge."

His bony cheeks, usually pale, were now two burning red circles. His violet eyes sparkled with excitement. With damp, light brown hair and fine droplets of mist gathered on the blond peach fuzz under his nose, she thought he looked like a young faun, a faun who had slept in the forest under a tree and was now covered in early morning dew.

"The caravan! It's here!" he exclaimed. "Two wagons on one side of the bridge and three on the other, with horses and everything."

"What are you saying?" she yelled, although his words echoed a familiar note. He used to run through the village, announcing...

"Gypsies! They're here! In Ratari!" he said, squealing those same words in the childish voice she had not heard for many years.

"Are you playing games with me?"

"No! I was helping my dad! He's off to the market."

"You saw them?"

"They had a fire going under a big black pot. A man was peeing under the witch tree."

"Gypsies are here?"

"I just said that! Wake up, rag doll! You think they'll be going around, begging food and telling fortunes?"

Rag doll? He said it. Again! This was his new name for her – his way of proving himself to be a man, or more perplexingly, to be more than just a friend. But each time he said it, his head wobbled just a teeny bit, and the long, sparse hairs on his chin twisted this way and that. He postured and strutted in a way that reminded her of Papa Novak's new goat, the Swiss Toggenburg everyone talked about. Lately, she found herself checking for the wattles on Miladin's elongated neck. And each time he called her rag doll, she was reminded of all the little tics she knew he would never outgrow.

"I wish Grandma was here," she sighed.

"She'd know what to do, wouldn't she?" he said. And then rambled on: "I saw lots of women in big skirts and kerchiefs. And I could hear babies crying."

"Babies? They had babies with them?" she said.

"I guess. I could hear them crying."

"How many?"

"How many what?"

"Babies! What else? How many babies?"

"How would I know?"

They paused and stared at each other for a long moment.

"You … think?" he began hesitantly.

"Do … you?"

She wrung her hands, but could not bring herself to speak the words out loud. In her mind, she could hear grandma's warning: *Words are powerful. Once spoken out loud, they assume a potency of their own. It is like breathing a spirit, a life, into your thoughts – once you turn them into words, your thoughts became alive. You must be very, very careful, Kata, what you say.* Here, Grandma would pause and look deeply into her eyes: *If you're not certain, you should test your words when you're alone. Close your eyes, and say them out loud. Pretend the voice you hear is not your own, but someone else's speaking to you. How do those words make you feel? Then you will understand the power they can have on others.*

"Let's whisper at the same time, to be sure, you know, we're thinking the same," Miladin said.

She recalled this well-rehearsed routine they had followed since they were little. Unable to resist the game, she moved closer to him, their heads almost touching. Then both whispered: "You think the babies are stolen?"

Just like in a school play. You've always been my favourite co-star, she thought, as they stepped back in unison, each searching for signs of dread in the other's face. But this game was more serious. Even now, she sensed that her friend was also unsure of the potential power of the words they had just uttered.

"You think they saw you?" she asked.

"Don't know. I ran across that bridge …"

"You must've been frightened," she said, teasing.

"I just ran and ran through the cornfield," he said. "I thought they'd be there, you know, stealing corn."

"They could've caught you, and nobody would've known," she said, playing along.

"Nobody would've seen them! Nooobody would've known what happened to me, just like Angela's baby. I could've disappeared just like she did. They could've blinded me, or broken my legs, or my neck, just like this."

Miladin was contorting his body, acting out the part. He had his neck twisted to one side, and made clicking noises to show what breaking it would sound like. Tongue stuck out of the side of his mouth, he tilted his head, hands grasping an imaginary noose. He began gasping as if he were being strangled.

Although they were the same age, Kata had always felt much older. And now he was carrying this game a bit too far, making fun of her, making her feel frail and anxious, and not 14. Usually, compared to him she felt like a sage who had already lived her life, observing herself from another world, looking down at an awkward, unsure, silly teenaged girl. She needed to sound wise and confident.

With her hands propped on her hips, she observed him with a sense of superiority: "You think they'd hang you?"

"Who says they wouldn't?"

"Let's go and see them, tonight! We can sneak out after everyone's asleep. I bet they'll be playing music and dancing by the fire. We'll hide in the dark, under the witch tree. Please, will you come?" Kata was too excited to curb her enthusiasm in front of him as she usually did, too anxious to notice his hesitance.

He stared at her, skeptical. "You serious? They could see us!"

"I don't care. I have to see them. Are you coming?"

"I guess."

"I'll meet you at the woodlot, at the dead soldier's corner. Midnight? You think your parents will be asleep?"

"You mean, you're not afraid, rag doll? You don't run by that corner any more?"

"Of course, not. Grandma used to say you don't have to be afraid of the dead ghosts, just the living ones."

"The living ghosts? You think there are living ghosts?"

"Grandma meant bad people who do bad things and blame it on ghosts, or on gypsies," she blurted out. "But if you're afraid, I'll have to ask... somebody else." She was pleased to discover that her words had the desired effect.

"I just thought you'd be scared, being a girl and all," he said and puffed out his chest.

"I'll see you tonight, then?"

"I'll be there, rag doll."

Miladin turned on his heels and jogged toward the gate, rolling his narrow shoulders, as if he were a heavyweight boxing champion.

* * * *

Kata returned to Grandma's room, the only place she could contemplate such intriguing news. She inhaled the smell of furniture polish mingled with the faint whiff of lavender sachets and thought it strange that two whole years had passed since Grandma's death, yet everything was going on as before. Even the lavender bush out in the yard, now woody and scraggly, still kept blooming, although no one had bothered to pick its fragrant, silver-grey leaves and tiny pale-purple flowers.

It's about time you clean up that farrago of trinkets! her mother's voice boomed in her head. *Throw away all that junk you've outgrown.*

Kata knew that, by everyone's account, she had outgrown most if not all of her collection. But she simply could not find a single item she could part with: the wicker trunk under Grandma's bed with newspaper clippings; her favourite books, some of which were fairytales she still read occasionally to ensure the characters did not get lonely; trinkets from various town fairs that took up a whole drawer in her grandma's dresser; miniature ceramic jugs and glass bottles that served as tiny vases for the wild violets and snowdrops she used to pick in the woodlot; necklaces and bracelets made of beads and sea shells; embroidered cotton tops; her first kiss – a lipstick imprint on the cut-off sleeve of a faded t-shirt; a tiny round mirror and a few crumbled sprigs of rosemary tied with a tuft of fuchsia wool which had failed to foretell a future husband.

Then there was her favourite, a gift she received when she was eight years old, on the day the bear danced. Although she could guess with a fair degree of certainty, she had never uncovered for sure the gift-giver's identity.

While some of the objects seemed to be losing their enchantment, this gift – nothing more than a large pink cookie heart hanging on a purple rope, made of cookie dough that never spoiled and was commonly sold by gypsy vendors – intrigued her and grew more mysterious each time she thought about it or its giver, especially its giver. Lately, she found herself peeking into the wobbly round mirror glued to its centre, examining her distorted features. These cookie-necklaces were special. During the town fair, every child and child-at-heart hoped to receive one: parents often bought them for their children; teenaged girls bought them for themselves and for their girlfriends as a sign of friendship; and teenaged boys bought them for a special girl.

Could this cookie heart possibly, possibly be from … him?

Kata glanced about the room, her treasure-house, containing all the riches she'd accumulated; objects most grown-ups referred to as a litter of junk and useless trinkets sold by lazy, thieving gypsies.

And now the gypsies have returned after six years. What could this mean?

Chapter XIII

The Corner Of The Woodlot

THE TWO SUMMERS since Grandma died had been rainy, and the girl who used to love summer was somehow glad that the cherries had turned wormy and the sun hardly shone. She found solace in daydreaming, imagining what it would be like to walk on the clouds in the crying sky and ask the unjust God why he took her grandmother away without so much as a warning. The villagers had said that dying from stroke was a blessing, sudden and painless. But that was little consolation to Kata. Even Grandma's voice in her head seemed to be fading. She found herself resenting people who laughed, who sang, who danced or played music.

Eventually, a sense of monotony set in. Nothing really mattered. Even acting in school plays, which next to reading and daydreaming used to be her favourite pastime, lost its meaning, for Grandma wasn't there to watch her perform.

Now, the return of the gypsies breathed new life into Kata. She became exhilarated by the prospect of seeing them again – as if they would somehow reunite her with her grandmother. As hard as she tried to dismiss this notion she understood to be absurd, her feverish enthusiasm refused to give way to reason.

* * * *

"Can't go with you, tonight," Miladin announced in a slurring voice, his words barely understandable. "Off to the market with dad. Sleepin' in the cart."

"You've got to," Kata pleaded. "You promised! I want to see them at night, when they play music and dance around the fire."

"Do your own spying," he said, head cocked to one side, one corner of his mouth drooping, his chin hair twitching in a nasty grimace.

"You've been at it again, haven't you?" Kata said, leaning in to smell his breath. "Drinking. Like your father."

"So why d'you wanna go?" he said, ignoring her comment. "Don' you remember Angela's baby?" He stumbled and burped before regaining his balance. "You think you're gonna see your gypsy boy, don' you?" he stammered, glaring at her with his puffy, blood-shot eyes. "Lorca? Univerees ... ity big shot? You think? A gypsy at a unive ... re ... esity, when pigs fly! Is what I say."

He turned and staggered off toward the gate, his shoulders waggling like his head.

A feeling of sadness and loss engulfed her. Usually she would have argued, insisting that he truly understand her point of view. But that was when his opinion had mattered. Miladin had changed to the point of no return. He was about to become the person he would have resented only a short while ago.

She considered calling on Maja, but quickly dismissed that thought. Her friend could be fully trusted with everything but this. She was a smart girl but cautious.

Kata stepped closer to the black-and-white portrait of her grandma and pressed her palm on the glass. She remembered many nights waking up and placing her palm on this cheek – in the darkness, the softness and warmth dissipating her fear. She recalled Grandma's words: *When people die, their spirit remains with their loved ones. It takes on the role of a guardian angel. As we pray to the saints, we can also pray to the spirits of our loved ones and seek guidance.*

Kata knelt on the pine floor where Grandma used to pray and settled her face into a reverent pose.

Dear God, she began, *I know I am not as good as I should be, but please don't blame Grandma for it. Please let her live in heaven for she is the kindest person in the world. And please let her find her Mihailo. And please, please allow Grandma to be my guardian angel.*

And then, a very strange thing happened. In the corner of her vision, she thought she saw her grandma's portrait smiling. A sense of comfort enveloped her, as it used to when Grandma sang lullabies or whispered prayers. She had feared that she had lost this feeling, forever. She closed her eyes tightly until darkness gave way to circles of glorious light, and began to pray. Grandma was smiling and God was listening, she was sure.

She wasn't sure, however, how long she remained in that posture. The prayers had turned into tears, and she thought that she must have dozed off right there on her knees. When she stood and looked around, the last rays of sun streamed through the cherry tree branches and into the room. This night was a risk she'd never thought she'd dare, much less on her own. Kata felt a strange effervescent energy and no longer wondered *if*, but rather *how* she should do what absolutely *must* be done.

* * * *

The yellow moon cast long silhouettes. Her gaunt shadow seemed to stalk her down the narrow path through the cornfield, breaking and bending only to grab onto her stealthy form. Every few moments, Kata looked back... sensing another pair of feet behind... another shadow. She was approaching the corner of the woodlot where a soldier had been killed during the Second World War. A young man, 19, pursued by Nazis, as he fled toward his parents' home a mere kilometre away.

A faint memory arose, something she'd overheard a villager say, long ago: *He ran through the cornfield, bent forward so they wouldn't see him... and just at the corner of the woodlot where the path curves, they fired so many bullets, his blood leaked like water through a sieve.*

Bathed in moonlight, Kata stood at this corner squinting through the scraggly tree shadows that swayed over the tall grass. It was midnight. She thought Miladin might show up, after all. He may have been testing her.

Then she spotted the cross. It was leaning to one side, almost hidden in the grass. A dry wreath she knew had to be *Ivanjsko cvece* hung on it. Kneeling, she tried to straighten the cross, and it shifted, just a little. But the lantern where she had seen candles burning was nowhere. Patting the grass, her fingers touched metal – scraps of the rusty lantern next to the cross.

Who was this solder running to his parents' house? And who was his mother lighting candles? No one ever mentioned her name. And why have I always thought of this soldier as some stranger? Someone I had been afraid of. Afraid of what? His departed soul?

A scene rose up, a fragment of a distant memory. It was the autumn after Angela's drowning. She and Maja had been walking home from school, passing the corner. A small candle had been burning in the lantern – with no one nearby. Then, at the far end of the long woodlot, Kata had glimpsed the slumped figure of an old woman. Now, she recalled something familiar she had not heeded at the time. The back of the woman's head looked as if a grey scraggly bird were perched on it – just like Nana Novak's hair bun.

Another memory fused to that one. She recalled visiting her grandma's grave shortly after the funeral. On her way out, she'd heard hushed voices, low sobs. She had turned back and walked among the tombstones, searching for the muffled sounds of mourning, wanting to help without knowing how. Two ancient-looking figures in dark formal clothing had risen from behind one of the tombstones, the man supporting the woman by the arm – Papa and Nana Novak.

"Help her on the other side, take her arm," Papa Novak had said to Kata. "She hasn't been well... all these years ever since our dear... son. She sits at that corner... lights candles... frightens the children." Kata had not made the connection at that time. She'd heard the words. But she had been missing her grandma so much that the words somehow slid by her, dissolved in the beat of rain on her plastic raincoat. But now, everything made sense.

Still on her knees, she passed her hands along the ground, flattening the grass, feeling the earth. *His soul departed here... blood drained here... his blood...* Kata now recalled odd fragments from Nana Novak's mumbling and grumbling. She'd heard it many times, but never paid attention to the meaning. Their son. The soldier was Papa and Nana Novak's son.

Fever flooded her body, a bubble of heat searing her chest. She could not inhale and, searching for breath, gasping for air, she ran in a frenzy. She fled through the woodlot, dodging tree trunks, feet catching the rustling leaves under the tree-shadows. Her head pounded as if some unknown instrument were strumming against every nerve, against every inflamed image, against the words ballooning in her thoughts...

In the rustling of the young leaves
in the growing grass
in the crowns of the slender white ashes
broad black locusts
grasping the sky…

In the crackling of the slender dry branches
from last winter's storm
in the fluttering of the invisible heartbeats
concealed in the black earth
and in the violet sky…

In the trumpeting of the armies
of the armies
in their razor-edged sickles
reaping the young hearts
crickets chirping hymns
chanting in the sky…

In the groaning of the blood-soaked earth
and in the empty graves
in the rustling of the young leaves
in the growing grass
in the crowns of the slender white ashes
broad black locusts
grasping the blood-soaked sky…

She ran faster, tears blurring the moonlit shapes flashing by, the same words, same tune, visions, rushing through her head.

Chapter XIV

The Gypsy Camp

WHEN KATA STOPPED running, she found herself at the other end of the woodlot. The strumming in her head and the chanting had stopped. She inhaled deeply, feeling light as if reborn with a sense of understanding, knowing. She now knew who the soldier was, knew why no one lit candles any longer. Nana Novak had passed away shortly after Grandma. Kata made a promise: she would bring a new lantern and continue to light candles under the cross.

All about her was calm, just the faint rustle of the leaves and the endless chirping of the crickets. Suddenly, in a shadow among a clump of trees, a stump seemed to move. It grew, stretched and shifted again. Miladin! Kata thought. He's come after all.

"Kata? Is that you?" But no, not Miladin. The tree stump spoke with Maja's timid voice. It waved its arms and teetered out of the dark – a gentle face bathed in moonlight, holding back tears while attempting to smile – like a child refusing to cry after falling off a bike.

The two gangly shadows bent and broke through the silhouetted tree trunks and into an embrace.

"What are you doing here?" Kata said, confused and relieved at the same time.

The story came tumbling out. Maja had seen Miladin earlier that day. He had revealed his plan not to show up, not to help Kata find her gypsy-boy.

"So you came instead? Aren't you going to get in trouble?"

"No. Nobody knows." And then added defiantly: "And I don't care if they do."

Hand in hand, they set out along the narrow path weaving through the fields toward Farmer Vila's land, the place where gypsies camped when they came to the village.

At the edge of Farmer Vila's land, Maja stopped.

"What's wrong?" Kata said.

"Roza said they're evil, the *vilas*," Maja whispered. "They kill people, especially children. Sacrifice them on the big stone slab."

"They didn't kill Farmer Vila. They helped her, enchanted her."

Everybody in the village knew the story. A farmer's wife, gone into the forest to pick mushrooms, had not returned that night. Believing she'd been eaten by wild beasts or sucked into the marsh, her grieving husband had gone into the village pub to drown his sorrows. He drank all night, rapt, he said, under the wicked spell of a gypsy dancer who, he swore, charmed the money out of his pockets – he, a lifelong victim of witchcraft. But his wife returned the following day. Her boat had sprung a leak. Unable to patch it before dark, she'd spent the night at Vila's Circle. But she was now a different person. Her husband claimed she had to be an impostor, no longer the obedient woman he'd known. She took charge of all farm matters with a new, steely determination.

Village talk had it that during the night in the marsh she had been under the *vilas'* spell. Soon after, she threw her husband off her father's farm and hired the local gypsies. Some villagers believed it was gypsy luck that turned the farm into such a profitable enterprise. Others swore they had seen *vilas* dancing in this woman's fields after midnight, sowing magic. And one summer, after a hailstorm destroyed most crops in the village while sparing hers, everyone agreed – her farm was enchanted. Fearing her wrath, the villagers kept their distance and nicknamed her Farmer Vila.

"Her daughters married gypsy men, didn't they?" Maja said.

Kata nodded: "That's why people don't like them."

"I heard that gypsies can be thrown out of their tribe if they marry a *gawdji*," Maja added.

"They married Farmer Vila's daughters. Grandma said that Lorca's in line to be the next chief. I'm sure he wouldn't be allowed to marry outside of..." Her voice trailed off.

"You still think of Lorca, don't you? You still think the cookie-heart was from him?"

"It was so long ago when I met him. He's at a university, far away in Spain. My God, what chance do I have?"

Maja took both of Kata's hands in her own. Her normally calm demeanour was overtaken by a sense of restless excitement Kata found a little alarming. While she had always hoped her friend would become more adventurous, now that it was happening she felt uneasy. At this moment, she would have preferred her usual guarded, astute Maja.

"And what if he was here? What if you saw him, tonight? And what if, just if, he asked you to marry him? Tonight. To run away with him. What would you do?" Maja's burning eyes pierced the bubble guarding Kata's hidden thoughts.

Her usual symptoms came on – stomach churning, head spinning. She thought that, if she had an anxiety attack and began gasping for air, Maja would know the reason, for sure. So she pulled her hands free and quickened her pace.

"Let's just get there. And can we not talk?"

Despite attempts to stay calm, she couldn't help envisioning herself in Grandma's silk dress the colour of ripe wheat. How it tickled her bare ankles and slid over her skin when she had tried it on, before Grandma's death. A wreath of freshly-picked daisies would support a long bridal veil.

Before long, they were standing on a hill from which they could see the main road that bisected the fields and continued over the bridge. On each side, a row of willows, lined up like the ghosts of ancient soldiers, guarded the bridge's crumbling pillars.

* * * *

The two girls huddled on the dewy grass at the top of the embankment, their backs against a broad willow trunk. In the valley, encircled by gypsies' tents and wagons, the last embers glowed in the campfire. Several horses, tied to the wagons, tugged at loose bales of hay. The incongruous collection of breeds, evident even in the moonlight, caught Kata's attention. She observed a few scruffy-looking horses and a couple of mangy donkeys. With its powerful build a bulky Belgian stood out. Its creamy mane and forelock gleamed against the dark chestnut coat, reminding Kata of the way Roza used to be – hard-working, ploughing through her day one chore to the next, propelling her upper body ahead of her wherever she went. Next to the Belgian was a shaggy Shetland pony. Kata recalled the many rides on the backs of these gentle ponies, when she was little and Grandma took her to the town fairs. Another form outlined against the night sky had to be a thoroughbred – with a graceful, muscled body and elegantly arched neck, a youthful version of the two racehorses Papa Novak tended in his stable. Its black coat and a flowing mane and tail gleamed with a purplish hue under the moon's soft glow. Could it be the famed Darley Arabian, the one Papa Novak talked about, had been reborn in this stunning creature?

One of the horses let out a prolonged, contented neigh. A shadowy figure crouched behind the wagons. Kata focused her gaze. Stories about gypsies stealing horses flashed through her mind. *Darley Arabian, stolen?* The man stood up and rubbed the coat of the black stallion in a circular motion, most likely with a currycomb or a coarse rag to remove the day's dirt and loose hair. Then he began grooming the stallion with downward strokes, from its neck toward its hindquarters, *the way I brush my father's horse, Kidran,* she recalled, feeling remorseful for her suspicious thoughts. Two male figures and one female stepped out of a tent and sat on the logs by the fire. Another man approached. He was tall, yet gnarled as a tree-root. He reminded her of stage props crudely imitating the human form. He poked the dying embers with a long, crooked stick.

* * * *

A gust of wind high up in the willow crowns, a rustle in the cornfields below... Kata squinted through half-closed eyes. A firefly flashed its lantern through the jagged overhang of the branches. It took a moment for her to remember where she was. The moon had vanished and the night was much darker. Maja slept, her head on Kata's lap. The firefly flashed again. Glancing in its direction, she glimpsed a male figure sitting outside the canopy. The firefly flashed once more, and she realized it was in fact a cigarette, no more than the length of a tree shadow away.

She paused, afraid to move. Then Maja lifted her face and gasped.

"Shhh," Kata whispered. "There's somebody here, close by."

Maja slowly looked around. Spotting the figure she gripped her friend's arm. "What do we do?"

"You can come out now, children," a voice announced in a slow, mocking tone. "Don't be afraid! There's no one here to hurt you. Come out, come out, wherever you are!"

Kata wanted to run, but she couldn't move. That voice. That mocking voice. The voice that reminded her of the contented rumble that always came when she stroked the head of her cat Remi. *His* voice – soft, yet with bumps and rough spots and now somewhat deeper. The girls tightened their grip on each other and stood up.

"I think it's *him*," Kata said, startled by the resonance of her own whisper.

"You girls might consider coming out," the man called again. "Don't be afraid. I just want to make sure you get home safely. I thought you were some village children spying on us."

Kata squeezed Maja's hand, petrified, no longer from fear but from an overwhelming sense of anticipation. *Oh, my God, what do I do?*

As if on cue, they walked beyond the shadow, shoulders pressed together. The man sitting on the grass stood, towering over them. His dark, shoulder-length ringlets shadowed his face. But Kata could discern the deeply-set eyes, a cleft chin, and the lips she knew were the shade of overripe cherries.

* * * *

Arranged by height like students lined up at gym class, the three figures walked along the narrow path through the cornfield. They were within sight of Maja's house.

"Now that you mention it, Kata, I do recall. I did have some of your cookies."

"How?" she replied playfully. "They were all gone, Lorca, there were none left."

"One of my little cousins stuffed a cookie in his pocket, saved it for me, crumbs and all. Just how my people are. Everything's shared."

"That's great!" Kata blurted out. "I wish I were one of your people."

"Maybe you should just watch me walk home from here," Maja said meekly. "So my dog doesn't bark her head off. Or I'll be in the biggest trouble."

"You sure you're all right from here?" asked Lorca in a fatherly tone.

"Yes," answered Maja. She turned to her friend: "Come with me half-way."

The two girls walked down the narrow path enveloped by the soft green and yellow summer grain about to ripen. Half-way, Maja stopped. She hugged Kata tightly, pressing a burning cheek against her friend's. Then she stepped back and whispered: "I didn't think anyone like him could exist. Ever!" She turned and ran toward her house.

Kata headed back toward Lorca, heart pounding. Alone. She would be alone with him.

"But you are," he whispered as she came close.

"Pardon?"

"One of my people. At heart, you are."

"Oh," was all she could say.

"When I saw you bring those cookies," he said, "I had such an urge to laugh. You were just a child, and you just wanted to share. It's a rare gift."

They entered the woodlot, walking side by side. Every once in a while she got a whiff of musky horse tang and wondered whether Lorca had been the man she'd seen grooming the stallion. As they walked, their arms came so near they almost touched. For the first time ever, she passed the corner of the woodlot without remembering the fallen soldier.

The brief silence seemed an eternity. She began to speak, saying whatever came to mind in the hope of concealing her still-pounding chest: "When I met you, you weren't that much older than me. But you acted as if you were my parent."

"Actually," he said, "I was two years older than you are now. So you realize how an eight-year-old appears to you. Am I right?"

Kata knew he was right but was becoming annoyed by his teacherly tone.

"You were so curt," she said, hearing the hurt in her own voice. "Almost rude. Refusing to talk to me."

"I thought of you on occasion," he said. "It even surprised me, when I caught myself. You reminded me of a ... cartoon character. Awkward and ..."

"And what?" she asked expectantly, glad that he had at least remembered her.

"And persistent. A few years later in one of my classes, we studied the Art for Art's Sake concept. And would you believe it? I began laughing as I pictured you with your cookies."

"A cartoon character, huh?" She was again an eight-year-old with bruised shins.

"As I said, my droning professor defined the doctrine that art is its own excuse for being, that its values are aesthetic and not moral, political, or social and so on."

Only half-understanding and not caring, Kata listened to his voice – disarming, hypnotic. Then she heard a tune in her head. *I could dream to his voice. I could stroll, run, to his voice. I could skip, dance, sing, to his voice ... pray ... sleep ... I could sleep to his voice.* She clenched her whole body to freeze the chanting.

"You were too young to understand. Wanted to make friends with me. But I couldn't risk getting into trouble, or getting my uncle or clan in trouble for that matter."

He paused, glancing at her, expecting a response? She continued walking without returning his glance. That would be risky. *Keep talking, keep walking, Lorca.*

"But you simply wanted to share. No motives, no social taboos. I named you ... Kata stands for Katarina, correct?"

She nodded, glad that the rhyme in her head had stopped. The only person who ever called her Katarina was her mother and that always in anger. She'd always hated it. Yet, when he said her name, it sounded different, somehow important. She liked it.

"So I named you Katarina the Giver," he said.

What exactly did he mean by that? She shot him a swift glance. Was she imagining it or did his eyes contradict his smile? She stumbled, but quickly regained her balance.

"The cookies were an excuse to talk to you," she retorted, as if he had wronged her somehow. "But you made it difficult."

She felt exposed, vulnerable. *He knows, he knows I'm dizzy just hearing his voice, just being near him.* She needed him to speak, anything to help calm her feelings.

"Had to return to school," he said, as if reading her mind. "But as for the rest, perhaps now you're old enough to know."

"I understood after Angela's baby," she said – and wished she could retract the words even as she uttered them.

"Ah," he said in a matter-of-fact tone. "That's partly the reason I'm ... we're here. With approval from the authorities ... Anyhow, that's a long story."

She glanced at him, hoping for more. But his eyes hardened and she knew he would say no more about it.

"Almost home, now," she announced.

They were at the end of the field, a short, rutted path away from her gate. In a changed, cheerful tone, he said: "So will you come tomorrow evening for my sister's wedding? You and your friend, I mean." Then more teasingly: "If you can get permission, that is."

"Permission?" Kata said, imitating Lorca's sardonic look.

Chapter XV

Jasmine

THE ARMOIRE AND the dresser drawers hung half-opened, their contents in a heap on the floor. Nothing Kata tried on felt right. She brightened when she saw Grandma's hope chest in the corner. But then realized that Grandma's clothing had been removed.

"What am I looking for?" She sighed and shrugged her shoulders. Drawn to the chest, she knelt and carefully piled its contents on the floor: white terry-cloth bedspreads, white sheets with white lace trim...

Her fingers wrapped around a garment and she sensed a familiar texture, a simultaneous crudeness and softness of the homespun cloth that had once filled this chest. To her surprise, the rumpled bundle was of homespun linen, its natural, greyish hue soothing to the eyes. Flattening it revealed a slip with wide shoulder straps Grandma used to wear under her dresses. She buried her nose in it and inhaled the faint whiff of lavender. She undressed and slid Grandma's slip over her head. It was a perfect fit – the cut widening below her arms creating a half-circle when she twirled. *This is it! I found it!*

Opening the dresser's top drawer, she foraged for the familiar package – the pink cookie heart. Gingerly, she removed the white wrapping and for the first time placed the necklace around her neck.

The cookie heart pendant covered most of her chest. She stepped into the guestroom and stood in front of the bevelled mirror. The image smiled back – a lopsided grin; long, dark, bedraggled hair and a large pink cookie heart with a mirror in the centre. Perfect for the occasion, she thought. Or was this it?

* * * *

"You girls hiding all the way up here?" Lorca called out. "If I didn't know your secret tree shadow I never would've found you." Kata and Maja stepped out from under willow's canopy into the softness of the twilight. "You ladies look ... lovely ... like moon fairies."

The two girls squeezed each other's hand in delight.

He peered at Kata's pink cookie-heart necklace and paused: "Is that ...?"

She nodded and smiled.

"You kept it all this time?"

"You're surprised?"

"Hmm. It was such an impulsive gesture. Seemed a fair trade at the time – a cookie for your cookies. Yes? Only later did I realize how it could be ... misconstrued."

For the first time he looked baffled, and she was glad. For a moment, he appeared awkward in his festive attire – a purple silk shirt, tight black pants, black boots with a prominent heel and a checkered *diklo,* the traditional gypsy neck scarf, knotted around his neck. And his long black curls tied in a ponytail. He cleared his throat, quickly composing himself. Assuming his typically confident stance, he waved a hand toward the gathering: "Come and meet the others!"

They followed him to a makeshift table. "What will it be? Some cherry soda?"

"We'll just walk around for a while, if that's all right," Maja said.

"Make yourselves at home," he answered, scanning the surging crowd. "I'll find my sister and introduce you."

Hand-in-hand, the girls moved into the gathering. After a few steps, they stopped and faced each other.

"Amazing. It *was* from him," Maja exclaimed.

Kata nodded triumphantly. As she glanced about, the sleeping caravan of the night before now transformed into a hive of activity, she also felt a change in herself. A feeling of comfort enveloped her. The cookie heart had been from him. Inhaling deeply the warm wind that had magically come to life, she sensed possibilities shaping. Had she not been part of his thoughts, his life, even of this caravan, in some miniscule way?

Maja pointed to one of two fire-pits, each with a few slow-burning logs alongside and a metal spit across. "Roasting a pig, just like for our weddings," she said.

Several men and women were gathered around the spit, in their everyday ragged clothes and bare feet, as another man approached them, bottle in hand. He grasped the cork in his teeth and poured a little of the liquid on the ground.

"That's a Romany ritual, an offering to the god of wine to banish bad luck," Kata said to her friend, as she watched them pass the bottle from one person to the next, taking long swigs, talking and laughing.

A group of fiddlers tuning their instruments waved Lorca over.

Maja nudged Kata: "I like the silky shirts the fiddlers are wearing. The blue one with yellow moons all over. And the one with honeysuckles."

"They're all dressed like Lorca," Kata added. She thought their boots were well crafted, like those the shoemaker from her childhood had made, except these were in fashion.

A man with a brimless felt hat sprouting a peacock feather handed his fiddle to Lorca. Leaning the instrument against his left shoulder and closing his eyes, Lorca drew the bow smoothly across the strings. He paused and drew the bow again, and again. Then he gently bounced the bow, producing shorter notes. He opened his eyes and adjusted some pegs, then repeated the whole routine.

"Wow! Look at those dresses!" Maja pointed to a group of women, some in long frocks and others in wide skirts with low-necked and tight-fitting bodices.

"Is that all you care about, dresses? Lorca is a fiddler. See? His father was a musician too. My grandma told me." Kata remained focused on the band and Lorca. In the din of the crowd, she could not quite hear his short notes. Then he handed the fiddle back and the two men patted each other on the shoulder.

As Lorca headed toward the fire-pit, a woman approached him. Her flowery frock was shaped like a bell from the waist down. A tight bodice outlined her generous curves. She clapped her hands as if glad yet surprised to see him and slipped her arm around his waist. She lifted herself on tiptoes and with her other hand, jingling with many silver and gold bracelets, she rumpled his hair as if he were a little boy, all the while laughing and chatting. They stood for a moment, talking and smiling, before a second woman pulled the first one away from Lorca and drew her back into the gathering.

"I like the big, looped earrings," Maja chirped. "You think I could wear a sash around my waist, like they do?"

Kata shrugged her shoulders. Didn't Maja see what just happened? The woman who'd hugged Lorca had a sweep of her dark, long hair pinned up with a posy of pink carnations. Did she have to be so beautiful?

As he wound his way through the crowd, Lorca exchanged a few words here and there. He patted the heads of the numerous children running ragged and barefoot around the encampment. The children threaded swiftly through the clumps of adults, disappearing and re-appearing among the women's frilled skirts – like eels through coral reefs from the pages of the *National Geographic* magazines Papa Novak kept.

Lorca crouched in front of two little girls cuddling corn-dolls, reminding Kata of her own from childhood. The dolls were fresh young ears of corn with long red-tinged corn-silk braided into a hair plait. After chatting briefly, he smiled and took his direction from the girls' pointed fingers.

As he entered the tent at the edge of the encampment, Kata's attention shifted to the children playing nearby. A boy of about seven lashed the air with a leather whip, while a couple of others wielded wooden sticks in a mock sword-fight. Two younger boys were wrestling, rolling on the grass, their excited shrieks making it unclear whether they were playing or fighting. A small group of boys and girls seemed to be competing in cartwheels, flipping their agile, slender bodies and walking on their hands, legs wobbly in the air. A girl of about eight held a baby in her arms, while continuing to play hide-and-seek with other children.

"We used to make dolls like that," Maja said, pointing to a toddler still unsteady on her feet, with chubby cheeks and shoulder-length curls, dragging a homemade doll almost as big as her. The doll's head consisted of a nylon stocking stuffed with rags, and the body a ragged skirt gathered around the doll's neck.

The toddler waddled toward an old golden retriever that lay on its side, yanking burrs from its tail. The girl dropped her plump bottom on top of the dog as if it were a chair tailor-made for her short legs. Then she spotted a woman in a flowery dress stirring a pot suspended on iron legs over a nearby fire. The toddler dropped the doll and headed toward the woman, whimpering as she lifted her arms in the air.

The woman crouched, hauled up the little girl onto her hip and continued stirring the pot. It was the same woman who had "draped" herself, as if she were a heroine in a romantic movie, over Lorca only a short while ago. Kata felt relieved. This was probably her child. She probably had a husband. But this could also be Lorca's child! And the woman? Lorca's wife? Kata was overtaken by sudden sadness. Why was she here? She remained standing next to Maja, idly observing the commotion about her as if it were a play.

Lorca emerged from the tent and walked toward them. He held another woman by her arm, as if he'd caught an escaped prisoner. Playfully, she tried to free herself.

"This is my sister, Jasmine," he said, chuckling. "Born under a jasmine tree."

"*Calo, pralo! Katar avas?* Speak Calo, brother! Where do you come from?" Jasmine's voice was clear as a church bell, her look mischievous.

"I mean," he said laughing, "she was named after the most sweet-scented, opiate-of-the-heart blossom." With arms fully extended, he held his sister by her shoulders, gazing at her admiringly. "Our guests don't speak Calo, my fragrant jasmine."

"In that case, let me greet your friends," Jasmine replied. Her smile was the same teasing one as her brother's. A long, black mass of curls enveloped her shoulders and cascaded to her waist, framing a scant white bodice. Countless folds of thin skirt fabric the colour of a ripe peach clung to her bare legs. Kata thought it strange that the vision from her childhood, the image of a beautiful singing fairy, had come to life, standing before her.

"This is our bride-to-be," Lorca announced, bowing in an exaggerated curtsy.

"Sit down, ladies," Jasmine said, lowering herself on the grass and folding her legs under her. "I'm really only bride number two. Your real bride, the youthful flower, is over there." Jasmine pointed to a young woman and man, dressed in festive outfits, sitting on a once-yellow blanket spread out on the grass, staring into each other's eyes, smiling and whispering as if no one else existed.

"The dresses," Maja cried out. "And all the hairstyles. All so amazing."

"They're waiting for the parents and the elders to close the deal," Jasmine said, carefully arranging her skirt. "When young people get married, our traditions are closely followed. I've done this before. It's my second time, getting married. And third for my *rom*, my husband-to-be. We're just joining in the festivities. Times are lean and life's a struggle. But we go all out when young people get married."

Glancing at Kata and Maja, Lorca laughed softly: "Hope you'll find our customs amusing."

"A little strange, almost eerie, to be here again," Jasmine said. "Last time we were here, there was a tragedy. You girls must've been young."

"You mean Angela's baby?" Maja blurted out.

"Yes! So tragic. My little Marco was just a baby. But he's a grown boy now. Seven years old. My gold and my heart, my reason for living!"

Kata examined Jasmine's features. Why does she look so familiar? Was it her likeness to Lorca? It was as if she had seen this woman's face in a dream. From the day the bear danced? Was it the three red roses tied to hold her hair above her forehead? Kata tried to recall the connection. But the next moment, her eyes were drawn by an elderly woman heading their way.

The woman was short and plump, shifting her whole weight from one leg to the other with each step. A large willow basket hung on her arm, grey hair pulled tight at the base of her neck. Kata stared in disbelief... Grandma's spirit... disguised... a gathered skirt almost to the ground... a loose shawl enfolding her shoulders... the round face with low-slung eyebrows... the confident air... Kata felt her thoughts teetering at the edge of a vortex.

Maja stood up and chimed a cheerful, "Hello."

"This is my great-grandmother, Goya," Lorca announced. "You can get acquainted. I'll go help with the food."

"I'd better help, too," Jasmine said, standing up. "Only the young bride and groom can play princess and prince tonight." She winked and walked away, flourishing her skirt with one hand.

With Goya squinting into Kata's face with Grandma's brown eyes, it was as if Grandma was standing there pretending to be someone else. She wished that she could say something, anything, a simple hello. But her throat was dry and her body frozen.

"Bread," Goya was saying, oblivious to the effect she had on Kata. "Fresh from grill. Pass it around."

Goya reached into the basket on her arm and took out a round loaf of corn bread. Then she peered at Kata again.

"You Kata? Yes?" Kata swallowed and nodded. "Your grandma's heart... soul." She spoke the last few words to herself in a low voice. "Your grandma, my *pen,* my sister in spirit. True shaman."

Two wrinkled hands crisscrossed with protruding veins were folded on the gathers of Goya's skirt. Gently, as if guided by some spirit, Kata lifted Goya's hand. She held it for a moment, amazed at how much it resembled... The last time she kissed Grandma's hand, it was cold and stiff and lifeless.

A group of village women dressed in black had gathered in the house. Their faces all looked the same – grey and sombre. They checked that the mirrors were covered. Kata was not allowed in the large dining room in the guesthouse. That's where the body lay. They had brought in Grandma's aluminum tub to wash the body three times. They took one of the last linen towels from Grandma's hope chest. Someone announced that Jovanka had grown the linen, harvested it, soaked it in the marsh, woven it into thread and made it into cloth on the loom built for her by her father.

Then the voices quieted and all Kata could hear was murmuring. Fragmented phrases arose from one particular voice: something about omens, magic and the blasphemy of it all. *What will Saint Peter say about her? She was a sorceress, like an old gypsy.* The voice doubted Grandma's soul rising to heaven. *Was it Nana Novak? Roza?* She even thought she heard laughter. Laughter? She wanted to ask why. But there was no one left to ask. Grandma was in there. She *was* the body Kata was not allowed to look at until it was ready for display.

The water from the aluminum washtub was spilled on the lawn, over the pink and white-tinged daisies. She remembered the exact spot where the water splashed – the dappled shade where Grandma used to rest after her morning chores.

Later, everyone was allowed into the dining room. Grandma was laid out on the large table that was at its full length as if it was Grandpa Mihailo's saint's day and at least a dozen of the villagers were expected for dinner. In fact, the last time this table was fully extended was on Christmas Eve, after the pig was roasted on a spit and left on the table overnight to be carved the next day, with cookie sheets under it to collect the drippings.

In her coffin, Grandma was dressed in the navy silk dress she always said she was saving for the day she rejoined her Mihailo. Wreaths of carnations and roses were strewn over the table. Kata had peeked at Grandma's hands clasped on her chest, holding the dark wooden cross she always kissed before taking a sip of holy water. She had leaned over ever so carefully to avoid crushing the flowers or ruining the fine dress that still smelled of lavender. Kata had pressed her lips on the back of Grandma's hand that now looked small and stiff, incapable of feeding the chickens or baking cookies or picking cherries. Grandma's hand was cold and lifeless and it froze Kata's heart.

And now, for the first time since Grandma went to be with her Mihailo, Kata had the desire to kiss the hand of an elderly person. It felt natural to lift Goya's hand and hold it against her cheek. Gently, she kissed the back of the hand.

Goya's arm enfolded Kata's shoulders and she found herself sobbing against the warm bosom. Eyes closed, she allowed the melancholy her mother warned against to flood her. She remembered standing on the wall of Kalemegdan fortress in Belgrade, overlooking the confluence of the Sava and Danube, as raindrops drowned in lazy swells. She imagined herself a raindrop, flowing away into unknown lands of unknown people who held all the answers to all the questions without answers.

Chapter XVI

Saint Sara

because my mother is a gypsy…

my love is like an ocean
deep and never ending
and all I ask of you my love
is your heart unrelenting

because my mother is a gypsy…

promise that you'll leave me
when you no longer love me

because my mother is a gypsy…

A CLEAR FEMALE VOICE lifted the notes, accompanied by the jangling of the tambourine and the rhythmic clicking of castanets. After every stanza followed the refrain, "Because my mother is a gypsy" in drawn-out notes that evoked both sorrow and joy.

One of the musicians waved at Lorca to join the group but he shook his head. Two men approached, grabbing his arms and pulling him upright. He tussled but they persisted. Goya placed her arm on Lorca's shoulder: "Must do your part, young man."

Lorca shrugged and made his way toward the musicians.

A young boy ran into one of the tents and in a flash returned with a fiddle. With a reverence beyond his years the boy handed it to Lorca. After tightening the screw at the frog end of the bow, Lorca pressed the fiddle into his shoulder and leaned his chin against the instrument. His bow gently caressed the strings, then suddenly dug into them, and then stroked them again with a gentle bounce. The tune, at first soft as a sigh, soon peaked to a bird-like trill. A second fiddle joined in, followed by a guitar. A female voice rose, soon joined by a deeper one.

It was the woman in the flowery frock, the beautiful woman with perfect curves, a perfect hair sweep, and now with a perfect voice.

The male voice? That was Lorca's. The most soothing baritone she'd ever heard. Not too loud or harsh. What had happened to the rough patches in his voice? She remembered those very well. She'd known them most of her life. Would recognize them anywhere. Except that they were gone. Kata covered her eyes. She could not face it, could not face the idea of that woman smiling into Lorca's eyes, singing to him, with him, draping herself over him.

The voices paused. The guitar and fiddles subsided, allowing a flute to emerge in clear, clean notes. And when the flute waned the female voice rose again, joined by the deep male one, the perfect one, Lorca's, and by the fiddles, the tambourine, and the wildly clicking castanets, enticing the listener to laugh and cry and sing at the same time. The dancers were soon on their feet.

Kata lowered her hand in time to see Maja tapping her foot to the music, swaying along with Goya and a group of women sitting on the grass. Most sang along while some joined in only for the refrain, infusing it with such passion that nothing else mattered. More food appeared, with people picking up pieces of hot roast pork in one hand and large chunks of bread in the other. Hungry revellers attacked large bowls of coleslaw and mixed salads. They munched and hummed to the music and occasionally banged pieces of cutlery together or against the glass bowls. Maja turned to Kata and with her mouth full mumbled something that sounded like, "This is amazing."

"Look!" Kata said shaking Maja's arm. "Look at them." She gestured toward the band. "Tell me what you see."

"Why don't you look for yourself?" Maja asked.

Kata glanced over. A group of people blocked her view, but a flowery frock was leaning against a pair of black pants, just like Lorca's. All the musicians wore the same type of pants. Was that woman's arm resting on the man's shoulder? The hand was gesturing, as if echoing the conversation, the heavily ornamented fingers flashing in a fast dance, bangles shimmering on her wrist. Kata couldn't see the man's face. But the purple shirtsleeve was identical to Lorca's. And then she glimpsed another purple shirtsleeve with yellow moons printed on it.

The crowd parted and she saw a peacock feather aloft, above the purple shirtsleeve with the yellow moons. The shirtsleeve with the yellow moons wrapped itself around the waist of the flowery frock. Kata sighed in relief. Lorca was heading toward her. She pretended to be absorbed in something else.

"Many of the customs seem the same as ours," Kata said to Goya.

"Two love birds sitting there? See?" Goya motioned to the bride and groom. "Met at gypsy fiesta. In Camargue."

Seeing the blank look on the girls' faces, she explained: "In Provence, in France. Beautiful. There is gypsy shrine. Every year in May, from all over Europe, from Canada, America, our people come to worship Saint Sara."

"You have a saint?" Kata exclaimed, while at the same time pretending not to notice Lorca sitting next to her. "Are your people Christian? My grandma said your people came from India, or from Egypt."

"I love your singing," Maja said to Lorca.

He smiled. Kata glanced at his face and their eyes met. She envisioned herself sinking into his embrace. *I could hide in his arms. I could sleep in his arms. I could die in his arms. I could ... die in his arms.*

"I heard that some gypsies are Christian," Maja said to Goya and Kata was glad of the interruption.

"We are an old, complex lineage," Lorca cut in. "Even we don't agree on our origins."

Goya raised her index finger with an air of importance. "Our Romany speaking, we keep. Our Romany ways. But much travelling, our life. Learn other speaking. Take on religion, ways of other people."

As the questions began, Goya talked over them: "Our Romany creed, never abandon. Our God, *o Del. O Del* is sky, or heaven, fire, wind, rain. Earth, *phu*. Always here. Before sky. Earth always here we call Divine Mother. One day, come *O Pouro Del,* ancient God. Suddenly, here, his a-co-lyte, *o Bengh,* the Devil. Now, *o Del* always Good, *o Bengh,* Evil. Both, *power*. Con-ten-ding. All around, in nature. Here." She spoke slowly, carefully enunciating each syllable and sculpting words with her hands.

Some men summoned Lorca again to help with chores but Kata did not mind. She was safe – as long as the flowery frock with her talking hand was "draped" over the shirt-sleeves with the yellow moons.

Goya continued. "*O Bengh* make two *papusha,* statuettes, from earth, mud," Goya continued. "But, *o Del* breathe spirit in them." She closed her eyes, and expelled air from her inflated cheeks, as if she were a drawing from the wind that came to life as breath. "So, *Damo* and *Yehwah,* or Adam and Eve, born. That one story only. Many tribe, many story how God come."

She nodded, to end the discussion. Then she raised her arms above her head and began to sway with the melody and to hum along with the singers.

Why had Grandma never mentioned Saint Sara? Goya's accounts were of a gypsy girl who was the servant of Mary Salome and Mary Jacobe living in Palestine at the same time as Christ. Suddenly the concept of a gypsy was no longer so mystical, nor evil as some of the villagers thought, an idea Kata had struggled with most of her life.

She knew gypsies believed in omens, magic. But now she found out they also believed in saints, and had their own. Seeing Goya so absorbed in her story, the flickering fire illuminating her untroubled face, Kata felt that her own belief in Christ and the Virgin Mary was not marred by her belief in omens, as some villagers claimed. Her fears about Grandma not making it to heaven were easing. She realized that Saint Sara would make sure all the good gypsies went to heaven, just like everyone else. And Grandma, although not a gypsy, was certainly good. Saint Sara would intercede to clear up any misconceptions.

"After Christ crucified, three Mary flee," Goya said, again picking up her story. "From Palestine. Sara call: 'Take me, take me.' At sea, big storm. Boat lose oars. Everybody drown? No. Sara look at stars. Show sign. She smell land on wind. 'Ha! Ha!' she say. 'I gypsy girl! Save saint. Three Mary I save, like dream tell me.' She come to Camargue. Use gypsy magic. Ha!" Goya chuckled, joyously, triumphantly, as if the saints had just been saved at that moment. Kata felt a sense of bliss.

"More story," Goya announced. "Sara beg in Provence. Beg poor fisher-folk, give dress to saints. Fisher-folk poor, but give. See, they poor, but share. We poor, but share. Share everything. Happy, sad, feast, famine."

We share everything, our happiness, our sorrow, Kata recalled Lorca's words from the night before.

She looked up at the pinkish clouds in slow retreat to unveil a pale night sky. Everything seemed so different, new and old. So many ideas that made no sense only a few days earlier were now taking shape.

She inhaled, deeply and freely, as if she were a swallow about to soar into the sky. How simple and rational everything seemed now that she understood the gypsy approach to spiritual as well as everyday life.

"Is this yours, miss? Miss! Is this yours?" A young boy was shaking Kata's shoulder, while a young girl was patting Maja's back, asking the same question, holding out a small object. Kata stared at the thin gold chain in the girl's hand, with a tiny oval locket just like the one Grandma had given her shortly before she died – the necklace Kata always wore. She passed her hand around her neck, but the necklace wasn't there. She glanced at Maja who seemed just as puzzled, staring at the tiny watch in the boy's hand that was identical to the one Maja had been wearing. The boy and the girl were hopping from one bare foot to the other, giggling and elbowing each other.

"Take it! Take it, it's yours!" the children exclaimed, each grabbing a hand and placing an object in it. Their lively, agile figures disappeared into the crowd.

"Show-offs. Their skill," chuckled Goya. "Ras-cal. That Jasmine's boy. Cle-ver. Like fox." She spoke something in Romany and wagged her finger in the direction where the two children had vanished. She shook her head: "They good. Yes, they good. Your jewel, make tight." She paused and added: "You, learn. We not easy to know."

"Is the story about Saint Sara finished?" Kata asked.

"Story never finish, child. Story live. Live in me, tell story. Live in you, listen to story. After, much after, you tell story. See?" Goya grinned, her long white hair straying from the bun, shrouding her shoulders.

She told about Sara who had also stolen the nails that held Christ to the cross and had taken away his crown of thorns. For relieving some of Christ's suffering, she earned the gypsies their right to steal small objects.

Then, with hardly a pause, Goya clapped her hands to the music: "Young bride and groom, see there? To be married."

She called out to the young couple and they approached reluctantly.

"I am Zara," the bride whispered shyly.

"Antonio," the groom chimed in with youthful confidence.

The girls gazed in admiration at the bride's saffron gown. A jewelled headpiece resembling a crown of gold ducats harnessed the waist-long black hair. The groom's silky shirt matched his bride's dress. The moonlight, the licking flames, and the glowing lanterns made the couple, Kata thought, look like a princess and prince from a fairytale kingdom. *Were they much older than her?*

"Find your *jumel*, bride, in Camargue," Goya said to Antonio. "There, many a lad meet his girl. Like me and my *rom*. God bless his soul in fragrant meadow heaven."

"Wow! You met your husband in France?" Maja loved romantic stories and looked at Goya with anticipation.

Goya nodded: "What night! Never forget."

Zara blushed and glanced at her fiancé. "We all know Goya's love story. The year was 1914, the second year the *gawdje* were allowed to be present inside the Church crypt on May 24. Up to 1912, only our people had the right to spend the whole night in it. The gypsies simply wanted to pray. Pray to their Sara, to *my* Sara." The shy bride's voice, filled with a mixture of restrained excitement and reverence, painted scenes of adventure and Kata ached to see and touch these mysterious, sacred places.

Maja clapped her hands. "Did you meet your husband in the crypt, Grandma Goya?"

"Oh, no, not in the crypt," Zara replied for Goya. "But we all know how Saint Sara helped her. Goya was fourteen, two years younger than I am now, and promised to a Hungarian *rom*. But she felt nothing for him." A swift glance at her fiancé promised passion simmering below her bashful surface. "You see, our families get together to give the future bride and groom the chance to fall in love."

Goya closed her eyes and smacked her lips in a pretend kiss. "So, I kiss him." She opened her eyes and puckered her lips as if sucking on a lemon: "Feel nothing. Again, I kiss, feel nothing. His family come to gypsy fiesta in Provence. To make wedding. I be married. At fiesta." Goya stared absentmindedly into the night, then continued: "I put on seven skirt, like bride. Go to crypt. Pray. To me, Saint Sara, Sara La Macarena, Virgin of Spanish *Gitanos*. My clan from Spain. I pray for love."

Goya closed her eyes and used her hands to smooth the air in front of her face. "I walk in crypt. Water seep, stone under my bare feet. Old altar. Bull sacrifices, wor-shipping *Mithra*, my father say. No. Much blood there. In centre, Christian altar. Right? Sara. Beautiful statue. Barren women pray to her. Blind. Crippled. Pray, pray. My beautiful Sara grant wish. Not all. Some. When she *see* you. When she *bless* you."

"Amazing," Maja chirped.

Goya sighed. "My wish – love."

Kata's head pulsated with a musical rhythm like that of a great throbbing heart, enveloping the fields and the trees and the sky.

An emboldened Zara took over the story as if it were her own. "And here was Goya, in front of the saint of the wanderers and the poor, Saint Sara. Pieces of garments left behind by others hung all about her."

Goya lifted her hand up and sighed, painfully: "Ah! Why I tell this? New world now. New story."

"Please continue, we'd like to know," Kata said.

"Pieces of garments?" Maja asked. "What does that mean?"

"*Dordi! Dordi*! Dear me!" exhaled Goya.

"Family and friends bring pieces of clothes from a sick person to be purified by contact with the saint," Zara said. "Some leave gifts of silk kerchiefs, pieces of cloth. Women rub the hems of the Saint's dresses, pray, ask for favours."

"I look up to Saint face," Goya said, moulding words with her hands. "Light, flame, candles. Sweet face smile at me."

She lifted her arms to the sky. "Saint smile at me," she repeated, her eyes brightening as if the miracle were happening that very moment. "Gypsy magic! Saint *see* me."

"Is this where you met your husband?" Maja prompted.

"That same night," Zara answered. "Yes. Not far from the crypt. We all think Saint Sara sent him to our Goya. Or her to him. Like me and my *rom*."

The musicians' melodies swung from sorrowful to happy, from sentimental to tumultuous, keeping the listeners in suspense and the dancers in thrall to the rhythm. The crowd of swaying bodies grew. The stomping feet and the snapping fingers and the shrill whistles picked up tempo until all Kata could see was a swirl of sideburns, half-closed eyes, peacock feathers, skin-tight pants, black boots, frilled skirts, silk shirts, and flowers falling from women's hair to be trampled beneath the furious feet below.

Hands cradling her face, Zara began her own story: "Late one night, I went for a walk, sorting out my thoughts. I knew my former fiancé's family would be arriving any day. I sat by the fire." Zara turned to her groom and whispered: "You must leave, Antonio. I must tell our story. I must tell it how I feel it." Antonio squeezed her shoulder and walked toward a group of men nearby.

"I stared into the glowing embers and I could still see my sweet Sara. I was bathed in her gaze. She'd *seen me, seen into my heart*. I felt someone watching me. I turned my head...and stared into the most beautiful eyes. *His* eyes." Zara gestured toward Antonio.

Kata felt as if she'd just been licked by a flame – that's how it had been the first time she saw Lorca, the day the bear danced, *his deep, green eyes the colour of oak leaves.*

Goya took over the story: "He hold my hand. Take me under tamarisk tree. Branches sigh, whisper. Happiness, I find."

Kata envisioned every detail of Lorca's face, lingering on the deep curve of his lips.

"I? Who I was?" Goya asked. "Gypsy girl, yes," she said, answering her own question. "But not virgin. No more. Lose my worth. Bring shame to my father. Bring shame to my clan." Her face lit up. "But love? I find. I know pa-ssion."

She stood up, propped her arms on her hips and commanded: "Never look another man's woman like that, my *pralo*, my brother! Men die for less!"

Kata and Maja looked around in fright, and Zara smiled, mischievously.

"Goya's lover," Zara declared. "The voice of her lover. Threatening. It was the same with me and my Antonio."

Goya nodded approval as Zara carried on. "'Will you marry me?' my Antonio asked, as if we were the only two people in the world. His next words were: 'Then take me to your father.'"

Goya looked deeply into Kata's and Maja's eyes, and confessed: "I look at my *rom*, my Sun, God, Love."

Kata felt light-headed. As Zara and Goya wove their love stories, Kata pictured Lorca. She imagined him wanting her, loving her among the wild flowers, jealously protecting her. She could see herself sitting on the grass, but felt as if she were in some unearthly state where her whole being vanished except for her burning face, and the warm wind rising in her chest and stirring that same low pit of her stomach, below the nauseated area of her belly button, that part of her body she would be afraid to touch, she was warned never to touch.

For a moment, Kata feared her usual panic attack, but it quickly passed. She felt bewildered and like never before utterly frightened by the new sensations. Worst of all – by a disturbing lack of trust in herself.

Goya tugged at her kerchief to let the silver hair spill down her shoulders. "My son born nine month later. Child of love."

"A woman who bears a child with a man she does not love will weaken the spirit of her people," Zara said. "Our children's souls must have a passion for life and love before they are born."

Goya waved her hand toward the band: "Look. Our dancers! Eyes fear-less, like eagle. Limbs swift, whirl-ing."

"Children born of love," Zara declared.

The women's voices rose and fell with the melody, peeling away the layers of ancient magic and answering the questions Kata thought had no answers, the questions of life and love, birth and death and existence. She felt possessed by the unpredictable run of musical notes mingling with the thumping of the dancers' feet on the trampled earth, by the glistening sweat on the smiling faces with eyes half-closed as if in a trance.

And now, Lorca loomed above her, hand extended: "Would you dance with me?" he asked.

Kata stared at him. Fear gripped her at the thought of touching him, holding him while in this feverish state. What if he were to sense her attraction to him; feel her burning face? What if he knew? If he knew how much she... *desired* him? The word sounded so unfitting, dirty. That was not her! That could never be her! Is this even love? Or pure lust, disgrace – those horrible words again? But he stood there, hand out. She tried to move. She opened her mouth to speak. But nothing happened. No movement, no voice. She became acutely aware of her own awkwardness. If she were to stand up, she would certainly draw attention to her spindly legs, her thin unwieldy figure. She shook her head in a "no" and continued staring at him, at the dimples in his cheeks and the deep curve of his lips. She noticed a glint of moonlight in his eyes and wondered if Lorca looked a little like Zeus under a moonlit sky. The notion that no woman could resist Zeus, the notion she once found absurd, suddenly became believable.

Chapter XVII

The Wedding

"NO WOMAN'S EVER worth the money a man pays for her. You hear me?"

"No matter what ducats a man pays for a woman. He's cheating, ha?"

"See that girl, there? Let me look at her teeth. How do I know you're not cheating me? How do I know she's not an old mare?"

"You think I would let you look into that girl's mouth? You old horse dealer. No wonder your woman doesn't love you. Treat women like horses, do you? When you learn how to treat a woman, come and talk to me, ha? You don't have the ducats worthy of that girl."

"And you don't have the girl worthy of my ducats."

"Now that I see what a mean old goat you are, I can't part with my girl for all the gold in Madrid! Look how sad she is to leave her dear mother. So the deal's off. I'm taking my girl home! Where she belongs!"

Jasmine sat on the grass next to Kata and Maja, clapping her hands in joy and along with other women encouraging the mother of the bride: "You tell him, *pen*, my sister, you tell him! I wouldn't give one of our women for a hundred of your men! Yes! You men have to learn how to *love* a woman!"

"That poor bride," Maja asked anxiously. "What's going to happen?"

"Just look at them!" Jasmine said, laughing. "Does that young bride look like she's sad to leave her mother? And does that groom look like he cares how much his father has to pay? They know it's a game."

"But why?" Kata stammered.

"It's the battle of wits between the father of the groom and the mother of the bride," Jasmine explained. "Nothing to do with the young couple."

"Brides are bought?" asked Maja.

"The groom must pay for the bride, yes. But it's just a game. An old custom. All the money is managed by the chief of the tribe."

"All those hurtful words. What about that?" Kata asked.

"Also customary," Jasmine said. "An age-old, man-woman struggle. The men from the bride's side join the men from the groom's. It's a bartering game, see? And the women do the same. This way, the whole pretend-squabble turns into the chance for men and women, husbands and wives, to fix their mistakes – yet preserve their pride. But the guilty mind" – and here she winked – "is always reminded of what's really meant."

"The bride's gown is so beautiful," Maja sighed.

Jasmine fumbled with the posy pinned to her bodice. She removed it and separated the sprigs of jasmine into two smaller bunches. She pulled a few hairpins out of her pocket, each ornamented with stones of varying hues. "Which one?" She held her hand out to Kata.

"Oh, no! Thank you, but I couldn't."

Jasmine lifted a dark tress falling over Kata's forehead. "Yes?" she smiled and pinned jasmine sprigs into Kata's hair. "Thick black hair, like a gypsy. A purple stone for you with white jasmine. Beautiful."

She leaned over to Maja and pinned her hair up as well, in the same way. "A pink stone for you, to go with your rosy complexion." Maja was beaming.

Goya and Lorca sat on the grass next to them. "Well, my moon fairies, the debate's heating up," Lorca announced. "The ceremony's about to begin." Turning to Jasmine, he added: "Are you ready, my sister?"

"Yes," Jasmine said, exhaling. She gathered her skirt, got up from the grass, and with a wide sweep of her hand at the sky declared: "Our universal church, the open heavens. My witnesses, the moon and the stars and all the people I love. While I breathe free air and feel the wind on my face."

"I have something for you, my fragrant Jasmine," Lorca said.

The same young boy who fetched Lorca's fiddle earlier produced another instrument.

"My sweet saint!" Goya murmured. "My *rom's* mandolin, from fragrant meadow heaven. My Lorca, since little boy. His great-grandfather's mandolin, keep with him, wherever he go. Make earth into heaven."

Lorca and the boy bowed to each other. Lorca picked up the instrument as if it were a precious object and glanced at his sister. The notes, barely audible, turned into a gentle trembling of air.

Kata leaned her head back. How well she knew these notes. Had known them always, as long as she could remember. The notes of her childhood that she heard late at night, while sitting on the windowsill. Jasmine's soft voice permeated the night air:

my dress in rags
jewels of stardust
my home gypsy carts

i sing and dance
for copper coins
and i sell cookie hearts

i'm a poor gypsy girl, just a poor gypsy girl
with no ducats of gold
but my heart and my soul, soar with a swallow
it can't be bought or sold

"It's been a long, long time. Since ... we've had peace," Jasmine whispered. She wiped a tear and flung herself around her brother's neck before lifting her face to the sky. "A new life. For my *rom* and me. I plan to give him my love and my body but not my gypsy spirit. That's mine and only mine to keep."

"And what would that be?" Lorca said, raising a sardonic eyebrow.

"My spirit?" she teased, twirling her gathered skirt flirtatiously, mimicking Lorca's wry smile. "My spirit is that of the earth and the sun, the wind and the rain, and the silver dust of falling stars, of course. As I've told you many a times, my *pralo*."

"I see the moon has turned pale," Lorca aid. "Dawn's almost here. They should be taking their bread and salt soon. Here they are. I think our *Romany boda*, gypsy wedding, is truly beginning."

An elderly man with a handlebar moustache approached the young bride and groom. His waistcoat was scarlet and black, dotted with metal buttons that resembled old coins. His wide black trousers were tucked into high black boots. A white shirt gleamed under his coat and he carried a long whip.

"Ahh!" Lorca exclaimed, "our chief!"

"Wow! He looks like a soldier," Maja said.

"The get-up, yes," Jasmine said, laughing. "The soldiering, no. Not for him. Or any of us."

As the chief neared, the bride and groom stood. The music, the dancing, the singing and the pseudo-quarrelling over the bride's worth came to an abrupt end. Everyone gathered in a tight circle. Kata slipped through the crowd to the first row of onlookers, only a few steps from the bride. The voices hushed and all eyes turned to the chief.

The chief appraised the audience, then turned to the groom and in a booming voice commanded: "Swear, Antonio, that you will leave this woman you want to make the mother of your children if you ever discover you no longer love her. Do you swear?"

The groom swore, repeating the chief's words.

Nodding with satisfaction the chief turned to the bride: "Swear, Zara, that you will leave this man you want to make the father of your children if you ever discover you no longer love him."

The bride also repeated the chief's words.

"As you love each other today, may you love each other forever," the chief declared with a tone of finality.

He then lifted a small flatbread high in the air for everyone to see. Breaking it in two pieces, he sprinkled salt on each, and handed them to the couple, saying: "When you are tired of this bread and salt, you will be tired of one another."

Then the bride and groom exchanged their pieces of bread. They ate the bread, slowly, gazing into each other's eyes.

The chief completed the ceremony by opening a simple switchblade he plucked from his pocket. The groom unbuttoned the sleeve on his left arm and exposed his wrist. The chief made a scratch on the groom's wrist. The bride pushed up the bangles on her right arm and thrust it out, allowing the chief to make a tiny scratch on her wrist as well. He placed her arm on the groom's, so each cut pressed against the other. He whipped out a white handkerchief and tied the couple's wrists together.

Kata felt Jasmine's arm around her shoulder. "No matter what happens from now," Jasmine said, "whether they live together as husband and wife until death, or go their own ways, they'll always care for each other."

The bride and groom entered a tent and the hushed crowd came to life, cheering, clapping, and throwing aloft handfuls of rice.

"The marriage union will take place now," Jasmine said. "I hope you girls don't mind hearing about these aspects of married life."

"Being chaste is not the same as being naïve," Kata said, surprised by the confidence in her own voice. Maja nodded in agreement.

"His is an old Spanish clan," Jasmine explained. "I wouldn't be surprised if they have four of their matrons showing chicken blood on a handkerchief tomorrow as proof of her virginity. When I first got married, it was my blood. I guess we'll see tomorrow. This couple seems to be following the old customs."

Jasmine straightened her tight bodice and the many folds of her skirt, bangles on her arms and ankles clinking. "Well, I'm about to take salt and bread myself. And here comes my *rom*. His cronies have been giving him advice how to act on his wedding night. As if he needs any."

Kata saw the man she thought looked like a gnarled tree, whose silhouette she had glimpsed the first night at the encampment. Jasmine introduced him as the man she planned to make the father of her future children. Kata was puzzled. She never imagined him as anyone's future husband, least of all wed to the beautiful, vivacious Jasmine. She saw him more as a *gnarled tree*, dried and decayed, *a symbol of suffering, an allegory for the transience of human life.*

Where had she seen the words that affixed themselves to Jasmine's *rom*? She closed her eyes to images surfacing like a photograph from the depths of emulsion in a darkroom tray. But this picture was not from the photo shop in the back of the school auditorium. It was from the art exhibit of the Dutch painters she'd visited with Aunt Agata. She could see the canvas in its full size, the power of light and shadow – *chiaroscuro*. As she gazed into the painting, she felt as if she could see through the eyes of its creator. The inscription read that the three graves in the middle could still be seen in the Jewish burial ground at Outderkerk near Amsterdam;

but the surroundings were the invention of the artist, Jacob van Ruisdael. *Jewish Cemetery,* circa 1670.

And here he was, the man whose shadowed silhouette she'd glimpsed from a distance the night before, her first night at the encampment. Her first night? It seemed so long ago. He placed his hands around Jasmine's waist and lifted her up, twirling her while she giggled like a child. He put her down and kissed her forehead.

"My *rom,*" Jasmine announced with a flourish.

Kata stepped closer to better observe him. He had thick, bushy hair he wore in an upright sweep, shorter than most other gypsies. For a moment, their eyes met – his deep-set and dark, harbouring a ferocity she'd never seen in a human face. His high forehead and high-ridged nose gave him a severe look. But below the cheekbones, his face narrowed, leaving an indentation in his cheeks as if he were sucking them in, his mouth appearing too narrow for the fullness of his lips. The broad top half of his face, sombre and intense, was set apart by a moustache clipped as if a piece of fur had been glued under his nose. And when he looked at Jasmine and she at him, they seemed alone in a perfect world. But the most striking feature was his indescribable sensuality. Kata suddenly understood how Jasmine could fall in love with someone like him.

Goya approached, wearing a blue satin jacket with embroidered flowers that gave her a festive air. Her hair was in two thick braids, one over each shoulder, a red carnation behind her left ear. Large gold hoops swung from her earlobes. She carried the same sort of bread as had the chief. Jasmine and her *rom, the gnarled tree,* stood waiting.

Goya broke the bread in half, sprinkled salt on each piece and repeated the same words the chief had used to marry the first couple. Jasmine and her *rom* exchanged their pieces and ate them. With the help of another woman, Goya raised a large earthenware jug high above the couple's heads and poured a shower of grain over them. Then, the two women threw the jug on the ground where it shattered. Goya picked up the broken handle and invited others to choose their lucky charms.

Encouraged by Goya's nod, Kata and Maja each took a shard of pottery. *What kind of magical power could this lucky charm bring?* Kata wondered. Goya's voice rose above the others as she addressed Jasmine's *rom*: "You promise to leave my Jasmine, my fragrant flower, when you not love her any more?" The groom nodded. Then Jasmine promised the same. Goya asked her final question: "Respect, be husband and wife, as many years as pieces of this vase?" The couple agreed.

"Is this marriage real?" whispered Maja.

"Goya is the tribal *Puri Dai*, grandmother," Lorca said. "A female counterpart to the chief. So, yes."

"Why is Jasmine's ceremony different?" Kata asked.

"Traditions. Many tribes and many customs. My sister chose the parts that suit her. It was Jasmine's will."

"What happens after the time runs out?" Maja asked. "What about, 'until death do you part'? Isn't marriage forever?"

"It is forever," Lorca aid laughing, "but only as long as the married couple wish it to be. When the time runs out, if it runs out, they could separate. Or break another jug."

The girls exchanged dubious glances.

"We love freedom, and freedom in love should be no exception," Lorca continued. "The notion of 'love' should not imprison. It should be boundless and invigorating as the blowing wind."

Kata was unnerved by Lorca's rare poetic demeanour. This was the second time she had noticed it; the first being when he had sung about love being as free as the wind.

"Imprison the wind within walls and you turn it into stale air," he said. "Chain 'love' to 'forever,' and you turn it into duty and possession."

Kata felt queasy. *Love must be free and invigorating.* The same stanza that sounded so enticing when sung now seemed ambiguous. Free to do what? Melt like butter under that woman's hand as she – bangles clicking and clanging – rumpled his hair? She envisioned him making that same declaration in a ceremonious manner, as if he were clan chief officiating at a wedding: "You must love each other freely!"

How would that apply to her as the bride, to him as the groom? At this very instant she did not feel free or invigorated by her love for him. She'd been puzzled but now she felt dismal and hopeless. At the same time, his words were far more enticing than any marriage vows she'd ever heard.

She felt a twinge of something she could not describe. Anxiety about his perpetual smirk? At this moment, his grin seemed bitter, as if recalling some hurtful memory. He glanced at her, but not in any special, meaningful way. Suddenly, all those phrases about love seemed hollow, as if he didn't believe what he'd said. *Do I belong in those stanzas? Could he ever see me in his lyrics about love?*

Kata felt betrayed, somehow. As if he excluded the present from his words, the moments that belonged to her. He excluded her. His cockiness, his smugness, his conceit, they all vexed her. She wished she could *raid* his thoughts and *invade* his heart and *infect* his spirit and make him pine for her. If only she had the gypsy love potion that worked wonders, according to Roza.

But the longer she stared at him the more quickly hope seeped away. *I am the only one who would pine and wither away like Narcissus. Yet there is no one like him.*

She suddenly felt as if she were drowning... like the stray bee she'd watched sink in the freshly-drawn honey being poured in jars... the honey her father harvested from beehives in the orchard. Could she ever fit in Lorca's life?

Chapter XVIII

The Blacksmith

AFTER JASMINE'S WEDDING, Kata continued visiting the camp as the festivities went on and on. This night she returned home early. It was not yet midnight, and here she was in Grandma's room. Her stomach churned with hunger pains. She had skipped dinner, escaping scrutiny of table manners: back straight; elbows off the table; fork in the left hand, knife in the right; no talking while chewing. She preferred the gypsies' easy-going approach to meals, sitting cross-legged or leaning against a tree, food in hand. But this evening, even the fragrance of warm cornbread could not raise her appetite, not after Goya's sudden words: "Madrid. Get message. Must go. Soon."

Kata needed to think. Needed to find her place in this latest complication.

There was a knock at the door: "Kata, open up."

Her mother? The only time she came to the guesthouse was to tidy up for visitors.

"You in there?" her mother called again. "Open the door."

Kata turned the large iron key protruding loosely from the brass lock. She pulled on the door handle and rattled the purple glass pane wedged between the green and yellow one in the row of rectangular inserts arranged across the door. That glass should be fixed, Grandma had warned shortly before she died. Kata knew it was her own fault that the glass was loose to start with. Gently, she pressed the palm of her left hand on the pane, and pulled at the door with her right. But the glass insert rattled again, like a distant school bell. She stared at it, memories from early school years surfacing.

Miss "Hygiene's" class. *Hygiene! Hygiene!* The teacher's voice barks in Kata's head. *Forgotten your handkerchief! Again!* Dead silence. Each student's hands resting neatly over a folded hankie, backs straight, all eyes on the single dot drawn on the blackboard. Shallow breathing. Kata holds her hands out, palms upturned, closes her eyes. Her heart pounds. The first slash burning the skin. More slashing. More burning. She opens her eyes. The ruler whizzes in the air. The door is ajar, only a few steps away.

She makes a run through the classroom doorway, down the long corridor, along the cement walk to the schoolyard gate, across the paved road, onto the well-trod path through farm fields that takes her home. She slows down and breathes freely. Then realizes she must get home fast and runs until all breath is drawn from her. In Grandma's room, she's safe at last. Grabs her handkerchief from the ironing board where she'd left it, and runs back out. She slams the door behind her and it groans and rattles and the glass inserts clink. She dashes down the verandah steps, across the lawn and bends down to fasten her shoelace. A heavy arm lands on her shoulder. Her mother's face looms above, screaming. A slash of a stick on bare legs. More screaming, slashing. Skin burning. "Run! Run!" Grandma yells from the barnyard. Kata is trapped, lying on the grass. Grandma is trotting, her footsteps unusually heavy, closer and closer. She is above her now, pulling on her mother, yelling, "Run, Kata, run!"

"Open up, Kata. I know you're in there."

Kata shook off the memory and unlocked the door.

Dare she look her mother in the eye? She must be angry. Otherwise, why would she be here?

She glanced at her mother's face. It was beautiful, even when compared to Jasmine's. Back when Grandma told the story about the nymph who hoped to soften Zeus' heart, Kata pictured her mother. When Grandma described the nymph loosening her dark, knee-length hair, Kata saw her mother's shining tresses. And when Grandma spoke of the nymph's turquoise eyes, Kata thought that even the nymph could not possess eyes more beautiful than her mother's.

Warily, she looked at her mother. To Kata's surprise, she saw no trace of anger.

"I know about your visits with the gypsies," her mother declared, sitting on Grandma's bed and sounding like one of the announcers reading the six o'clock news. "Miladin said you're planning to run away with your gypsy boy."

Kata stared at the laced fingers in her lap as if she'd never seen those hands before. What could she say? She was mute. Was the play about to begin? Scenes about to start evolving: the screaming, the striking, the hysterics? She knew her part in the drama. Even if it had been a few years since the last performance. And while she had no lines to memorize since she preferred to play her part silently, the plot had always remained unchanged.

The turquoise eyes were still, not a flicker.

"I came to see what you've been doing there, at the camp." The statue remained frozen. "You've been going there every night, haven't you?" Kata took in a shallow breath. Her stomach turned rancid. "You seemed quite at home. Aren't you going to say anything? Do you feel at home with them?"

Kata looked up into her mother's eyes and nodded, amazed at the calm she saw there.

"I haven't been much of a mother to you." Kata winced. This play was different than the others. "Have I?"

The thought that she should run to her mother's embrace and shout: *But you could be, you could,* flashed through Kata's mind, then fizzled.

"Come and sit next to me."

The statue clambered onto the bed.

Her mother lifted an arm as if about to embrace her. But instead, her hands fidgeted with a fold of skirt.

"I've got a confession to make," she said, looking down at her hands. "Seeing you with them like that, I realized. I've got to tell you. I never thought I'd have to. That it would come to this."

Kata was startled to hear a touch of guilt, and became wary of the calmness. To the point where the statue might disintegrate. But she realized that if she let her guard down, all hell might break loose.

"After your grandpa died, gypsies worked for us, helping Grandma. But then you know that."

Still fiddling with her skirt, her mother talked about the winter before Kata was born, the winter Grandma broke her hip and needed extra help with the farm chores. Kata listened to the distant voice, about a distant time when her parents had teaching jobs in town and came to the farm only on weekends, before they moved back to run it.

As her mother described that bitter winter, Kata wondered what kind of a teacher she'd been. Could she recite the botanical names of plants? Did she have a beautiful singing voice? Did she ever slash her students with a ruler? She must have been a better teacher than she was a farmer as she performed all farm chores resentfully – never seeming comfortable with other farm wives. Grandma always sheltered her as if she were incompetent or fragile – as if she might break under hard work.

"One of the men was a blacksmith, an expert with horses," her mother said. "He was thin, tall, with a wiry build. Full of energy. An unusual-looking man." She smiled. "I thought him rather unpleasant until I got to know him. Then I realized he had a certain charm. Magnetism you could call it."

Kata thought it strange that her mother talked about a man other than her father. But then she never talked about her father. He was just there.

"The blacksmith stayed for a week, and then another. He said work was slow in winter. His men could cover for him."

Kata felt tired, her eyes heavy. Her mother stood up as if ready to leave but then abruptly sat down again. "I must tell you, Kata. Or I may never again find the courage."

She rose and began pacing. Then stopped right in front of Kata.

"There was this intensity in his eyes," she said. "When he looked at me, he burned a hole in my soul." She uttered these words urgently, as if she'd been waiting an eternity to release them. "Kata, I see that intensity in your eyes," she said.

She placed her hand under her daughter's chin and lifted her face, looking long and hard into her eyes. For a moment Kata felt as if she would crack under her mother's gentle touch. But at her mother's next words, she jumped off the bed and backed away.

"Kata, he was there, at the camp. That's when I realized I must tell you."

"Tell me what?"

"I think you know."

"Know what?" Kata shouted, not believing her nerve.

"He's your father, Kata. He's your father."

For a moment, they stared at each other in silence. Then her mother moved toward Kata as if to offer an embrace. Kata stepped even further back.

"He slept in that room over the barn. That was my special place. As a child, I used to hide up there when I was sad or lonely. It felt so high, the view so long." Her mother looked at her as if expecting something more. Then shrugged her shoulders. "I don't know what else to say. I just thought you should know."

"Did you love him?" Kata yelled.

"What does it matter now," her mother said with a wave of her hand. But the twist in her lips told another story. Her china doll face wrinkled up, as if she'd taken a spoon of Grandma's wormwood fermented in *slivovica* that still sat in a bottle on the kitchen shelf.

"I need to know. Did you *love* him?"

"I... really don't know," her mother said. "I think it was more a need, loneliness." She paused. "I can't say it was love. Perhaps it was. Who's to know?" She stood for a moment, lost in thought. "I could see myself loving a man like him. In another life, maybe. Not in this one." Her face twitched into an almost-smile.

"Desire, some called it," she said, grimacing. "What did they know? Disgrace. Shame. Lust. Pointing a finger is all anybody knows."

She looked straight at her daughter. "You've always been different. When you were only four, one night you woke up screaming. You said somebody was killing the peacocks in the gate. You wouldn't stop. So Grandma got us all up and we lit a lantern and took you to the gate to show you that the peacocks were just made of copper. Well, the next day we found out that a young woman in the village had died in the night."

"Angela's sister? Is that who it was?" Kata voice was trembling.

"Yes. Yes it was. How did you know? We never talked about it again. Thought it was better left alone." Her mother shrugged. "I never thought I'd say this. I think it's your gypsy spirit. Use your gypsy spirit wisely, Katarina. Use it wisely."

She turned and walked out of the room. The glass door rattled behind her and the loose pane looked ready to fall.

* * * *

The gnarled tree is my father, the gnarled tree is my father, whirled in Kata's head. She buried her face in the feather pillow and felt herself sinking into Grandma's embrace, hearing her whisper: *All is well that ends well.*

"But there is no end to this story," Kata barked at the empty room. She went to the dresser and opened the top drawer. Beneath all the trinkets, she spotted the corner of her old school notebook and pulled it out. List of Puzzling Questions Without Answers, she read aloud from the cover. She inserted a finger under the cover and lifted it, only to snatch it away and stuff the book back in the drawer. None of these questions mattered. Only one. The one that now superseded all others.

Am I the child of love? A woman must love her man with her whole heart and soul. Or am I only ... only a child of lust ... or desire? Those ominous words loomed again. *My spirit, weakened by lack of love? By this out-of-control thing called desire? Is that all I feel for Lorca? How would I know what love is?*

Kata saw her face in the mirror across the room. The expression resembled her mother's as she told Kata that loving the gypsy would have been hopeless.

"Perhaps it was love," Kata murmured, repeating her mother's words.

She crossed the room and stared into the mirror. "Tresses like horsetail, like a gypsy's," Roza used to say when braiding Kata's hair. She ran her fingers through hair that hung past her shoulders, stuck out this way and that, and wiggled itself out of every hairband she owned. She liked the blackness of it, even the red highlights caught by the sun. But she often wished it were more like friends' hair, silky like Maja's, or buttery blonde like Lena's.

She disliked the figure in the mirror, wishing she could reshape it like putty – skinny legs, inconspicuous breasts, high-bridged nose, ears poking out of the coarse hair. She stared at her own eyes again, light green with yellow specks. Not turquoise like her Mother's, not leaf green like Lorca's, not ice-blue like Van Gogh's, and not black like her father's – at least the man she'd thought was her father. And then she remembered that *the gnarled tree,* her biological father, also had dark eyes. Her own eyes did not resemble those of anyone she knew, only the green marble she'd traded to Miladin many years ago for a bubble-gum card of Richard Chamberlain.

Nor could she see the intensity described so emphatically by her mother. Yet the thought of having this special intensity made her feel strong, defiant – the way she had felt when Papa Novak found music in her voice.

In the mirror, Grandma's spinning wheel was silhouetted in a dark corner. Kata wished that she could fall into a deep 100-year sleep, like the princess who pricked herself on a spindle. Then she could wake up some day, after all the confusing questions without answers had been resolved.

Chapter XIX

Under The Gypsy Moon

THE DEAD SWALLOW under the blue hyacinth lifts her wings and sweeps toward the sky. I run, try to catch up with her. Her shimmering feathers grow longer and longer, taking the shape of a woman. The swallow/woman turns her head and looks at me with her turquoise eyes – long dark tunnels. They are now my father's eyes, burning holes in my soul, beckoning me to run faster, faster. Not catching up with the swallow/woman's eyes, with my father's eyes, is worse than death. She raises a flute to her lips and blows an ominous tune: "Sleep my little baby, sleep in the night, sleep in your cradle, under moonlight…" I scream: "No! Not Angela's lullaby!" Two figures run toward me. But this is no longer a dream.

She stared at the approaching figures.

"Kata? Is that you?" Lorca's voice, surprised yet somehow warmer than usual.

Sheepishly, she stepped out of the shadow.

Her mother's warning echoed in her head, *Stop hallucinating, stop running from reality*. Now, those instructions seemed futile. Where did reality end and unreality start?

After the previous night's exchange with her mother, these visions flowed in and out of her mind, awake or asleep: the dead swallow's eyes, the nymph's turquoise eyes, her gypsy father's eyes, one and the same staring at her in the darkness… And now the vision of Angela sitting under the mulberry tree and singing her lullaby. She wrote down the images as if they were scenes in a play. First thing in the morning, she rewrote them again and again, organizing the sequence, filling in the details. She hoped to dissolve the visions and watch them drift away by the end of the day. But they stalked her. It was now past midnight, and here she was at the top of the hill overlooking the encampment where she thought she could finally escape. Still, in the darkness, scenes from her dreams of the previous night marched on like an army conquering new lands.

"Do we all know each other?" Lorca asked.

The reality of her connection to him struck her. *I am a gypsy, just like him.* But it was the man standing next to Lorca who caught her off guard. She never expected to see him here. It was Stefan, her frog-prince she once pretend-kissed a long time ago.

"Hello Stefan," Kata muttered. She looked past Lorca into the darkness at the silhouetted figures moving among the tents beyond the smouldering fire, searching for a glimpse of her… father.

He must be here somewhere. Then she saw Jasmine approaching. *He must be nearby.*

Jasmine sat on the grass, legs folded under her skirt as usual, and began examining the bottom of her foot.

"I can't find it," she said, turning her sole toward the moonlight. "But I can feel it. That darn thorn. Blackberry."

"Picking berries with your husband?" Kata asked.

"Just us girls."

Is that what gypsies did on their honeymoon? And where could her husband be?

"Probably staring at you," Lorca said laughing. "That thorn you stepped on." With an exaggerated flourish, he performed a low curtsy and recited:

Bajo la luna gitana,
Las cosas la estan mirando
Y ella no puede mirarlas.

Jasmine narrated the translation ending each line with a question:

Under the gypsy moon?
Things are staring at her?
Things she cannot see?

"Reciting poetry, again," Jasmine said, smirking. "Garcia Lorca, his namesake."

Stefan grinned: "The first time he met Angela, he rhymed off those very same verses. Sure got her attention, my *pralo*. Have to say, I wished I could've made such an impression on her."

Lorca knew Angela? And Lorca reciting poetry? Kata was baffled and slightly uneasy. She had found comfort in his ordinary brooding stance. Now, for the third time since she had been welcomed to the camp, he appeared strangely boisterous, carefree. Three times – like the bad omens. She suddenly felt queasy.

"He's memorized Garcia's every line," Jasmine said. "That's why he is Goya's favourite. Always has been."

"And you expect to find a thorn in your foot by the light of the moon?"

Ignoring Lorca's mockery, Jasmine turned to Kata and continued: "The love of Goya's life she told you about? Well, that was our *boro dad*, our great-grandfather. He was a close friend of the poet."

"Was he from Spain?" Kata asked. "The poet? Like your clan? Is your husband also from Spain?"

"Yes. We keep close ties. Last time in Granada, we were in Sacro Monte. Went to the *cueva,* cave home of Lola Medina. At one time, Lola was the most celebrated gypsy dancer of all."

"Your husband is from Spain as well?" Kata persisted.

As if not hearing the question, Jasmine continued: "Our Goya discovered a plaque with an inscription: 'In this *cueva* Federico Garcia Lorca wrote many of his gypsy poems.' Goya just stood there, eyes closed, swaying to the rhythm of her own humming. She would've been happy to remain there forever." She leaned over and lightly patted Kata's hand: "But for her gypsy spirit calling her to follow the winds."

"Goya was a dancer in Sacro Monte," Lorca said. "That was before our *boro dad* was killed."

"Killed?" Kata said, while recalling Grandma's words: "We've both lost our husbands."

"Taken to the *Sremska Mitrovica* concentration camp in 1942," Jasmine answered. "The last Goya knew of him."

"Perished in the Holocaust," Lorca added. "One of the half-million gypsies."

These last few sentences clung to Kata like magnets. She had heard stories about gypsies stealing children, stealing horses, robbing graves, using black magic or the evil eye to cast spells and even cause people to die. But she couldn't remember villagers talking about gypsies being killed by the Nazis – except for Papa Novak. He'd once said to Grandma:

"Our people were slaughtered by the thousands, my dear, we all know that. But our position was different. We weren't sought out like the Jews and the gypsies. We were targeted for refusing to cooperate with the Nazis and so we were called White Jews. Many of our people were killed in retribution for fallen Nazi soldiers, or for hiding our Jewish friends."

At the time, Kata had been uncertain what all this meant. She thought of the schoolchildren in Kragujevac who were killed by the Nazis. Do the reasons matter? Was her grandfather killed for hiding his Jewish friends? Why did they have to hide? As she grew older, facts trickled in until the big picture emerged, the millions of Jews killed, not just the grownups but also children – linking with the *five and three zeros* killed in Kragujevac. And now the gypsies as well. The gruesomeness loomed over her, enormous and unfathomable.

"Goya still talks about the time they spent with the poet, as if it were yesterday," Jasmine said. "The golden years of her life, as she put it, before the wars began."

"Goya's seen much death in her life," Stefan said.

"Yet does not mourn," Lorca said, his carefree demeanour gone. "Instead, she honours her loved ones in her stories and songs. But Uncle Grizzly's death crushed her. Her last grandson."

"We'll find the truth," Jasmine declared. "It's Goya's wish. She must know before she joins the love of her life in the fragrant meadow of heaven."

Lorca turned to Stefan: "After Grizzly's death, your letter, your belief in our uncle's innocence meant the world to us, my friend."

"Your uncle's death was no accidental drowning," Stefan said. "It was murder of an innocent man."

"We can't bring our uncle back, but we can clear his name," Lorca said. "To be suspected of such a hideous crime – of killing that baby. Or that young woman, Angela."

"Until that crime is solved, everybody's guilty. Every gypsy in this clan. The police are still looking for ..." Stefan looked at Jasmine and stopped mid-sentence.

"There is only one way," Lorca said. "Find the truth."

* * * *

What do I know about my father? I found nothing at the camp. It's all talk about wars and death. And here in the village, more talk about wars and death. And gossip about Angela's baby.

That night Kata dreamed she was in a school play. She stood on the stage and stared at the audience. They were her neighbours, in their raggedy work clothes, not like the audiences she saw at the Belgrade theatre, all dressed up and cultured, as Grandma used to say. And the villagers were laughing.

As far as she could see were faces contorted in laughter, an endless mosaic of gaping mouths of crooked teeth and dark gaps. Why where they laughing at her? The scene was evolving as it should. Her part was silent. It was cast that way – a new version of the old play. Suddenly she realized she was an imposter. This part belonged to Angela who was now staring at her – eyes deeply recessed burning through the matted hair shadowing her pale face; one side of her skirt torn away; dried blood from a neglected wound on her calf dribbling down to her foot – just as Kata had seen her by the well all those years back. She held a baby in her arms.

Kata stepped closer in disbelief.

"Angela, is that you? And your baby? Thank god! I thought you were dead!"

"Only the truth can set you free," Angela whispered.

"It's all your fault! You made that holy water that wasn't holy!" the village chorus yelled. Kata sat up in bed, drenched in sweat, heart pounding, orange and blue circles pulsating in the darkness before her.

Chapter XX

Do Not Speak A Dead Man's Name

I'LL LOOK HIM in the eye. He'll see it. See the intensity in my eyes. He'll know.

No he won't, silly. How could he?

I'll tell Jasmine. He's her husband. She'll help.

No, no. Bad plan. She could hate me.

He might be by the fire, where I saw him the first night at the camp, poking the embers with a stick.

Kata stumbled along the path through the fields. With no moon, the skies were sooty. As she emerged from the cornfield, Kata thought she heard footsteps and looked back at the path behind her – it gaped like a tunnel. She shuddered and broke into a full-out gallop toward the encampment.

I need to see him. Talk to him.

And say what?

Anything. He is my father.

That means nothing to him. Your own father never talks to you. Never looks you in the eye. Why should the gypsy be any different? You know nothing about him.

From the edge of the embankment she stared down at the campfire, mystified by the angry commotion below.

Unwilling to walk into the cluster of raised voices, she picked an apple from the fruit basket she'd brought as a gift, and bit hard into it. She paused, stopped chewing, and listened: there was moaning, then sobbing in the darkness.

"Who's there?" she called out.

A slumped figure under a tree shifted. Kata ran over and kneeled next to the woman curled on the grass. She unwrapped the shawl from the woman's head and gasped: "Jasmine?" Voluminous hair concealed the woman's face. Kata gently brushed it back with her hand.

Jasmine looked up, bewildered, murmuring in another language. Then she grabbed Kata's hand: "Come with me."

The two stood at the top of the hillock and looked down at the furious, yelling assembly of gypsies that encircled something, someone. Jasmine tugged at Kata's hand and they charged down the hill.

Seconds later, they stood in the midst of the angry crowd. Two men, one on each side, held a third under his arms, supporting his limp body and dragging feet. A burlap sack was pulled over his head. He was propped up for a moment, towering awkwardly over the two men, then allowed again to slump, bloody knees scraping the dust. The crowd shouted at him as he was flung, like a pile of rags, on the trampled patch of earth that had served as the dance floor two nights before. He lay motionless.

"Is he dead?" Kata gasped.

"He wishes. He'd be better off," Jasmine spat. "Wait here," she said. "This will only take a minute."

Jasmine approached the turbulent crowd. Arms propped on hips, she lifted her head high, and looked around. Silence fell and all eyes turned to her. She grabbed the top layer of her skirt, now streaked by dust, and in one swift motion tore away a strip of the fabric. Kata stared at Jasmine's hardened face.

Cheers went up as Jasmine waved the piece of cloth above her head. She shook the hair off her face and approached the figure slumped on the ground. She lifted her hands above her head and snapped her fingers. There was a moment's silence. Then fingers snapped, hands clapped, and feet stomped, swiftly joining in a tempestuous rhythm. Jasmine swished her skirt while arms and hands became one sinuous flow of movement.

"*Cante jondo Andalusia*, a deep song of Andalusia," murmured the crowd. The words followed the beat of pounding feet. Kata went back to the day the bear danced. She closed her eyes and saw it all again. The flamenco dancer is Jasmine. Her partner, *the gnarled tree*. She opened her eyes. He seemed so much younger then, but it had to be him. But now Jasmine danced alone, her body and arms swaying as if in pain, arching over the slumped figure, her face smeared with tears, lips held firm above a quivering chin.

Jasmine paused over the man on the ground. She extended a hand over his covered head for a moment. In one quick motion, she pulled off the burlap sack. The crowd roared and Kata gasped in recognition. She stumbled through the crowd and stared into his down-turned face, searching for his eyes, for the intensity in his eyes. But they were shut.

"*Drabengro*, evil man of poison," Jasmine shouted as she threw the fragment of skirt over his head. The crowd had quieted.

"You are condemned!" She hissed before she spat on him. "*Devla mar tu!* God strike you!"

"*Devla mar tu, Devla mar tu*," an angry chorus repeated, as every adult present approached and spat on him, followed by a ceremonious nod.

Jasmine brushed her hands against each other as if indicating a job well done and one she was glad to be done with. "*Mokado*, magically unclean," she snapped. "The father of my future children, *no more*!"

The words hung in the air for a few long moments before they sank into Kata's mind. "The gnarled tree is my father," she heard herself whispering.

Jasmine turned and swiftly began walking away from the crowd. Kata caught up to her. "Your husband?" she blurted out. "But why? Your wedding. The way he looked at you. He loves you."

"Her too. He loves her too, I guess," Jasmine said disgustedly. "That woman over there." She pointed to another shouting group. They were encircling a young woman whose hair was being shaved off, long dark tresses carpeting the ground beneath her.

Kata recognized her as the one who had draped herself over Lorca the night of Jasmine's wedding. The one who had so seductively fingered his hair. Kata sighed in relief. This woman probably meant nothing to Lorca. Then she thought of Jasmine. This woman would be hard to compete with. Then she noticed the same little girl who'd sat on the old golden retriever the night of the wedding. The toddler, in the arms of another woman, was screaming and waving her chubby hands toward her mother who now lay in a crumpled heap on the ground.

"Under that willow tree. They made love," Jasmine scoffed. "The day after our wedding." She motioned in the direction where Kata usually hid under the tree shadows. "And I didn't even know until today."

Kata took Jasmine's hand into her own and stared at it. It was limp and cold, like her grandma's dead hand. But Jasmine's face was bright red, smudged with sweat and tears, her eyes burning with anger. Kata felt fear, cruel and cold, seeping into her – fear of love, loss, betrayal, naked fear stripped of all promise. She lifted Jasmine's cold hand and pressed it hard against her own face, then fell into Jasmine's embrace, into their rhythmic sobbing.

Goya approached: "*Dordi, dordi,*" she murmured, enfolding both women into her arms, into the heady scent of smoke and burning logs and baking bread. "What one woman do to another," she murmured. "But she, *Mokado*, be pitied, for life. No dance. No friends."

"Ha!" Jasmine said, breaking the embrace. She'll hide under a kerchief. Until her hair grows back. That's all. But this heart? Broken. Forever." She struck her chest with a clenched fist and moaned in pain before quickly turning and walking back up the hill.

Kata was about to follow, but Goya motioned her to stay. "She talk to *Ravnos*, Spirit of the Sky."

Goya sighed, as she sat on the grass. "My Jasmine. My fragrant flower. He good. But he have curse, *Bari Hukni*, the Great Lie."

"What's going to happen to him, to them?" Kata asked, sinking down next to Goya.

"Jasmine? Find love, some day," Goya said, sadly, as if she herself had been wronged.

"What about him?" Kata persisted.

Then she recalled Goya's words: *Kris, you pro-miss to leave Jasmine when you no lo-ve*... The wedding seemed so long ago, long before Kata knew of her own ties to this man. Yet barely a week had gone by. She had never before spoken his name, although Jasmine had told it to her, written it in the dusty patch of soil in the grass. Then she had gotten up laughing and twirled her skirt like a schoolgirl. She had spoken it with such love that his name, Kris, somehow became hers, belonged to her. To Kata, at the time, he was simply the gnarled tree from the painting. But things were different now.

"What about Kris?" Kata asked again, unnerved by the sound of her own voice uttering his name for the first time.

Goya looked at Kata intensely. "Speak his name? Never. To me. Here." She waved her arm at the encampment. "We not speak dead man's name!"

"A dead man's name?" Kata cried out. "Is somebody going to kill him?"

"Take on *wafdo bok*, bad luck, from him? Nooo," Goya scoffed. "He not take life. He take woman's heart." She grasped the fabric on the left side of her chest and scrunched it up in her fist. "He have no name. Dead man."

Kata felt fire ants crawling up her legs, arms, face. She thought of jumping up and shaking them off, but could not move. She tried to lift her hand and brush them off her face, but her hand remained at her side, propped on the cool grass. Down below, a scraggly old man was bent over Kris, trying to lift him. Kata recognized the old man. He had a limp. She'd seen him shovelling horse manure, scrubbing iron pots. Always alone, sad and alone.

Lorca and Stefan emerged from a nearby tent. They passed Kris, still slumped on the ground without a glance. They did not even pause to help. As they approached, Kata glared as if seeing them for the first time.

"That old man always eats alone. Outside of the camp," she said to them, aware of the accusation in her voice. Kata wished she could ask them why they didn't help Kris, why they did not help the old man, but she could not, not after what she just learned. Yet, she felt hollow, betrayed.

"Condemned by the tribe, the old man. Long ago," Lorca remarked casually and Goya spat on the ground in the direction of Kris and the old man.

Stefan added: "Does chores no one else likes."

Lorca motioned toward the noisy group below. "That's his wife and children, there," he commented flatly, as if none of what just happened concerned him.

"He still lives with his family?" Kata asked.

"They'll have nothing to do with him. Not even his mother," Lorca said. "The tribe takes care of them, though."

"Let's see how Jasmine's holding up," Stefan said.

"Coming?" Lorca asked Kata. Goya nodded approval, and the three headed up the hill. They sat on the grass next to Jasmine. The shouting below had subsided.

"Our codes apply to all of us," Lorca said, tenderly encircling Jasmine's shoulder.

"I thought we were for life. I thought I could change him," Jasmine sighed, gathering her skirt and straightening the fabric with her hands.

"You were brave," Stefan said. "Dealt justice yourself."

"Why not?" she said. "I am a married woman. I've borne a child. Why ask another? You can't break what is already broken. This heart." She held her fist at her chest and struck it to emphasize her words, her face twisted in an ugly grimace that made her a stranger. "I stood by him. Took him into our clan. Even his own people had doubts."

"He joined us to be near you, sister," Lorca said. "To regain your trust. Not to get away from – "

"Stop it, Lorca!" Jasmine yelled. "Stop it, now! He joined us to save his own skin. I know it now. I know it in this heart." She stood and brushed her hair off her face. "He is her father, Lorca. And we are all fools. I can see it now. All the deceit. All of it. Otherwise, why did she come to us, why? If he wasn't the father."

Jasmine knows about me?

"That young woman came to our camp," Jasmine said. "Begging for help. Why?"

What are they talking about?

"She was in trouble, Jasmine. Angela was in trouble. She came to us because we're gypsies. Because she thought one of our women could, would ..."

"Give her an abortion, Lorca. I know. This whole village knows why she came to us. The gossip is still out there. But there was more. Everyone thought he was the baby's father."

"If he was, Jasmine, what stopped him from admitting it? Angela was not a gypsy. So, by our law, he'd done nothing wrong. Not like now."

"But not by my law, Lorca. You think I would've forgiven him? Never! Cheating is cheating. No matter the woman, a gypsy or a *gawdji*."

"We must believe one of our own. Kri ... s," Lorca caught himself. "He has a weakness. But he is not ..."

"No, Lorca," Jasmine cut him off again. "Angela came to our camp and begged for an abortion, because he, Kris ... Yes, I said it, Kris. I am not afraid of *wafdo bok*, bad luck. No dead man's name can bring me any more bad luck than I already have. Or condemned man's for that matter. Everyone thought Kris was the baby's father. Isn't that so?" She looked at Stefan, who shrugged his shoulders.

"He swore he wasn't. And I ... we all believed him," Stefan said, "But if that happens to be a lie, God help him. I will kill him with my own bare hands."

"I always thought it was you, Stefan," Jasmine said. "I thought you were the baby's father."

"You know that's not true," Lorca cut in. "Stefan told me he wasn't. You've known that all along."

"Yes, but I suspected. We all know how you felt about Angela. We've all seen your side of hell. Searching for that poor baby. Besides, you've never looked at another woman, since. Not like my serpent."

"I need to know, Jasmine," Stefan said. "I need to know."

"So do I, Stefan. And this *vardo,* caravan, is not going anywhere until I do. Even if it kills me."

"We came back here to get some answers, and we'll get them," Lorca declared, as if whole burden were his alone.

"God help me, if it means handing one of our own to the police, so be it," Stefan said, glancing at Jasmine.

"He's not my *rom* any more," Jasmine snapped. "I'm not his *jumel.* I need the truth. He is his own *o Bengh,* his own Devil."

Kata felt nauseated, confusion descending like a dense fog. She could not inhale, could not think. Images swam in her head, voices mingled, one moment hinting at possibilities and the next holding them up for all to see above dark, bottomless chasms. *Not me. They're not talking about me. It's Angela. He, the gnarled tree, is the gypsy, the blacksmith the villagers talked about? He is Angela's baby's father? That means ... Oh, God. No. That can't be.*

Chapter XXI

Kris

"GO AWAY, GIRL. Out of my path."

"Where are you going?"

"I said, step aside. What d'you want from me?" His voice rumbled, sturdy yet with a tremble like the huge bass she had seen him play; with a tinge of sadness, a hint of vulnerability.

"I have to know where you're going."

"Why? What's it to you?"

"I have to know."

"Stop following me."

"You're hurt. You'll die. You can stay with them. They'll let you."

"I'm no good. Cursed."

"I must know where you're going."

He laughed, but it sounded more like a horse neighing. "I'm accused of many sins. Innocent of most. Guilty of some. Guilty like hell of others. Go away, girl."

"I will follow you if you don't tell me where you're going."

"Have it your way."

Kris lowered himself onto the rock at the side of the rutted path and placed his injured right leg carefully out in front of him. Using both hands he lifted it gently into a more comfortable position, his makeshift crutches nearby.

Kata pulled out a sandwich from her straw bag and offered it to him. He looked at her, surprised, then shrugged his shoulders and took the food. He picked up the sandwich carefully, ensuring their hands did not touch. She looked at his callused hands and wished they had touched. Wished she knew how they felt: scratchy, hard. Did they smell like horses? She'd seen him grooming Darley Arabian. Or perhaps like the copper pots he fashioned. Was Kris still a blacksmith, and if so, where? She did not see any gear. What else did he do? He was a jack-of-all-trades, Jasmine had said.

Kata sat on a hump of soil on the other side of the path, skirt pulled over her knees, chin propped on her hands and eyes alert. It was dusk, but she could see his eyes. They were not black as she'd first thought. They were brown-green, dark and shiny like bottle glass.

"How do gypsies get green eyes?" she asked.

He stopped chewing and looked at her but said nothing. He took another large bite, so large that she wondered if it would fit into his mouth. But he continued chewing, slowly and unwillingly, with a look as if the food was bitter.

She knew the bread was fresh, and the *kajmak*, a type of cream cheese she'd spread on it, was delectable, must be melting in his mouth. After he finished the sandwich, she pulled out a bottle of sour cherry juice and handed it to him. He picked up the bottle, again avoiding her hand, and shook his head in wonder.

"I am glad you liked it," she said and returned to her throne of hardened soil. She hoped he would say something – even if only to complain again about her presence – so she could listen to his voice. But he remained quiet, his sunburned face solemn. The deep creases running from the sides of his large nostrils down the corners of his mouth burrowed into the bottom of his unshaven chin. He raised the bottle to his mouth, threw his head back and began to drink. Each time he swallowed, the liquid gurgled like a spring and his large Adam's apple jumped up and down as if a rock was trapped in his throat. When he finished, he rolled the bottle towards her. "Now, scoot! It's getting late."

He got up from the rock and stood on his left leg. He placed his crutches under his arms, leaned his weight on them, and lifted his left leg. A dry cracking sound broke under him, echoing in the still evening air. The broken crutch flew. He stumbled, groaned in pain, and the next moment he was slumped on the ground next to the rock.

"Oh no!" Kata cried out. She ran over and lifted his head. "I'll get somebody from your camp. They'll help you."

"Get outta here, girl. Now!" he growled. "I'd rather die. With dignity, if there's any left."

She grabbed his crutches and stuffed them under her arm. "I'll be right back. Don't go anywhere," she said, and ran off.

As soon as she was far enough to think clearly, she threw the crutches into the cornfield and paused. Only one was broken. He'd probably try using the second one and worsen the damage. Go to the gypsy camp and get help? No, he'd rather die, he said. He can only crawl, so he can't get very far. There was an old pair of crutches stored in the attic over Grandma's room. She ran.

* * * *

"What are you? Saint Sara?" Kris groaned.

"I am Kata, your …" She stopped. She couldn't say it. Not just yet. Instead, she lifted his head from the pillow she had smuggled out of Grandma's room.

She glanced around the hut she'd quickly swept up and tried to make homey. The farmer who once used the hut to guard his watermelon field had slapped together a bed from warped boards. An oversized burlap bag – wheat sacks sewn together and stuffed with dry cornhusks – served as a mattress.

"Here, take these," she said while stuffing two aspirin in his mouth, and tilting a glass of water to his lips.

"I'd rather have a drink from that other bottle you brought," he said.

"That's for the wounds. A disinfectant."

"Not wounds. Just a swelling. That'll do my stomach more good."

"All right," she conceded, reluctantly tilting the bottle of *slivovica* to his lips. He took a few eager gulps before she yanked it away.

"That's holy water, by God," he exclaimed.

She pulled out her mother's old kerchief and sprinkled *slivovica* on it. "I'll put this on the swelling."

"Don't waste that holy water, girl. Hand it over."

After he refused to roll up his pant leg so she could place the wet kerchief on his knee, refused to let her check the shoulder he injured when he fell on the rock, and refused the food she had smuggled out of her house, she finally gave in and handed him the bottle.

He gulped the liquor as if it were water, exhaled a loud "aaaah" and passed it back to her.

"That'll do for now," he said.

She hid the bottle in a corner, out of reach. Gingerly, she sat on a rickety chair near him.

"You in pain?" she asked.

"Nah," he snorted.

Kris seemed comfortable enough, except that his feet were hanging over the footboard, even with his head propped up. His eyes soon closed and his breathing became even.

She placed her hand on his forehead. He was burning up, and she hoped the aspirin would soon take effect. The evening seemed chilly, so she unfolded the blanket she'd brought and spread it over him. Then she snatched it off for fear his fever would get worse. She left the wet kerchief on his forehead and returned to her creaking chair. Then blew out the kerosene lamp before someone noticed the light.

Chapter XXII

The Talisman

"THE NEW MOON is out," Jasmine announced, pointing to the thin sickle moon, so pale that Kata had not even noticed it. "I'm off to pay my respects." Jasmine raised her face to the sky and blew a kiss to the moon. "Time for cleansing. Who's coming with me?"

Kata wondered how Jasmine could be so cheerful. Had she forgotten all about Kris? Another thought came to mind. *My mother might be looking for me. Probably not. She no longer asks questions.*

* * * *

A group of women stood at the embankment looking down at the marsh, Kata among them. She recalled her visits to this same area with Grandma, who used to leave tall hemp stalks to soak in the shallow part of the water.

The marsh looked sinister under the star-strewn sky. Wobbly willows leaned against each other like drunken old men staggering home from the village pub. Their gigantic shadows hovered along the embankment stretching into the valley below, reaching for the pools of still water.

The women began removing their blouses, then their bras, plump, round flesh lustrous in the starlight. Gathered around the gentle spring flowing toward the marsh, they cupped their hands and collected the water. They splashed their breasts, chanting in Romany, laughing and chatting.

Jasmine was standing in the middle. "*Pani*, the Spirit of Water, dissolve my betrayal, wash it away. The pain in my heart, flow away." She splashed water on her chest, closing her eyes.

One of the women raised her cupped hands filled with water to Jasmine's chest and let the liquid trickle through her fingers. "He's no more. Has no place in your heart."

"This was his special place," Jasmine whispered. "He used to go for long walks here, at night."

Kata stood aside, in wonderment. She spotted Zara, the new bride she had not seen since the wedding night. Zara seemed different, emboldened. Gently, Zara grasped Jasmine's shoulders and spun her around. Jasmine laughed. Other women began splashing water on Jasmine's face, her hair.

"This heart was his," Jasmine placed both hands over her left breast.

"Let him go. Wash him away," Zara murmured.

Kata began to unbutton her blouse and felt her fingers turning numb. The thought of exposing breasts barely the size of green peaches terrified her. Zara embraced Kata's shoulder. "Do as you please," she said.

"*Dik ta shoon*, watch and listen." Zara motioned to her face: "Eyes, for seeing. Lips for talking. And these" – she pointed to her chest – "for suckling our babes. See?"

Kata smiled. She felt as if someone had just lifted the veil off her face and for the first time she could see how silly she had been all these years.

Again, she glanced at other women's chests – some large blubbers of flesh hanging down to their owner's waist, some narrow and pointy, some more rounded. She searched for a pair of small ones, smaller than hers. As a young girl about her own age turned around, Kata spotted them – each barely a swelling with a perky nipple. The girl held her back straight, proudly parading her nakedness, giggling and splashing herself with water. *It's now or never.*

Kata unbuttoned the bodice of her dress and pulled her arms out. Kneeling by the spring, she collected the water in her cupped hands and took a long drink, savouring the coolness in her throat. Then she unlatched the front hooks on her training bra and stared at her chest – two brown nipples curving slightly upward stared back at her. She splashed water over her face and felt it trickling down her chest, cleansing the tension, the fear. She continued splashing while the women formed a circle and began chanting.

Jasmine took Kata's hand and pulled her into the lively loop. She felt as if she were in a fairytale participating in a secret ritual – chanting to the new moon in a language she did not understand, chanting to the gypsy talisman, the luck-bringer.

Shonuto nevo ankliste, tal amighe bachtalo, Zara recited.

"The new moon has come out, may she be lucky for us," Jasmine repeated. Other women joined in.

Kata closed her eyes and listened. Through the chanting voices, words whispered in her head – *only the truth can set you free* – Angela's plea from the dream. Then she heard her own voice, as if disembodied, add: "May she help us find Angela's baby." She repeated the whole incantation: "The new moon has come out. May she be lucky for us. May she help us find Angela's baby."

She continued chanting, and then suddenly realized that her voice was the only one. She opened her eyes. The women were all staring at her, wide-eyed. She felt exposed, embarrassed. She fumbled, pulled her garments to her bare chest. She had to run away. Then she looked at Jasmine who was nodding at her and smiling.

Jasmine resumed the incantation. The mantra turned rhythmic. All the women repeated the same words, over and over again: "May she help us find Angela's baby. May she help us find Angela's baby."

Chapter XXIII

Roza's Ducat

IT WAS CLOSE to midnight, and the man in the moon was in a watchful mood. Kata stole toward the gate and carefully opened it, reciting the peacock chant. As she entered the courtyard, a shadow shifted and vanished under the broad linden crowns. A dull *thunk* followed as if someone had tripped over the wooden bench beneath, and then a gust of wind ruffled the leaves and muffled all sound.

There was laughter ... more like a horse's snort. A figure broke through the shadow, her face mottled with dark and light patches, a long braid resting on each large breast, hands wrapped in an apron. Roza. She extended one hand as if to touch Kata. From her bunched-up apron, dozens of cookies rained down and fell to the grass, followed by a small loaf of bread. Kata stepped back. Eyes trained on Roza's face, she continued stepping back slowly until she felt the verandah step scrape her calf.

"Here," Roza said, panting. "My ducat. Pure gold. Take it." She moved closer, hand still extended. Kata saw a tiny coin held tightly between her fingers.

"No, Roza. That's your dowry to your Alex. Your dear mother gave it to you. Remember?"

Anger distorted Roza's face, but her voice was soft and thick like mud. "Take it. Put it in water. Drink a glass every day."

"No Roza."

"Take it!" Roza stepped closer and grasped Kata's arm just above the elbow, her grip a clutch of iron. "To dispel a love potion. Never fails. You stay chaste, girl. Stay chaste! Evil eye on you to dispel, gypsies' evil eye." Her grasp loosened just long enough for Kata to wiggle free. She ran up the steps. "Or you'll wind up like poor Angela. They cast their evil eye ... put a curse on her ... stole her chastity ..."

Inside, Kata turned the lock and clanged the iron safety bar into place. She stood behind the door, breathing hard.

It had been a long time since she'd spoken to Roza. Kata had managed to avoid her. But the woman out there had been following her, she now realized. Those footsteps and eerie cornfield rustles in the night were not imagined.

She stepped close to the window and pulled the curtain aside, just a sliver. Roza was still standing between the two cypresses guarding the verandah, hand extended toward the moon, gazing at the tiny coin, her precious ducat.

Chapter XXIV

Only The Truth Can Set You Free

W*HOSE VOICE IS that? Kris is talking to someone?* Kata peered through the boards of the makeshift door. She could see nothing. The voice stopped. There was a muffled sound, a shuffling. Nudging the door open a crack, she squinted into the darkness. The shuffling resumed, the voice mumbled. She opened the door and entered cautiously.

Kris was sprawled on the bed. Through the tiny window, bluish moonlight cast a beam across his head hanging off the mattress. His mouth was a gaping hole. His chest heaved. He moaned, then lifted one arm and let it drop, thrashing his arms at an invisible attacker.

Kata lit the kerosene lamp. She took two aspirin from the bottle, her heart racing.

"You look horrible, worse than a dead man," she whispered. "And Jasmine still cares about you."

She placed one hand under his head and tried to lift it. His hair was coarse, like a horse's tail, like her own hair. The similarity startled her. She grasped a few strands and rubbed them between her fingers, the way her mother checked the quality of fabric, and heard a faint grinding sound.

"You're hurt," she said. "Hated by your people. Once, they loved you. And you are my ... my ..." She stepped away, pressed her back against the boards of the hut.

Are you Angela's baby's father too? The thought flashed through her like electricity. She moved closer and shook his shoulder. "Kris, wake up."

He mumbled and groaned in pain. Then opened his eyes and stared in confusion.

Ask him? How?

She poured a glass of water, slipped the aspirin into his mouth, and shook his shoulder. "Wake up."

"You, again," he said and reached for the glass. He spat the aspirin onto the floor but gulped the water. "Get out. Now, enough. Enough hell. Out!"

She pressed her back against the door. His hair stood up on his head even bushier than she remembered. His cheeks shone in the semi-darkness as if made from fist-size balls of beeswax her father stored in the cold cellar, all lined up on a shelf, for what purpose she never knew and never mustered the courage to ask. Besides, even if she did, he would have stared somewhere above her head, waved his arm and said: "Idle minds asking questions they have no business asking."

"Give me those crutches," Kris said. "I'll get ya outta here."

He propped himself on his elbow as if about to get up, and winced in pain. She opened the door just a crack, for a fast escape.

"Hand over that bottle, girl. An' get out," he growled. "An' don't come back. You hear me?"

"Here, drink yourself to death," she snapped and pushed the bottle into his hand. She retreated to the open door and listened to the *slivovica* gurgle down his throat.

"Ahh! Holy water, by God," he sighed.

"I knew you'd say that."

"Out," he spat through clenched teeth, clutching the bottle to his chest.

Kata slammed the door behind her. The hut rattled, and for a moment she feared it would collapse and bury him.

"Go ahead," she yelled. "Die. See if I care!" She stepped out into the narrow locust grove shielding the back of the hut from the path. She turned and glanced back into the rustling cornfield that was once a watermelon patch, many summers ago, before the summer of the dancing bear. Or was it the same summer, not long before the baby's disappearance? She winced. She could remember Miladin's warning.

"Run, he's coming."

The watermelon farmer had been gruesome. She now knew it was the right word for him, the word she could not think of at the time. Even her own fear of him had been repugnant. It sickened her. All she had to do was recall the glint in his eye, the smirk that lifted an upper lip under hairy nostrils as if he smelled something foul. He said she could come to his watermelon patch any time. And eat all she wanted. Grandma's back was turned when he told her that. *You can have allya want.* With every recall of those slurred words came the foul odour of decomposing carp he carried with him, along with that bloat in her stomach as if she'd just swallowed a mouthful of sludge from the marsh.

So he had known that she and Miladin snuck in and stole his watermelons, eating them in the dappled shade of the locust patch. Did he watch them? See them crossing the bridge? From the open field, the bridge was fully visible. Why did he not chase them? Everybody knew he shot at one of the boys from the village. Roza's brother. Missed, luckily.

Miladin hid the knife they used to cut watermelon under a rock by the big locust tree – the knife she'd smuggled out of her kitchen. Grandma looked for it everywhere, and then said she must have lost it while picking young summer cabbages for salad. After the farmer told Kata she could have all she wanted, she never went back to the watermelon patch.

Run, Miladin's voice yelled in her head. But her legs felt numb. She could not inhale. The air was stagnant; the air she hoped would finally reach that chamber in her lungs that always seemed starved of oxygen. She turned back and sat on the makeshift bench propped up against the hut.

That farmer would kill you, Kris. I will not let you die.

The night was quiet and the moonlight so weak that she closed her eyes.

They say that handsome one, tall, wiry build, was there when the bear danced. You know, the blacksmith.

Kata cringed. Where did that come from? That voice. Grandma's.

He helped me, worked on the farm when I broke my hip. A good man.

Maybe he was the baby's father and Angela went to see him. Kata shook off the villagers' gossip from long ago.

If the baby's father was a gypsy, you think he'd murder his own child?

Kata jumped from the bench and began walking away on brittle legs, as if they were Kris' useless crutches. She clenched her head with her hands to stop the words from expanding.

You think he'd murder his own child...

But the villagers' words kept swelling in her head. Light flared. A spring day in the forest; that longed-for spring sunshine from childhood. Or was it early summer? She was not sure. And all that shimmering freshness and woody dampness after rain, of that she was certain and smelled it now, this very moment. It permeated all her senses as powerfully it did then. She must have been four, five years old? Grandma was calling her.

"Over here, Kata! Hurry! You may never have a chance to see it again."

Kata stared into the tangle of leaves and grass on the forest floor. Shocked, she saw the pile shift, as if it were alive.

"A nest of snake eggs, hatching," Grandma whispered.

Then Kata saw the young snakes unfolding, pushing their limbless bodies out of the cracked eggshells. The writhing mass expanded magically, like dough that filled the bread bowl to the rim and climbed over the edges.

"God's miracle," Grandma had said.

And now, like the nest of hatching snakes, the words, "you think he'd murder his own child," writhed in Kata's head. They ballooned, heavier and fatter until they filled every crevice in her thoughts, ready to burst.

You think he'd murder his own child …

A voice arose from the hut. She tiptoed to the door and listened. *What is Kris saying?* Gently, she pushed at the boards, and they gave way, just a crack. She closed one eye and pressed the other tight against the gap. He looked horrible, distraught. He thrashed his healthy arm and mumbled.

"Are you Angela's baby's father? Are you?" she yelled into the parted boards. "Go ahead. Die. See if I care."

She pushed at the door and it screeched, like the wounded peacock from her dreams. Her hand jerked back. Hesitantly she stepped in, edged closer, and gently shook his shoulder: "Kris! Wake up. You have to tell me."

"O'ly … 'ruth … can … free," he muttered.

"Gibberish, nonsense." She raised her voice. "That's all you can do. Nobody cares about you. Nobody. Not even me."

Oh, God, what am I doing yelling at him? He's half-dead. She poured a glass of water, lifted his head with one hand, and brought the glass to his lips. To her surprise, he drank it. She poured another one and he drank that too. He opened his eyes.

"Ahh," he sighed, as if he had just gulped mouthfuls of *slivovica.*

"Kris?" she called out.

He stared with his huge eyes, stared somewhere beyond her, through her.

"With magical … eyes … burn …" he mumbled, voice faltering then rising before trailing off.

Kata stood over him, head turned away from the stink of stale *slivovica*. His eyes rolled in his head and landed on her, vacant. His head remained still.

"Vila ... burning holes in your soul," he announced, in an eerily clear voice. She knew he was delirious.

"O'ly truth ... set ... free," he went on. She waited. Will he say it three times? The way Grandma told the story? "Only truth ... you free."

He repeated the same words three times, as in the story. She knew the story by heart – the one Grandma learned from the gypsy who helped her with farm chores the winter she broke her hip – learned from him, Kris. It tells of the *vila* with magical eyes who lures the guilty into confessing their sins by playing "only the truth can set you free" on her flute, while peering deeply into their eyes. The guilty would be charmed into telling the truth under the spell of the music and the *vila's* gaze. Grandma believed that the words, "only the truth can set you free" held magic power.

Kris rambled on and she could fill in the pauses, groans, missing words. A story evolved in her thoughts, its shape sketched in part by Grandma's voice and his muttering.

Chapter XXV

Angela's Baby's Father

TELL THEM, MY *girl. You must tell the truth,* Papa Novak's voice echoed in Kata's head as she ran toward the spring by the marsh.

No, he is not a murderer. Angela's baby's father? May be. But what does that matter? He is my father too. The blacksmith was a good man, Grandma had said.

"I will not give you to the police, Kris, I will not," she said, panting between short breaths. She stopped and looked around – the moon was pale and the sky strewn with clouds like torn rags. Her mother had lied to the police – said she didn't know about the goings-on at the gypsy encampment. Kata had nothing to do with the gypsies. Her daughter spent all her time at home, helping with the chores. Papa Novak said he'd go with her mother into town the next day and talk to the lawyer. He asked the police not to talk to the girl without legal representation. This all sounded serious. She needed legal representation? Had she done something wrong? Strangely, her mother wasn't angry. Just worried. Those little fine lines around her eyes were as sharp as paper cuts.

"We know he's hiding somewhere around here," the policemen had said. "All we ask is that you tell us what you know."

* * * *

"You all right?" Jasmine said, taking Kata's hand. "What's wrong?"

"Goya said I'd find you here... Didn't you know? The police are looking for... Kris," Kata stammered through the rushing river in her head. Other voices floated in and out of her thoughts. She heard them one moment and, before she could make sense of them, they were gone, like the swishing of bats' wings at dusk.

"I know," Jasmine replied. "They talked to us. Asked questions."

Lorca and Stefan approached.

"Maybe, just maybe, something will come out of this, after all," Lorca said. "Maybe we'll find out what happened with our Uncle Grizzly."

What about Kris? Kata felt tears welling in her eyes. *Has everyone forgotten about Kris?*

"We owe it to him, to us," Jasmine said. "He raised us after our parents' death."

"He was everybody's uncle, in a way," Stefan said. "Even his bear's."

"His bear's?" Kata said, wishing someone would say something about Kris, and realized that no one would.

"He found a cub, abandoned, motherless," Stefan said, chuckling. "He raised it, named it Grizzly after hearing about American grizzlies. Himself as well."

"Thought the name added fierceness, adventure," Lorca said.

"All year round I looked forward to your visit," Stefan said. "And if you didn't show up, my whole summer was ruined. I didn't have many friends."

"Angela was your friend," Lorca said.

"Once, in grade four, we came here and listened to the frogs," Stefan said. "Then her father found out and all hell broke loose. After that, she avoided me. Even in winter, I come and sit by the frozen marsh, remembering."

How peculiar it was, Kata thought, hearing Stefan. She could have imagined him picking a fight with someone. Or getting drunk. Or trying to date somebody's daughter without her parents' approval. Or simply wasting his life away as most villagers claimed. But she never pictured him at this embankment listening to frogs.

"It's about time you stopped blaming yourself, Stefan," Lorca said.

"Let it go," Jasmine said. "Let's put our heads together and try to figure out what happened, once and for all. I'm ready to face anything now."

"Those few days the bear was dancing here in Ratari, I'd been drinking," Stefan said. "Then I'd come to the marsh to finish the bottle. Sometimes fall asleep."

"My *pralo*. Sleeping off his hangover under the bush like a true gypsy," Lorca said, laughing quietly.

"That night I woke up to a loud splashing in the water." Stefan said, rubbing his eyes. "My head was throbbing."

"Angela was your age, only 14, when she had her baby," Jasmine said to Kata. "We thought you could remember something, anything. Any hints at who the father could've been."

"Angela baby's father?" Kata blurted out.

"Yes."

She knows about Kris and me? Kata heard a noise, as if a distant flute was playing in her head. She cringed: "Me? How would I know? It's all gossip."

"Your grandma was a healer, knew more than anyone else what went on in the village," Jasmine said. "I just thought ..."

"You weren't that much older when you had Marco," interjected Lorca, and Kata breathed a sigh of relief.

"That was different," Jasmine replied. "I was in love."

"And what makes you think she wasn't?"

Jasmine shrugged her shoulders: "She was such a sad young woman. People who are in love have an aura of happiness no father, no matter how strict, can subdue. I sensed unrest in her."

"You only met her a few times," Lorca persisted.

"But I felt her *pena,* her torment." Jasmine grasped the fabric covering her chest and scrunched it up in a fist as if about to tear it off.

"It could've been fear of gossip, of her father's disapproval," Lorca said.

Jasmine nodded. "I suppose. Who am I to say, either way?"

"If anyone knew her, I think I did," Stefan declared.

"Had her baby at fourteen and at sixteen, she was dead," Jasmine said bitterly. "Sixteen years old."

"Once, I asked her to come to a school dance with me," Stefan said, pacing. "She said she'd like to, but never showed up. And then, she was taken out of school."

"You did see her after that," Jasmine said.

"At the market a few times, with her father selling vegetables and watermelons. I hung around, tried to catch her eye. Her old man simply went mad! Came after me with that wooden cane of his."

"Did you ever talk to her again?" Jasmine asked.

"Yes ... but never found the right way to tell her ... how I felt."

"How were you to know, my friend?" Lorca said, patting him on the shoulder.

"I had the chance and lost it." Stefan placed his hand over his eyes. "Once I ran into her and she was angry, screaming: 'I hate him! More than I hate life! More than I hate God for putting me on this earth.' I tried to say something but she turned on me: 'Don't you ever talk to me again! I hate you! All of you! You're all the same.' And then she ran off." He sighed. "I should have gone after her. Instead, I did nothing."

"You can't change the past, my friend," Lorca said. "But you must try and remember. For her."

"A few months later she had her baby," Stefan said.

As if startled by a predator, a flock of ducks took flight from the marsh, quacking and flapping their wings. Stefan stood up and waved his hand in their direction. With his palms to his temples, he shouted into the sky: "God! If only I could remember the face. Damn you God for pain, for guilt! And most of all for taking her away from me."

All eyes fell on him. Lorca was the first to speak.

"If you could remember whose face?" Lorca said.

"You saw somebody?" Jasmine yelled. "Stefan, you never said anything about that before!"

"I was drunk, wasted," Stefan said. "Couldn't be sure of anything." He lowered his head and continued: "Earlier that day, I saw Angela. She was in the crowd that followed the dancing bear, looking at the baubles at one of your carts, at the roadside. I was surprised. She never went anywhere after her baby was born. I headed her way. But she took off, ran through peoples' backyards. So I dove into the bottle. That's why I can't really be sure of what I saw."

"You did see somebody, didn't you," insisted Lorca. "That was the night before Angela's baby disappeared."

"See those ducks in the marsh?" Stefan said. "That night, it was a splash that woke me up from my drunken stupor. Except, it was much louder. And I don't remember seeing any ducks, that's the trouble. I saw a man, though."

Jasmine's eyes widened. "Think hard, Stefan. What did he look like? Something must've stood out."

"It was a clear night. Full moon. Not like now. It took a moment to realize where I was. Then I thought I'd heard a carp jumping. I looked across the fishing pier, and saw a man way out there, shuffling through the reeds in and out of the shadows."

Stefan passed his hand over his eyes as if brushing off cobwebs. "It all looked strange. As if some ghost was staggering around. Later I realized he must've been walking along the pier. I thought I was *seeing* things. My head was pounding as if somebody was hammering nails into it. And then he was coming out of the marsh – a scraggly, ghoulish shape. Sounds crazy, I know." He shrugged his shoulders.

"Another drunk like me, I thought, or the devil coming after me. I could hear my mother's voice: 'If you keep drinking like that, the devil himself will find you.' He was too far away to see me, and I was glad. I hid in the shadow. Closed my eyes to ease my pounding headache. And when I opened them again he was up on the embankment."

"So who was it, Stefan?" Jasmine cried. "Did you recognize who it was?"

"I stepped out of the shadow and looked at the moon. It was huge, shiny, like I've never seen before – it was staring at me. I stared back and I swear ... I swear I saw the man in the moon! The devil stopped and turned his face to the moon. And then he waved his stick at it. For a moment I thought I heard him swearing – at the moon? What kind of devil waves his stick at the moon? I looked at his face, but all I could see was – the man in the moon! I think I didn't really care to see the devil anyway, so I was glad he hobbled away."

"Did you tell this to the police?" Jasmine asked.

Stefan laughed. "Tell them what? That I was drunk? That I saw the devil walking in the marsh? That I saw the man in the moon? Which part of my story would they find funnier? As if I am not the butt of enough jokes already."

"You said you heard him swearing at the moon," Jasmine said. "Think back, Stefan. What did you hear?"

Stefan shrugged. "Strange how the voice carries in the quiet of the night, I often thought. Tried to remember the words. But I was wasted. I could've imagined the whole thing – it seemed so unreal."

"Kris used to take his late night walks here," Jasmine said shakily. "When that knee of his acted up, a walk helped, he used to say. Carried that cane of his around with him."

"Jasmine," Lorca said, "are you saying that Kris ..."

"I don't know," she said. "We'd come and sit here late at night. He said there was magic here – the willows casting their shadows, the marsh like a mirror in the moonlight, the fishing pier in the distance." She looked at the others. "Funny, I can talk about him and feel nothing but an empty hole in my stomach. As if I'd been hollowed out by termites."

Chapter XXVI

The Vila's Circle

GRANDMA'S BLACK-AND-WHITE PORTRAIT on the wall seemed lonely in the semi-darkness, Kata thought, as she clutched the reed flute against her chest – the flute her grandma gave her long ago, the one she had received from the gypsy blacksmith. Kris? From Kris?

Does she dare blow into it? The last time she'd played it was the night after Angela's baby disappeared. She'd flung it out into the darkness. Yet some time later it had reappeared in the back of Grandma's drawer, behind the cookie heart.

She examined the flute, twirled it between her fingers. She recalled something else – she had hidden it in a safe place at Vila's Circle, in a cleft in the large flat stone, the one called the altar. It had been the last time she went with Grandma. How did she come to be holding this flute?

She used to be able to play any tune she wished. All she had to do was close her eyes and recall the melody. She would blow gently into the flute, and magic would do the rest – fill every crevice in her ears, the air bubbles about her, with its enchanting tune – as it used to when she submerged her head under the water in the sunlight-warmed aluminum washtub. She'd shut her eyes tighter and tighter, and the water infused with jumping sunrays would evolve into a flowing melody, drawing colours in her vision. The flute could do the same.

The first time she discovered that the flute was magic was at Vila's Circle. She scoffed at the memory. How naïve she used to be, how easily she used to believe in everything, even magic. Yet, that evening at the marsh dancing in the moonlight was magic. *Maybe my magic is back.* She closed her eyes so she could recall a melody, a soothing melody.

sleep my little baby
sleep in the night

Kata shook her head. "No! Not Angela's lullaby!" she yelled. "I want a happy song." She closed her eyes again.

sleep in your cradle under moonlight

She envisioned Angela sitting by the pig puddle next to her grandfather's well, leaning against the mulberry tree. She opened her eyes. *Is the melody trying to tell me something? If I can play it on my flute, perhaps I can find Angela's baby.* She lifted the flute to her lips, spaced her fingers, and gently blew.

She winced at the grotesque sound that had emerged. Worse than the screeching peacocks. Worse than the screeching gate. It was painful. As if someone screamed in pain. In fright, she threw the flute across the room. It hit the wall, the floor, bounced and settled into a corner. The tune, the lullaby in her head, became more audible as if somebody had just turned up the volume.

"Stop!" she yelled, squeezing her head, palms cupping her ears. "Stop the lullaby! Stop the dreams! The voices! Stop!"

Something, someone screeched again. She stared. There was no one. She was alone. The rooster crowed. It was dawn.

* * * *

Go back, retrace your steps, and you'll find it, Grandma's voice urged every time Kata lost something. But magic? How could I look for magic, Kata wondered as she walked the wobbly dock, stepping over rotted boards. She paused, her eyes absorbing the rosy eastern sky reflected in the pools of water between the clusters of bulrushes that dotted the marsh. Dew glistened everywhere.

Kneeling at the dock's edge, she felt below it for the metal hook and unlatched the old dinghy. The boards creaked as she stepped into the boat. With her foot, she pushed away the tangled fishing net atop a beat-up aluminum pail, releasing a whiff of dry fish scales. She rubbed her foot across the bottom, searching for a clean spot to drop her straw bag. Seeing the oarlocks on the boat's gunnels, she slung her bag over the hook so it rested on the dry wood at the side.

A mental inventory of her bundle proved satisfactory: a light blanket, a few slices of bread spread with lard and sprinkled with red paprika and salt, a couple of rose-pears she'd picked up under the tree and knew were sugar-sweet and pink inside, a few small cucumbers she'd pulled off the vine, and a large bottle of water. And a straw hat Grandma had woven for her a few years back. Grandma would have approved – she always made sure Kata wore her hat in the strong sun.

As she pushed off with the broad oar, a small chunk of wood rot crumbled and fell onto the stagnant surface. It drifted and sank into the murky depth, into some debris below. She scanned the marsh for the wooded hillock on the far side, where she and Grandma had gone to pick mushrooms and collect snails. She could not see it, but knew that she would spot it once she was a bit farther out in the open.

A flutter of wings startled her. A brownish bird flew out from under the dock. It cheeped and carved a smooth arc in the sky, then swooped down and vanished behind a clump of reeds. *A swallow? Do they nest in the marsh? They usually stay in the barns. What kind of a bird is this? Grandma would've known.*

The wooden blades propelled the creaky vessel with surprising smoothness, gliding through the white-blossomed lily pads that reminded her of cream puffs she used to make with Grandma. Her stomach rumbled. She reached into the bag and pulled out a pear. A cream puff would have been better.

She scanned the expansive blossoming surface in the distance, glimpsing an outline of the old growth forest. She veered off, bypassed a growth of reeds, and when she looked up, the forest was nowhere in sight. "Hidden by the bulrushes," she murmured. Placing one foot against the right edge of the boat's bottom, left against the left edge, she briefly stood to scan the marsh. She sat back down to resume rowing and watched frogs jumping aside, bugs on the surface skidding away, lily pads parting before her. The sun had risen high and it was steaming hot. She slapped on her straw hat and continued, arms getting weaker, the muggy air sticking in her chest. *Keep rowing. The old forest is near. I know it's near.*

A splash in the bulrushes sent warm liquid trickling down her face. She yawned and wiped it off. The oar in her right hand seemed stuck. She tugged at the handle to free the blade. The boat heaved, as if an invisible limb was hoisting it up from beneath. A tangle of twigs poked through the smooth greenish surface an arm's length away. It led to a huge mass of entangled roots embedded in mud, concealed under the shade of a gigantic willow. She pushed her hat back and stared at the sparse row of willows lined up along the embankment. Beyond the willows, a gentle slope rose toward a tall grove.

The boat was wedged in, and it would not budge. The water seemed too deep for walking to the shore. Swim? No. She and Maja almost drowned at a small stretch of beach on the banks of the Sava where some of the village boys, led by Miladin, learned to swim. Besides, this is where Grandma used to collect her leeches and starve them in a jar of water so she could place them on her legs until they swelled up and fell off – her foolproof remedy for lowering high blood pressure.

She unlatched the oar and stuck it into the swamp, searching for bottom. The blade stopped half way up the handle – not as deep as she'd thought. The oar popped out of mud as if it were a suction cup. She stuck it in at another spot, and it slid in a bit deeper, then stopped. Standing, she lowered one leg over the side of the boat and felt for the tree trunk below the surface. She set her foot on the slimy limb and tried for a firm grip, the duckweed twining itself around her calf. She turned to lift the other foot out of the boat and small-step along the log to the shore, only a few steps…

The glittering surface blurred and a dull thump reverberated in her head plugging her ears with cream puffs. A hush filled the warm liquid greenness about her, stuffing every crevice, and she sank into the soft, comforting stillness… a sunray reaching all the way into her quiet world. She reaching for the sunray…

* * * *

The smell of the marsh filled her nostrils. The hot sun beating down on her skin beneath the faded fabric was comforting. She sized up the steepness of the embankment above her and quickened her pace, stomach grumbling. She entered a sparse woodlot of locust where clumps of blackberries loaded with ripe purple fruit dappled the shade. She stuffed handfuls into her mouth.

She resumed her climb. The woodlot became dense and the air cool. There were fewer patches of sun and after every few steps the light dimmed. Soon she found herself in a light fog. She stopped and looked around, shivering. Would she ever see the world she left behind? The world with warm sunrays?

She began walking on spongy ground studded with decomposing tree stumps, stepping over fallen trees, their broad trunks covered in moss. This was the right place, she knew, the forest she and Grandma walked through on the way to Vila's Circle. Grandma was retelling her story about the First World War.

"Dead soldiers, everywhere. Like fallen tree trunks. I turned them over, looked at their faces, looked for my brother's face."

Kata could see it – Grandma bent over a fallen tree trunk, grasping the underside. "I found him," she said and Kata glimpsed a smile through the tears rolling down the furrowed cheeks. "So I could bury him. Save him from the vultures, the wolves, fighting over his eyes, his heart. He was nineteen years old. Nineteen. My big brother."

And when Kata glanced around she saw an army of fallen trees, scattered on the infinite forest floor. She stepped over one and paused. Could this be the tree that reminded Grandma of her dead brother? She tried to roll it, but it was heavy and would not budge. The forest was getting denser, darker. Kata felt her heart sinking. *Will I be lost, forever among the dead soldiers?*

A spear of light pierced her shaded world. Her eyes followed it up into the green oak crowns, then back down into the undergrowth at the forest floor, where a patch of sun settled over a mossy bed. She lay on its velvety tufts – sinking into the softness filling every crevice of humid air, sinking, sinking.

"Here? Was it here, Bako, you saw a *vila*?"

"Yes, dear. In the mist, in the sunrise."

Kata peered into the mist at the silhouette combing the long black hair that hid her face and much of her body as it billowed down into the tall blades of swaying grass.

"Were you scared, Bako? That she would blind you, or make you go mad?"

"Just a little, dear. But they also help people. Just look at Farmer Vila."

"Did anybody else get enchanted?"

"Many women, even your mother. She went into the forest and returned the next day to elope with your father."

"You think she was enchanted?"

"Must've been. Married against Mihailo's wishes – disobeyed her own father."

"Anybody else?"

"Goya was, dear. Told to take care of her people, to become a healer."

"The *vila* spoke to her?"

"Through her thoughts, dear. Helped Goya to understand her calling."

"How would I know if the *vila* is good or bad, Bako?"

"You'd know. Just follow your own feelings. And always think for yourself. Don't let anybody put thoughts in your head."

"Are we almost there, Bako?"

"Yes dear. This is *Vila's* Circle. A sacred place."

"Is this where they dance to the moon? After midnight?"

"You see that circle of rocks?" Grandma pointed to large boulders arranged along the edge of the clearing. "Twelve of them. See how flat the tops are? How smooth and clean, free of moss? Well, how can a rock stay free of moss in a forest like this one, you may ask? Only if somebody was to dance on them, night after night, that's how." Her voice was distorted; she spoke like an exuberant child. "And see the stone altar in the middle, my little swallow?" She pointed to a larger stone block in the centre, so large a person could sleep on it. "That's where the offerings to their deity are made."

"Offerings of what, Bako?"

"Oh, could be of mushrooms or wild roots, could be of animals, even humans," Grandma said with a carefree giggle. "People have vanished, for good."

Kata winced. There was something eerie about the whole place. About Grandma.

"The marsh swallows up a person every once in a while," Grandma said with an impish glimmer in her eye. "Makes them confess their sins. Only then are they set free."

"Set free? I thought they get swallowed by the marsh!"

"Only if their sins are not forgivable, dear," Grandma chuckled. "That's up to the head *vila* to decide."

"The one who plays the flute and has turquoise eyes?"

"I don't know about the colour, dear," Grandma said. "She peers deeply into people's eyes. Burns holes in their souls. Makes them tell the truth."

"How do you know all this, Bako?"

"Some say she is a young girl who met an untimely death," Grandma said winking. "Some say she's an old hag. And some say she's a beautiful young maiden – like you, my little swallow."

Kata glanced about. Something was not right. All about her was mist and fog and Grandma was not her usual self. She was much younger, but Kata knew it was still her, had to be her. She was the only one who knew all these things. Told them to Kata, long ago. Yet there was something unreal about it all.

"Wait here," Grandma said, as she walked deeper into the forest, carrying two burlap sacks, one for the mushrooms and one for the Roman snails.

Kata ran into the circle of boulders. She lay on the warm altar stone and closed her eyes, basking in the sunrays, intrigued by odd bird songs.

A flock of swishing wings glided by in a swirl and an entire army of reed instruments rose from their mossy bed, their tune turning shrill:

sleep my little baby
sleep in the night…

Tall, billowing women, their faces veiled by Zephyrus' wind, were closing the circle of light. Kata reached into the deep crevice below the altar stone and pulled out the only perfect flute. She raised the sleeping flute to her lips and blew. Sweet singing voices melded as one, drowning the ruthless melody:

only the truth can set you free
only the truth can set you free
only the truth can set you free

"I made that holy water that wasn't holy," Kata whispered.

"Childish pranks, dear," Grandma's voice echoed from somewhere deep in the forest. "That's all forgiven my little swallow." And the sweet melody grew, filling the air all about her.

"Kata, Kata!" Her mother was leaning over her, shaking her arm. "Say something, anything. So I know you're all right."

"Where am I?" Kata whispered.

"In your bed. Well, in your Grandma's bed. Roza insisted we put you in your grandma's bed. To get better quickly, she said."

Roza? Kata tried to focus. But everything seemed foggy, in slow motion.

"She found you this morning, way out there in the bog, hoisted on a tree root."

Her mother brushed Kata's hair from her face: "The old fishing boat was wedged nearby in the bulrushes, so she put you in and rowed back." Her mother shook her head: "Way out there near the old forest, what's left of it, anyway."

Kata wondered why her mother was here in Grandma's room.

"Brought you home, on her shoulder, like a sack of potatoes," her mother said, forcing a chuckle. "She's waiting out in the yard to see that you're all right."

Roza?

"I was surprised, too. She hasn't been here since the funeral."

Funeral?

"Well, Grandma's funeral, you know, long time ago," her mother said. "What a night. What panic! After the storm I came here to see that you were home. But you weren't."

Kata stared at her mother standing in the doorway. *You were enchanted? Long time ago?*

"What was that? You said something?" her mother asked.

"No," Kata answered and stared steadily at her mother's face. *You've aged – fine wrinkles rising when you speak, when you pucker up your rosy lips, rising like tadpoles with wiggling tails.* She felt a rhyme beginning to gel, making her nauseated, as if she would tumble into a dark pit.

Roza pushed her way through the door, rushed toward the bed and dropped a palm on Kata's forehead. "Burning up!" She scowled, as if it was somebody's fault. Snatching the faded kerchief off her own head, she dunked it into the glass of water on the night table and with the water dripping from the cloth, slapped it on Kata's forehead.

"Heading out? In the marsh? Where to?" Roza scolded. She glanced about, bewildered. "Got to go. Bake a chicken for my Alex. Good thing I went to check on him, bring him breakfast. Alex's son, his boy. Fishing in the marsh, he was. Yeah! Otherwise, we could've pulled a dead body out of that marsh, ha, Olga?" She snorted and stormed from the room.

Kata listened to her mother's name. *Was it the way Roza said it?* As if she'd heard it for the first time.

Her mother waved goodbye and said to Kata: "That poor woman. After all these years still thinks her son's alive. Changes her story as time passes, as if he's growing up." She paused, then added: "Her son would've been what… about five or six years old now?"

Kata heard Maja chime a cheery "hello" to Roza. She stepped into the room and ran to her friend. Kata sat up in bed and took the wet kerchief off her forehead. Some vague memory slid by like a minnow. It was at Vila's Circle. The women, with veiled faces, their eyes behind a shroud of Zephyrus' wind, Maja's eyes…

"You were there," Kata whispered.

Maja leaned over and hugged her friend: "You still have a fever." She passed her fingertips lightly along the swelling on Kata's forehead. "Pretty big bump."

Her mother brought a bowl of fragrant soup and placed it on the night table, followed by a glass of water along with tea and some cookies. For a moment Kata felt as young and cared for as when she was a child and Grandma fussed over her.

Her mother lifted the bedspread and rubbed her hand over Kata's calf: "These polka dots on your legs will fade in time, not to worry. Got to eat, though. Doctor said you've lost a lot of blood. Lucky you were hoisted on those roots, or that goddamn vermin would've ..."

She stopped mid-sentence and looked at Kata, worriedly. Then she sat on the bed and fed the soup to her, and Kata let her – all the while knowing she was capable of feeding herself.

"You were there," Kata said after her mother had left the room. "At Vila's Circle."

"Go to sleep. I'll come back later, when you're better," Maja said and got up to leave.

"Don't go," Kata said, grabbing Maja's hand. "You were there, at Vila's Circle."

"Stop that," Maja said, pulling her hand away. "You're scaring me. The forest is not there any more where you and your grandma used to go. It burned down. Don't you remember? After your grandma died. Just a patch left now."

"I hid my flute there. Last time I went there with my grandma. Remember?"

"That's what you told me. It was a bad flute. It's just as well it was burned."

"I found it. Under the altar. Where I hid it. And it wasn't a bad flute. It lost its magic, that's all."

"Then where is it? Let me see it. Show it to me."

Kata patted her chest and peeked under the bed sheet. But she now had her nightgown on, and the clothes she had worn to the marsh were nowhere. Somebody must've found it. Roza? Her mother?.

"That forest burned down," Maja said frowning. "And there is no such a thing as Vila's Circle. Never was. Just a bunch of stones. So people made up stories. And now there is not even that. Just a highway running through it."

And she stood up and left the room.

"But you were there," Kata said as the door shut. "If you would just try, try to remember."

Her mother came in and placed another wet kerchief on Kata's forehead.

"What were you doing there in the swamp? You've been gone since yesterday. Never mind. You rest now." She began tidying up the room. "And in such a thunderstorm. As if the earth was cracking." She picked a bundle of wet clothes off the floor. "An old hut caught fire out by the bridge. Struck by lightning, they say. Went up in flames like a pile of matches."

The glass insert in the door clinked as her mother stepped out of the room. It reminded Kata of something, but she couldn't remember what. She picked up the glass of water next to her bed. That reminded her of something too, as if she'd forgotten to do a chore, to go somewhere. For a moment she felt panic, then gave in to an overwhelming need to close her eyes and sink into gargantuan bales of hay rolling in gentle wind.

Chapter XXVII

The List Of Puzzling Questions

AFTER A NIGHT of rain, the clammy tang of wet cinders was not unpleasant. It was an ordinary scene, as if someone simply had a bonfire. It didn't seem that anyone bothered to clean up the site. Besides, there wasn't much to clean up. Strangely, the locust grove, only steps from the hut, was not even singed.

Kris must've escaped. Someone must have saved him. He couldn't have died here. There would be some evidence. But there was none. No one mentioned anything. Not even Papa Novak. He was the one who first saw the fire and ran for help. By the time the villagers arrived, there was nothing more than a pile of coals.

Where could Kris be? How can I find him? I need to know the truth and he's the only one who can help. Kata stepped carefully around the mound of ashes and charred lumber. *Mother said nothing about Kris, yesterday. Only that the hut had burned down. Did Mother know that Kris was in it?*

Kata sat on a nearby log. Veiled by an expansive carpet of dew all was washed clean: the locust woods behind her, the cornfield on one side, and a field of purple clover on the other. Soft sunlight flooded the area. A golden glow suffused a pile of wet cinders and Kata saw sunlight winking. She stepped onto the mound and with her foot shoved aside the ashes over the sparkle.

"*Slivovica*. Holy water, by gosh," she exclaimed, then cupped a palm across her mouth to stop more of Kris' words from escaping.

She picked up the empty bottle and wiped it clean in a patch of clover. It was just an ordinary green bottle but she knew she'd keep it. She returned to the rubbish pile and spread the debris around with the tip of her running shoe. A rigid, cylindrical object turned underfoot. She bent and pulled it out. It was just a wooden stick. She was about to toss it into the pile. But a closer look revealed a number of holes, evenly spaced, gaping through the grey mud.

* * * *

Standing by the well her grandfather built, Kata submerged the stick in a pail of water. Air bubbles escaped as she rubbed off the grime. It was a flute. She shook it dry and examined it. The squiggly engraving at its base was slightly charred but still recognizable. Could it be the same one? No. Impossible. But how did it get there? Then she realized that it must've been Kris's flute.

Some day, Kata, you will find answers to your questions, not all, but some. Every once in a while an answer will come to you when you least expect it, Grandma had told her.

Was this one of those times? While she'd been looking for solutions, she'd found only bewilderment. Was this what Grandma called "creative chaos," when everything was so perplexing and many ideas crowded one's thoughts? And didn't she tell Kata that often something clear emerged from this pandemonium? *After a dark night, comes the morning light.*

Kata slipped the flute into her bodice and walked carefully to Grandma's room, mindful not to dislodge the intricate puzzle of her thoughts. She opened the top dresser drawer. Without looking inside, she hid the flute where the old one used to be, behind the white parchment paper covering the pink cookie heart. Next to it was her green notebook containing the list of questions she stopped keeping after Grandma died. She opened the back cover and read the last note she'd written:

> I will never write another question because there is no point. Nothing ever came of it, and nothing will. The list has too many questions and no answers. For example: God. Are You there, up in the sky? If You are, You are not listening.

She grabbed the pages by the top corner, ready to tear them out. She paused to listen. Was it the squeaking gate she heard? Or a screeching peacock from one of her dreams? She closed her eyes to better recall the scene – peacock fans spreading out against the lushness of the tall grass and enormous roses reaching to the sky. She peeked through the iridescent plumes into the turquoise eyespots of the long peacock train, and the roses behind it parted. She stood in the infinite green expanse. This was her own place, she knew, a collage of her own thoughts spanning from the beginning of her world to the present and somehow into the beyond. The beyond was littered with questions. She opened her eyes and looked down at the open notebook.

> **List of Puzzling Questions Without Answers:**
>
> *Why do bullies want to fight?*
>
> *Why is Miladin's father so mean?*
>
> *Why couldn't Apollo foresee Hyacinthus's future?*
>
> *Why did Nazis kill thousands of schoolchildren in Kragujevac?*
>
> *Why did Grandpa Mihailo allow himself to be killed?*

Why does my father not look at me?

Why was Zephyrus so jealous that he killed Hyacinthus?

Why do my parents fight?

Why do people accuse gypsies of stealing babies?

Why does Zeus always have to get his own way?

Why do people have bad dreams?

Why could no woman resist Zeus?

Why didn't Lorca want to tell me his name?

Who gave me the cookie-heart necklace?

Why do people have to die?

Why did Angela drown in the well?

Who stole Angela's baby?

Why does God let bad things happen?

Who stole Angela's baby?

Why does my mother get so angry?

Who stole Angela's baby?

Why did my grandma have to die so soon?

Her eyes rested on the last item. The notion that perhaps God didn't exist crept into her mind and shadowed all else. Otherwise, why would He allow Angela's baby to be stolen? Or killed? Or Angela to drown? And now, why did her own father, Kris, have to be condemned? To be suspected of fathering Angela's baby? Of killing it? And to vanish so Kata would never find him again? And to hurt Jasmine so badly, as if a worm had hollowed out her insides? And why do the gypsies have to leave, refusing to let her go with them?

She felt that tomorrow and every day after, she would have nothing to look forward to, nowhere to go, and no one to talk to. The caravan was leaving at dawn. The decision seemed sudden. Did they discover something? No one mentioned Kris. As if he'd never existed. They simply said it was time for them to leave. Lorca had to be at the University of Madrid for his first teaching contract and needed time to prepare. A course on Garcia Lorca's poetry. She might never again see Lorca, or Jasmine, or Goya, or any of the women, men and children who welcomed her into their camp night after night, some of whom she felt closer to than her own family. She would gladly have joined them. But they told her she must remain among her people. They insisted that some day she would understand. They told her to treasure God's love in her heart, and everything would unfold as it should.

And Lorca? He said he didn't want to ruin her life. She knew that all he had to do was ask and she'd marry him on the spot. But he believed she was too young and needed to choose her own path in life. She couldn't even tell him how she felt. He'd only offer his usual teacherly advice. Why did he treat her as if she were a child?

"Goya believes he has an old soul," Jasmine had said the night before, when they were saying their goodbyes. "Perhaps it's because he's to be our next chief. Our tribal head is usually chosen later in life, after having attained wisdom. But with Lorca, we've always known he'd be the one."

"Sometimes, when I think of Lorca," Kata confided, "I imagine an ancient spirit, wise and all-knowing. I'd devote my whole life to him, just to be in his presence. Yet, when I am near him, anything I do is somehow imperfect, not as it should be."

"He wants you to grow up among your people," Jasmine had said. "He knows you wouldn't be happy just being somebody's wife. You need to find your calling. You're only fourteen."

"So were you and Goya when you married. And my grandma was only fifteen."

Jasmine's words had echoed Papa Novak's. Kata was becoming annoyed by these voices from her past. She preferred to replay the last few moments with Lorca. If only she could stop time and simply live in that bubble with him.

"The caravan leaves at dawn, Kata. We don't say long farewells. Until I see you again..." Lorca's voice flowed through her thoughts. His dark green eyes were on hers. He'd bowed, as if he were Hamlet. Then he'd smiled, with just a twitch of mischief deepening the dimples in his cheeks, the gleam of moonlight in his eyes.

"In four years you will be a young woman," he'd said. She wondered what that meant. Should she allow herself to hope? Interpret his words as encouraging?

Kata had absorbed his presence and would keep it with her forever, she knew. But she also knew she was seeing Lorca perhaps for the last time. And for the very first time she realized what Grandma meant when she had said: "When Mihailo left me he broke my heart." She remembered one of Grandma's last words: "I might be going to him soon, Kata. I might be seeing your grandpa Mihailo. I've been talking to him." Kata let her tears flow, without wiping them or her runny nose and without pushing aside the damp lock of hair drooping over her forehead.

Drawn back to the list in her hands, clumped eyelashes blurring her vision, she read the first question and on down the list, feeling as if the pages of a mysterious book written in a foreign language were finally being translated. It was as if she could hear meanings, as if she could hear the earth and the sky, the birds, the trees and Zephyrus' wind; and through the receding fog could glimpse the answers. *The sun rises every day, the sun rises every day,* Grandma's voice whispered. Kata picked up a green pen, and carefully wrote: *Will my Lorca ever return?*

Chapter XXVIII

A Flash Of Lightning

THE CHERRY TREE branches lashed against Grandma's bedroom window. Kata jumped out of bed and stepped out into the darkness just before dawn, wind gripping the faded summer dress she'd forgotten to remove the night before, her sweaty body turning chill. She crossed the verandah and stood on the steps that were flanked by two cypresses twisting in the wind. Above her, churning purple clouds were as low as the tree crowns.

This is the torment of madness – the words imprinted in her mind – as Van Gogh's *Cypresses* came to life all about her. *The heavy leaves writhe like flames, their movement countered by the reverse spirals of windswept bushes and clouds.* She knew by heart the inscription for this painting, telling of the dark curving brushstrokes that revealed the rhythms of the painter's turmoil, his search for physical release from mental torment.

"The inscription is untrue," she muttered. She saw no evidence of madness in his canvas. Just the power of the colour and the curve and the unrelenting movement in the hidden truth of his world, propelling her to seek the truth in her own – the truth about Angela's baby. *I must know it. I must.*

She calmly received Angela's anguish within herself. The need to run through the narrow escape in the painting, far beyond the turbulence around her, supplanted all else.

But as she looked up into the sky, her escape vanished in the whipping wind. Lightning flashed in the distance. She ran, her bare feet pounding the worn path. Raindrops grazed her burning cheeks, washing her feverish body, pummelling the sticky dust.

Forks of lightning... thunderous rumbling... the marsh was calling...

The stench of decomposing carp floated on the damp wind. An old man stood at the edge of the marsh. He lunged at Lorca, hands around his neck, shaking him, choking him. Lorca was calm, face serene, despite the handcuffs on his wrists. One policeman tried to wrest the old man's hands from Lorca's neck. Another yanked on the old man's arm and pulled him away.

"You killed my granddaughter, didn't you? Admit it! Admit it! Right here and now!" A crooked cane hanging on his arm, the old man shook his knotted hands, and pointed his trembling finger.

"I'll break your neck, you godforsaken filth! You an' your *pralo*, here ..." The old man growled like a caged animal, trying to free himself from the policeman's grip. He pointed at Stefan.

"Farmer Vila's grandson. I should've done away with you long ago. When my sweet Angela first set her eyes on you with your gypsy blood, I knew there was trouble. Disgraced my daughter, my innocent swallow! You filthy pricks. Got her pregnant. Did you take turns raping her? She wouldn't admit, but I knew! Betrayed her father. Me! Betrayed me! Policeman! Policeman! Let go of me. Put your goddamn cuffs on the guilty. He's a gypsy too. Just as guilty as the other."

In one yank, the old man tore himself from the policeman's grasp and charged at Stefan. With a quick jerk of his shoulder, Stefan freed himself, eyes unwavering as glass.

Kata stood frozen – a detached patron watching a play. She felt disconnected. As if all this were just a scene in a drama. She was simply part of the background, part of the sky and the marsh and the stray raindrops slashing through the wind.

She saw Papa Novak standing near Stefan. He seemed small, his white hair pasted to his skull.

Angela's father continued to shout obscenities, each more vile than the one before: "Throw the filthy pricks in the dungeon 'til the skin rots off their backs. Better yet, throw them to the wolves. Tie them to a tree and let the vultures gouge out their eyes. Tear up their hearts. Give me a knife so I can carve out those godforsaken gypsy hearts and fry them. I'll eat them for breakfast…"

The old man's rant pounded in her head, melded with the apparitions from her visions and dreams. *Where had I heard these words before? When?*

A bubble of memory burst. The old man had come to her house a few days after Angela's baby had disappeared. He had asked Grandma whether she knew the whereabouts of somebody. A son? A grandson? Then the shouting had followed. She thought that Goya's name was mentioned, but was not sure. She was not allowed to listen to grownup talk. She didn't dare ask any questions, everyone was very upset. During those frightening days, much of the talk was in hushed tones. Now, Grandma's words rang clear: "That's Ivan, Angela's father. The man's gone mad. He's ready to blame the moon, never mind everyone else. But who could fault him? This is a tragedy beyond belief."

Kata's eyes landed on Lorca. He was gazing into the distance, beyond her, through her. She heard the rushing river in her head, drowning all other sounds. She was at the edge of the gorge, about to drop into the waterfall, into the chasm below. She closed her eyes, succumbing to the magnetic pull. But the noise subsided and Lorca's voice rose above the falling water:

under the gypsy moon
things are staring at her
things she cannot see

She opened her eyes. She knew these lines well. They had been coiling in her dreams, faint images of those unseen things snaking through her visions. If only she could make some sense of them. *What am I not seeing?*

She heard another voice, clear as a church bell: *Keep up your list of puzzling questions, Kata. Some day, answers will come to you.*

And another: *Your gypsy spirit, use wisely, Kata.*

And yet another: *His eyes were intense, as if he were burning holes in my soul…*

A flutter of wings on the marsh caught her attention. At the far end of the decrepit fishing pier, the dead swallow lifted her wings. The shimmering feathers grew longer and longer, shaping the figure of a woman. The swallow-woman looked at Kata – with Angela's sorrowful eyes. She raised a flute to her lips and blew.

sleep my little baby
sleep in the night
sleep in your cradle
under moonlight

and if the moon hides
beneath its lore
sleep under the stars
my angel's soul
and if the stars hide
when swallows fly
chase the swallows
into the sky

chase the swallows
my angel's soul

sleep in the stardust
of gypsy lore

The lullaby fell in all around, filling every crevice of the marsh, like fog. And then, at the end of the pier, Kata spotted the dancing bear – hopping and skipping and bouncing to the song. The bear turned and smiled, but his face was that of the old man. Kata felt shivers rushing through her. The bear waved, beckoning her to follow, as the swallow-woman soared toward the still-bright moon.

Stefan pointed to the shiny globe low in the sky. "If only that old man in the moon could give us a sign."

Angela's father swung his cane. Stefan dodged the blow. Ivan lunged at him and swung again, but Stefan jumped out of reach. Ivan raised his cane and shook it at the moon. "You saw nothing! Nothing!" He shouted. Then he bowed low and made the sign of the Cross.

It was him? Him? ... the watermelon farmer, Angela's father, one and the same? The man limping along the fishing pier – whose face Stefan could not see the night Angela's baby vanished – had to be Ivan, had to be ... Angela's father.

Kata ran towards the old man. She brought the flute to her lips and blew. And the perfect tune floated on the marsh air:

only the truth can set you free!
only the truth can set you free!
only the truth can set you free!

She stared into Angela's father's eyes, into the sunken eye-sockets shaded by bushy, mud-coloured eyebrows – and recoiled in anguish. She was seeing *him* ... seeing Ivan ... through Angela's eyes as she sat by the pig puddle singing a lullaby to her missing child. He looked up and their eyes locked. Kata felt a strange surge of heat coursing through her, her thoughts penetrating his – *burning holes in his soul.*

He stopped shouting, stood up straight and thrust out his chest, ready to address his hapless audience.

The story has ended and the plot is about to unravel, announced a voice in Kata's head.

Kata wished she could check where the voice came from. Was it something she read? But she could not shift her eyes from the old man. Breaking eye contact could cause him to forget his lines. At long last, the old man remembered his true lines.

"Come, come now, old woman!" he said, peering intensely into Kata's face. "If I didn't know better I'd say you're that vila…

"What choice did I have? Had to save 'er from those gypsy scoundrels. If I didn't get to 'er in time they sure would.

"What's that you say?

"Me? You're accusing me, her father?

"I've no fear of you or your flute or your eyes. I gave 'er what she wanted.

"What did you say?

"You say I raped my own daughter? My own flesh and blood?

"Careful now, old woman. You're beginning to vex me.

"I saw her talking to those filthy gypsies. Twirling 'er skirt, prickly little ass squirming like a worm on a grill, asking for it. I say she wan'ed it. I am 'er father. Nobody was gonna give it to 'er like me. Nobody was gonna have 'er but me.

"You what?

"You can call it rape all you want.

"I say she liked it, she did, I say.

"Oh, sure, she screamed and cursed and yelled. Like my wife when I gave it to 'er. The little stuck-up whore. Called me scum. Said she'd rather die than marry me. But she married me alright. I made 'er squirm, like all the others. They all like it, I say.

"You heard 'er screams, you say?

"Ha, ha, ha! You wicked, wicked old woman!

"You'd scream too, in joy. Frisky she was, I admit.

"Yeah, she was frisky after 'er old man. My own flesh and blood.

"You say I killed my own grandchild, my own daughter?

"Yeah, yeah, never thought of it that way. My grandchild my daughter.

"You wicked, wicked old woman. Don't you go putting fancy ideas in your head.

"You're angering the old man. What choice did I have? Just a few drinks. Playing with 'er, tickling 'er, I was. Come to Grandpa, I said. She giggled and wiggled like a worm. Liking it. Like they all do. Didn't kill 'er. Not me. Nooo... nooo... Turned limp like dishrag... Goddamn. What's a man to do? It's those goddamn thieving gypsies. Poking 'round till they find something. I had no choice. Goddamn Grizzly was on to me. I should've wiped out the whole damn lot so they don' come hounding me, over and over. Had to protect my family. That's my duty, isn't it? Protect my family.

"I dumped her little body in the marsh, you say?

"Better than giving 'er to the wolves to rip up 'er little heart, or to vultures to pluck 'er eyes out. She's safe in the marsh, I say.

"All the little pieces in a few cement blocks. Her little soul in heaven. Lifted itself into heaven to be with dear Jesus! Darted up, up, like a swallow! What more could I do? I sent 'er spirit straight to Jesus! Well done, eh? Not a trace. Those murderous gypsies can poke all they want. Let's see if they can poke from the jail cell! Yeah, once they're in jail, she's safe. Yeah!

"... Right over there, in the marsh, 'er little body safe with dear Jesus! Here, I'll show you."

The two policemen gaped at the old man, and then at each other. Stefan and Lorca stared at the old man, then at the police, then at the hushed gathering of gypsies that had quietly appeared, huddled in a group.

Kata saw her dog, Samson, jump in the marsh and swim toward the end of the pier. He climbed the tip, shook himself, and crouched down. Placing his chin solemnly on his paws, he stared intently into the pool of water just in front. Then he gave a low, mournful whine.

Pointing his finger to where the dog lay, the old man strode into the marsh. His eyes fixed on the distant pier, he sank deeper and deeper. For a moment, he stood still, as the dark sludge rose up to his chest. Then he turned to face the group on the embankment behind him. He slowly sank lower. The water surface reached for his neck, his gaping mouth, the tuft of grey hair atop his scalp. The water churned about him as if a school of carp had rolled in mating.

A flash of lightning... a crack of thunder... all was darkness...

Chapter XXIX

One Leap

(Summer 1967)

THE WHIFF OF burnt tobacco was comforting, reminding her of Goya's clothing that so often carried the scent of smoke from campfires. More and more often, Kata found herself drawing a breath through the brown pipe as if she were smoking it while holding the flute across her chest, close to her heart.

After that night at the marsh, she thought her flute was lost forever. But on the day when she'd sat in Grandma's room for the first time since that night, she was drawn to the top drawer holding the pink cookie heart. And there it was, her flute, on top of the cookie heart. Who could've placed it there? Her mother? But no one said anything. So she left it at that. What she did with her time didn't seem to matter. Nothing mattered. Not until she found out. One way or another, she needed to know.

"I've been going though Goya's things," Jasmine had told her. "I want you to have something from her. She cared about you very much. I want you to have her ceremonial pipe – it was one of her sacred possessions – supposed to be passed on to me when I got sworn as shaman. But somehow, every time I look at it, I sense that it belongs to you."

Jasmine had said that it was Angela's brother who ran toward the group with a rifle that early dawn at the marsh. No one saw him coming. He fired several shots. "We're all grateful that you're..."

Kata needed to know about the others.

"Goya was also shot," Jamine had said. "She is with her husband in their fragrant meadow of heaven."

Lorca had been hit as well. He had an operation, but the bullet remained lodged in his brain. Removal could cause more damage. He was still in a coma. He had been flown to a hospital in Madrid to be near family. There was hope, but more surgeries would follow, and it could be many months before any conclusive results.

The village was stunned by the old man's confession. The usual greetings between the villagers were replaced by snippets from Papa Novak's retelling of the events from that night at the marsh:

"A man murders his own offspring. Is there a more despicable crime, I ask?" a villager would exclaim while lifting his hat to greet a passerby.

"No, there isn't, my brother! Here's a man who desecrates his own daughter and his own granddaughter – his own blood," the other would reply.

"Possessed by a devil? No, no, he is the devil itself!"

"And to think we've lived with him in this village, all these years..."

"That's the epitome of evil! The epitome of evil, if I've ever seen it!" Papa Novak would recap. He was a shadow of his former self. But as always, the villagers commended Papa Novak on his good deeds – this time on his success in convincing Stefan to pursue his studies at Belgrade University.

"Smart young man, Stefan is," the villagers remarked as they nodded to each other in passing, "He'll make our village proud!"

Kata edged one step at a time toward Grandma's armoire mirror. How strange was the image she saw there. Yet, she was getting used to it. At first, every time she looked in the mirror she thought it was the glassy eye of a dead chicken staring impudently at her. It was her own eye – well, not exactly her own. But it was glassy, just the same. It was better than the dead chicken's eye. In fact it was made of glass. Even the match to her own eye colour was pretty good – almost the same light green, but without the yellow specks.

It was still strange to be able to touch one's own eye while it was wide open, and feel nothing but a cold, still surface. The eye felt no burning or tears even when she touched it with onion juice smudged on her finger. Sometimes she felt this eye was watching her even when she was asleep, because the eye did not sleep. It never closed or blinked. It just stared and stared. But if she closed her working eye – she had labelled the glass one as an ornament, like a jewel, so she didn't look monstrous – all was darkness.

She thought she must look strange regardless, because people usually stared at her. Maja was with her when the doctor said that medical research was advancing and that some day Kata might get an eye that blinked. Whenever Maja thought that her friend was sad, she would remind her of what the doctor had said.

One good thing, Kata pondered, was that she no longer had to fear marrying Miladin.

"Who on this earth would marry a maimed girl, no matter how much land she brought?" Miladin's grandmother had said.

Miladin's visits were rare and brief. He no longer ran wherever he went nor rode his broom "horse." He speed-walked, his legs bending in different directions when he walked and when he stood. His head still wobbled unsteadily on his thin neck, but it gave him an air of superiority, as if he were assessing others. She would catch him staring at her, at her glass eye, with his head tilted to one side as if trying to see her from a different angle. But as soon as she looked at him, he would avert his eyes and rush away.

Jasmine had said that she needed to be near Lorca. She could not write to Kata about his progress, but he would want Kata to move on with her life and not worry about him. He was like that, and Jasmine had said that she needed to honour what she knew would be his wish. Kata agreed. Lorca would have wanted things done his way.

"I can do something for you," Jasmine had offered. "I'll send you a message, a sign. If you look at the post on your gate, you'll find..."

But Kata already knew how it was done. "I saw them on my gate post once. You'd do that for me?"

"Did Lorca tell you about that?" Jasmine had asked playfully. Kata felt their bond strengthening across large distances, solidifying like spider's silk – delicate, and yet wondrously life-supporting.

"Yes," Kata had answered. "There was a circle with a dot in the middle on our gate, which meant that visitors were welcome. I found one on Miladin's gate. It was a plain cross that Lorca said meant 'stay away.'"

"Well, that should tell you how he feels about you. Gypsies share their symbols only with other gypsies."

Kata almost gave in to the temptation to confide in Jasmine about her own gypsy roots. But then she thought of Kris, and resisted.

Her love for Lorca had evolved to a higher plateau – she no longer hoped to marry him, or anyone else for that matter. After all, who would marry a one-eyed girl? Still, once in a while when she felt that her glass eye was not watching, she would retrieve the pottery shard from Jasmine's wedding and imagine what it would be like to have a large vessel shattered above her own and Lorca's head, she in Grandma's silk dress the gold of ripened wheat and he in his long-sleeved purple silk shirt, tight black pants, and a *diklo* tied around his neck, looking into her working eye as he did the night of

Jasmine's wedding when she refused his invitation to dance. This time she would not refuse. She would not be afraid. But she knew this would never happen again.

"After Lorca's surgeries, I'll give it a few months," Jasmine had said. "You're our sweet sister, my *pen*, forever, after what you've done for us. If I can't do it myself, I'll get the message to somebody and a symbol will be left on your gate. Let's keep them simple. Usually, a triangle means a difficulty and a circle stands for good news. So it'll be one or the other."

"What if you forget?" Kata had asked.

"I won't," Jasmine had said. "There's only one reason you wouldn't hear from me." She had studied Kata's eye with a long, meaningful stare.

Kata thought that if Lorca's second surgery was to take place in the fall, with recovery time and possibly more surgeries, she could expect to hear from Jasmine by early spring. It was now May, the most enticing time of year. It had been a cool sunny spring, and the tulips and hyacinths had been blooming gigantic, heavy blossoms as they hadn't since Grandma's death.

She checked the gatepost every day, but no sign from Jasmine. Saint Sara's day was approaching, and she had devised a tiny shrine of her own, secretly, to avoid the scorn of her family and friends. After all, no one knew the full story. No one knew about her being a gypsy, not even Maja who came to visit every day, and whose friendship Kata treasured.

She realized that she was too old to play with dolls, but she secretly dressed one in seven skirts, each of a different colour. She thought that Grandma must have prayed to Saint Sara, the saint who understands a woman's heart. Every few days, she made a tiny wreath of fresh wild daisies and placed it like a halo on the doll's head. She prayed to her effigy of Saint Sara, pleading for Lorca's recovery. But still, no sign on the post.

Saint Sara's days, May 24 and 25, came and went. The whole country celebrated Tito's birthday on May 25, the baton carried by youthful runners from one end of the country to another, ending in Belgrade. Parades and other festivities saturated the town of Obrenovac and the surrounding towns and villages. And still no sign.

It was now June. The tightly-wrapped peony buds unfurled, burgundy and pink and pure white, their heavy, rumpled blossoms and musky scent. The school year-end was approaching.

Disheartened at the thought of a long summer with no news about Lorca and no gypsy caravans, Kata spent her spare time reading Dostoyevsky – sometimes enthralled by the rhythm of thoughts and events, and other times disenchanted by the futility of all human actions and aspirations. As June advanced, utter despair and fear gripped her heart. She realized that her hopes for Lorca's recovery were unrealistic. She saw her optimism as delusional as a single glass of liquor to an alcoholic, pacifying one's fears only to reveal them the following minute, more dismal and hopeless than the hour before.

She withdrew from everyone, staying in Grandma's room, which her mother kept threatening to redecorate. She hid from the warm, glorious days and the sun-dipped green leaves and the twittering swallows darting about, stuffing bugs into webbed pink beaks poking out of mud nests.

She thought of her birthday, a few weeks away. She hoped the day would be rainy. She could not face a day of sunshine. It would be too sad to think of all the people she'd loved and lost, some forever and some most likely forever. Far too much to bear on a hot summer day when surrounding fields turn into Van Gogh canvasses, into a mélange of gold.

It was the last day of June. She had risen early, waking from a vivid dream of the day she stumbled on a rock and broken a pitcher. She had dreamed the face of the gypsy woman who had taken her hand and lifted her off the ground, the woman whose voice had been sleeping in Kata's consciousness all the years since. Had she seen this woman again? Heard her voice? Seen her face and flaming hair? But the sun had all vision that day, and Kata had retained only the deep eyes and a halo of auburn tresses – and a strand of that comforting voice.

The day the bear danced seemed long ago, yet the identity of this woman was a missing piece of a puzzle that had to be pressed into place for the full picture. Kata felt as if a part of her was missing with it.

She realized it was too late. Too much time had passed for the feared triangle or the hoped-for circle. The only possibility left was the one needing no sign, the one that had drained Jasmine's eyes of all optimism.

Kata went to Grandma's dresser, picked up the pink cookie heart necklace, and for the first time since Jasmine's wedding hung it around her neck. And then she heard the voice from her memory harmonizing with the one from her dream.

"Give me your hand," a woman leaning over her beckoned. Kata tried to look up but blinded by the sun could only squint. Two large, almond-shaped eyes and a halo of reddish-brown hair framed by the sun loomed over her, a flowered skirt kneeling in the dust. Kata placed her hand into the warm grip. "You have a strong hand, little girl … sign of strong character. You will have many adventures." That compassionate, drawn-out speech enunciating each word slowly and carefully, as if to engrave them upon Kata's memory.

"Jasmine! It was Jasmine!" Kata cheered in the childish voice she'd left behind on the day the bear danced. She felt as if the million pieces of a broken puzzle, like the shattered fragments of a pitcher smashed in the dust, were suddenly reassembling themselves into a meaningful whole. She ran to the front gate and stared at the post. A circle had been drawn in charcoal. A sprig of jasmine with plump white flowers and yellow centres covered in dew sat atop the post.

Kata opened the gate expertly, without any squeaking, and left. Her vision rested on the expansive landscape ahead, *irresistibly drawn into the distance by the diminishing columns of trees, the well worn-path paved with ridged dry earth, broad, wavering slightly off centre, the receding plane balanced by the horizontal grids of the fields* – Meyndert Hobbema's *The Avenue.* She smiled to herself, pleased that she so easily recalled the synopsis of the painting.

The sun rises every day, echoed Grandma's voice.

God was all around, watching, listening…

The dancing bear turned and smiled, playing the charmed flute, beckoning her to follow, to follow the wind swirling in the wheat fields and the swallow darting high in the sky.

Acknowledgements

An excerpt from Chapter XIII was published in the anthology, *Gathered Streams*, Hidden Brook Press, 2010.

The stanzas quoted in Chapters XIX and XXVIII are from Federico Garcia Lorca's *Romancero gitano*, translated, *Gypsy Ballads* by Robert G. Havard, Aris & Phillips Ltd., Wiltshire, 1990.

Although *Summer of the Dancing Bear* is a work of fiction, the inspiration stems from my childhood experiences growing up in the former Yugoslavia. During the harvest, gypsies often worked on my grandmother's farm. On many evenings I was privileged to listen to their music and watch them dancing around the campfire and sometimes even join the children dancing among the adults – some of the best memories of my childhood.

Regarding this work, the following contributed to my knowledge of Roma traditions and history and offered anecdotes and insights: David Crowe and John Kolsti, editors, *The Gypsies of Eastern Europe* (M.E. Sharpe, Inc., 1991); Patrick "Jasper" Lee of the Purrum clan, *We Borrow the Earth: An Intimate Portrait of the Gypsy Shamanic Tradition* (Thorsons, 2000); Robert G. Havard, translator, *Gypsy Ballads, Romancero gitano* by Federico Garcia Lorca (Aris & Phillips Ltd., 1990); Carl W. Cobb, *Lorca's Romancero gitano:*

A Ballad Translation and Critical Study (UP of Mississippi, 1983); Dieter W. Halwachs, *Burgenland-Romani* (Lincom Europa, 2002); Jan Yoors and Andre A. Lopez, *The Gypsies of Spain* (Macmillan Publishing Co. Inc., 1974); Rupert C. Allen, *The Symbolic World of Federico Garcia Lorca* (U of New Mexico, 1972). A number of stalwart classics offered broader insight into customs and religion: Irving Brown's *Nights and Days on the Gypsy Trail* (Harper & Brothers Publishers, 1922); Juliette De Bairacli Levy's *As Gypsies Wander: being an account of life with the Gypsies in England, Provence, Spain, Turkey, and North Africa,* (Faber & Faber Limited, 1962).

* * * *

My heartfelt thanks to my family for their love and unwavering support: to Mirko, Adrian, Sarah, Austin, Michelle and Marijan. To my siblings for sharing the history of the family that bends reality – whose untold story has been an inspiration – and the history of the country that no longer exists. To Svetlana, Mile, Goga, Anita and Izidora. To Ratko, Ceca, Marko and Gabrijela. To Vladan, Dragica, Stefan and Predrag. To my friends Vesna Lopičić, Albert Dumont and Silvia for their encouragement when I needed it most. To friendships not forgotten, Pat, Ed, Tanya, and Matt. To Antonio D'Alfonso. I would also like to thank my colleagues at the Canadian Authors Association, Bloorwestwriters, Toronto Writers Co-op, Writers and Editors, the Algonquin Square Table, and all those who have read my work and provided valuable comments. My thanks to the staff at the Toronto Reference Library, the U of T Library, and York U Library for assisting me with research on Roma history. My special thanks to my friend Jackie for her encouragement. Many thanks to Paul Butler and Elizabeth Abbott for their enthusiastic support.

My thanks to dear friend Jane Munro whose support I treasure, and to Gordie Munro whose strength of spirit will always inspire me. My gracious thanks to my editor Lindsay Brown and my Editor-in-Chief and publisher Michael Mirolla not just for believing in me but also for their vision in taking me to the "finish line," and for some of the best editorial advice and encouragement a writer could hope for, and to Connie McParland for her support and guidance, and to all for welcoming me to the family of writers at Guernica Editions, a staunch proponent of multicultural voices for over 30 years.

Author Bio/Previous Publications

Bianca Lakoseljac is an author and educator with a special interest in women's issues, the environment, and social justice. She holds a BA and MA in English literature from York University, and is the recipient of the Matthew Ahern Memorial Award in Literature. Bianca taught communication courses at Ryerson University and Humber College.

She has served as judge for literary contests such as the National Capital Writing Contest, the Dr. Drummond Poetry Contest, the Canadian Aid Literary Award Contest, as well as contests of the League of Canadian Poets and the Writers Union of Canada.

She is past president and special project chair of the Canadian Authors Association, Toronto Branch; a board member of the Book and Periodical Council and the League of Canadian Poets; a member of the Writers Union of Canada, and PEN Canada, among others.

Bridge in the Rain, a collection of stories linked by an inscription on a bench in Toronto's High Park, was published in 2010 by Guernica Editions in Toronto.

Memoirs of a Praying Mantis, a collection of poetry exploring environmental issues, horrors of war, and legends of High Park, was published in 2009 by Turtle Moons Press in Ottawa.

Summer of the Dancing Bear, a novel set in the former Yugoslavia and exploring the rite of passage of a fourteen year old girl befriended by a gypsy clan, published by Guernica Editions in 2012, is Bianca's first novel.

Flower Power, a historical novel inspired by the 1967 Art Symposium in Toronto, is her work in progress. She is also working on a sequel to *Summer of the Dancing Bear.*

Her short stories and poems have been published in journals and anthologies such as: *Canadian Woman Studies,* Inanna Publications and Education, York University, 2007; *Canadian Voices,* BookLand Press, 2009; *Gathered Streams,* Hidden Brook Press, 2010; *Migrating Memories: Central Europe in Canada,* Central European Association for Canadian Studies, 2010, among others.

Bianca was born in Obrenovac in the former Yugoslavia, and has lived in Canada since the age of 19. She divides her time between Toronto and Woodland Beach on Georgian Bay and has been an environmentalist all her life.

Also featured in Guernica's Essential Prose series:

THE TENANTS OF THE HÔTEL BIRON

Laura Marello's novel "brings us a perceptive and unique understanding of the people whose lives crossed in the Hôtel Biron: Rodin, Claudel, Picasso, Satie, Matisse and other fascinating characters from that time. This is a compelling story on a real and imagined Paris – the ravishing bohemian Paris of the early 1900s." – Award-winning writer Jennifer Clement.

LEPER TANGO

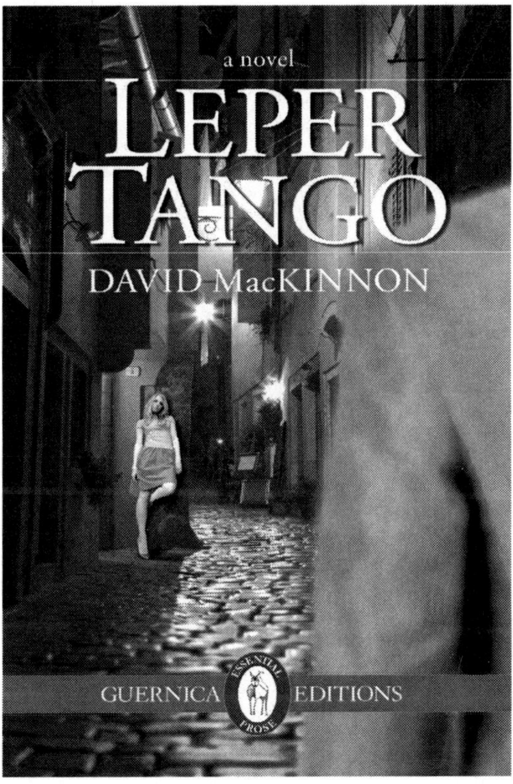

Leper Tango recounts the lunar trajectory of Franck Robinson – a self-confessed member of "the despised and despicable sub-species of skirt-chaser known as the john". During one of Franck's regular free-falls into the Parisian night, he meets Sheba, who moves from being Franck's favourite hooker to being Franck's obsession. Leper Tango is a confession of an unrepentant man whose stated life aim is to screw an entire city. The author, David MacKinnon, presumably the alter ego of Franck, is also a jack-of-all-trades and vagabond spirit.

Imprimé sur Rolland Enviro100, contenant 100% de fibres recyclées postconsommation, certifié Éco-Logo, Procédé sans chlore, FSC ® Recyclé et fabriqué à partir d'énergie biogaz.